The

Stuff What Actually Is

The Stuff What Actually Is

A Novel

J. A. Nunn

GFB

This is a work of fiction. Names, characters, organizations, places, events, and incidents are either products of the author's imagination or are used fictitiously.

Published by GFB™, Seattle
www.girlfridayproductions.com

Produced by Girl Friday Productions

Image credits: cover © Adobe Stock/Tony Marturano, Adobe Stock/Andrei Korzhyts, Library of Congress, Envato/Wirestock, Shutterstock/Olga Popova

ISBN (paperback): 978-1-964721-48-4
ISBN (ebook): 978-1-964721-47-7

Library of Congress Control Number 2025902905

First edition

To "Ces," one naive but well-meaning
Haffa-Taffy and ever my guiding light.

And to the brave men and women of color who have been
willing to fight for a country not always willing to fight for them.

"He is convinced—and what immigrant isn't?—that all Americans are crazy."

—Sigrid Nunez, *A Feather on the Breath of God*

"Only connect."

—E. M. Forster

"The past is never dead.
It's not even past."

—William Faulkner

AUTHOR'S NOTE

This story is based on the actual experiences of my father, a British immigrant, drafted for service during World War II. It is the story of his discovery of the America beyond the borders of his experiences growing up in an all-white immigrant Los Angeles neighborhood and working part time as a lifeguard at the beaches and public pools (both primarily off-limits to people of color) and at the Beverly Hills Y, where he likely got his job through peripheral connections in the local underworld made by his father during Prohibition.

I wrote this book as an exploration of the more positive aspects of America and Americans, the obstacles we must overcome to maintain and strengthen our democracy, and of yet one more journey of discovery and assimilation into the fabric of this "one people out of many" country—no matter what may have brought them here.

Although novels don't often include an author's introductory note, since the story's overriding themes of social integration and acceptance are highly personal ones, the publisher has asked me to provide some helpful context. This is a work of historical fiction, and while I hope it will entertain, I also endeavor to enlighten and educate within these pages. (I myself learned a lot from the many hours of research I did before and during the writing process.)

To accomplish especially these last two goals, I have tried to be as true to the then-contemporary places, people, and social and historical environments and events as I have been able. For example, the vocabulary of some of the characters and some of the perspectives behind those words, therefore, have been written with these things in mind. The contemporary reader may take exception to some of those choices. I know that some of the offensive, race-related words themselves may shock, in or out of context. They shock me. Those words were intended by the character who speaks them to shock.

My intention is for that repulsion to inform the modern reader's understanding of an unfamiliar time, place, and set of circumstances. Words of irrational hatred, and the sentiments behind them, though thankfully encountered somewhat less often more recently, are unfortunately still with us. They are among the bigot's array of offensive weapons, intended to both shock and to disarm the recipient, simultaneously turning the bigot's internal fears of the "other" into aggression against that which they do not understand, while denying the need to attempt any level of understanding as to why they perceive the mere physical appearance of "other" or "different" as a threat.

The protagonist Gower's impressions of the America beyond Poppy Peak—before he entered the Army—were primarily informed by the fantasy versions of his adoptive country he encountered at the cinema down the street. Drafted and sent to the Jim Crow South, he is forced to face "The Stuff What Actually Is" and, as E. M. Forster so concisely put it, "Only connect."

PROLOGUE

As they waited for Joey's boys to unload the goods, the two more or less still friends leaned up against the railing of the pier. Soon bored watching the transfer, they lit up a couple of cigarettes.

"So . . . you gonna finish telling me, or what?" Harvey said after a few minutes.

The other man looked up. "What?" He'd been staring at his brother's lighter, occasionally flipping it open, then shut again—the overhead sun glancing off "105 Bttln Co C 1942" and several pairs of initials, all crudely etched into its tarnished, silver-plated surface—except for Wendell's perfectly applied "WG."

"OK, *OK!* I admit it!" Harvey went on. "You've got me hooked. Your war stories are better than I thought."

"Didn't think anything interesting could ever happen over there?"

Harvey tilted his head back and blew some smoke into the air but miscalculated the breeze coming in off the Pacific and got a face full of his own exhaust. His throat double-clutched before he could continue. "Did you bring the nig . . . That *colored* guy back alive, or what?"

His friend stared a while at a particular pair of the rough-edged letters. “It’s a long story.”

“Your story’s already long,” Harvey huffed. “What difference does it make? ’Slong as it’s good.”

Before reburying the lighter in his trouser pocket, the other man forcefully closed the Zippo with a last, loud *clack*.

CHAPTER ONE

The Welsh Kid

1

The sound of an unseen door clicking shut set Gower in motion. *Finally—the place is empty.* With an armload of laundered towels from the boiler, he shouldered his way through the swinging doors and into the members' locker room for the very last time.

Something caught his eye—a vacant spot on the wall where his "Our Staff" photo had been smiling back at him only hours before. *Well,* that *was fast.* He stepped a little closer. *Been here . . . What? Two years . . . ? Sure gonna miss this place.* His eyes settled on the pleasant but hard-to-read mug of Hey-Gee Nakamura. *Especially this guy.*

A gaggle of talking silhouettes bubbling across the frosted-glass entry opposite only added to Gower's sorrow. *Friday afternoon regulars heading for the lobby and the "Good Life" beyond it. Gonna miss them, too . . . Well,* most *of 'em.*

Whenever Mr. Scobbs let Gower fill in at reception, his

envious eyes followed members Aaron "Mugsy" Levine and the other swells as they stepped out into the early evening—cars and drivers ready to take them home, or to a restaurant, or to a nightclub deeper into Beverly Hills. Living the American Dream. *Someday—catch a few breaks in the ring, work my way up the rankings—that could be me,* if *I make it back alive. . . . Sure shoulda signed up for the Navy—like Wendell did, right after Pearl Harbor, 'steada hoping I wouldn't get drafted. What a dope.* "Join the Navy and See the World." *Wendell's gonna be sailing the Seven Seas while I'm stuck in some foxhole somewhere, waiting for the war to find me.*

His already-lowered spirits got pinned against the ropes when a recent hit seeped in over new speakers Mr. Scobbs had ordered. Gower hummed a few bars. "Stardust," he announced to the empty room. Wendell had played it on his violin for Mom's birthday. She'd said she liked the melody. Gower wasn't sure she'd like the words, though. *She's not gonna want to be reminded about loneliness and her two sons being away for . . . Well, who knows? Maybe forever.*

The laundry cupboards restocked, Gower indulged his habit of practicing some work for the ring. Between short, crisp jabs at the steam-and-sweat-sopping air, he picked up discarded towels from the floor and the benches while bobbing and weaving against an imaginary foe, pausing only to fling tossed-aside linen casually over a shoulder, more or less toward the hamper. He worked on a couple of new moves Mugsy had been showing him, there at the Y and over at the gym on Figueroa—not far from the only home Gower could remember ever having—pressed up against the ragged, northeast corner of the City of Angels, on the immigrant side of Poppy Peak.

Mugsy recently insisted on giving Gower a ring name. The ex-amateur champ from Brooklyn claimed he did it because *"Folks like it when a fighter reminds 'em of the Old Country."*

Gower sidestepped a bench as he went through a couple of new combinations for use against upper cuts. *"The Welsh Kid"! Ha! Even gave me a robe with the name sewn on the back!* Despite reminding his mentor more than once that his parents brought him to the US when he was only three—and that he was only half-Welsh—Mugsy insisted on the moniker. *If that guy can smell money, the truth isn't gonna stop him from getting what he wants.*

When Gower finished at one bank of lockers, he switched to defending against shadow southpaws. *Maybe they'll let me box in the Army.*

Inevitably, Mugsy's favorite tune drowned out the piped-in variety. *"Jeezuz, kid! Lefties are killing you! You're leavin' yourself wide open! You don't even know what hitcha, 'cause you keep making the same stupid mistake!"* As near Gower could figure, his "stupid mistake" was having "no brains and no heart."

The novice knew he'd developed the very dangerous habit of overprotecting against a right hook—even when facing left-handed opponents. *"If you keep looking for stuff what ain't actually there, Kid, you're gonna miss the stuff what actually is."*

And more recently, maybe no luck. It'd only been a week or so since Hey-Gee Nakamura shared the latest rumor. "Word is, Mugsy's looking to take some Italian kid under his wing."

'Course, the guy's a lefty, Gower thought. *If I know Mugsy, he'll send Moose and some of the other boys out to twist promoters' arms*—literally—*to get this guy on the bill!* The news had Gower worrying about his future in the ring once the Army was through with him. *Assuming I make it back here in one piece—and Mugsy stays out of prison.* Unfortunately, the

only thing Mugsy couldn't seem to stay out of was the papers. Gower grinned at the thought. *Palling around with the stars and the starlets. "The Hollywood Hood!" A gossip columnist's dream.* To help shed some worries he'd rather leave behind, the last-day locker boy moved on.

At the sinks was a half-smoked cigar with some life in it. Wiping the butt on his trousers, Gower took a puff, then immediately regretted it. *Jeezuz!* When he'd more or less recovered, he drew the smoke in again—as if he'd been doing it all his life. "The next stiff who steps in here with me is going *down*!" he said, jabbing the smoldering stogie at the mirror. But the guy staring back—broken nose squiggle down a round, dark-haired head atop the squatty body of a Welshman—looked as if he'd taken one to the gut. There would be no more trying to knock some guy down in the ring. *Starting tomorrow, I'll be training to kill . . . Could I do it?*

Violent death was no stranger. Gower had seen it before. *That Saturday night. At the Jungle Club, bussing tables. Watching from the kitchen door.* A couple of Momo's boys showed up, claiming Jimmy Shine vouched for them. So, they let them in. *But Luca smelled a rat. Told me to keep an eye out.* The two goons passed among the tables, smiling and nodding, greeting folks here and there, heading toward the dance floor. Gower's brother, Wendell, had been leading the band. *"Moonlight Serenade." Just another night at the Jungle . . . Till they got to Johnny Three-Cheeks's table. They smiled at Johnny, too, then drew their .38s and shot him dead. Three, four times, they shot him. Took one just below the eye. Blood everywhere.*

Gower daubed at a smudge on the mirror's face, his reflection recalling it all. "Luca's boss made me and Harvey clean it up." His voice echoed in the tile-walled room.

"Mervyn . . . ? Is . . . that . . . you?" It was Scobbs, the Y's general manager. As usual, his words came in whisper-soft spurts, rough around the edges. Hey-Gee spilled the beans to Gower his first day on the job. *"It's cuz of mustard gas. In the trenches. Somewhere in Belgium, they said."*

In a panic, Gower doused the cigar butt under a tap before hurriedly tossing it around the corner, onto the gang shower floor. "Yes, sir, Mr. Scobbs," he said, waving vainly at the smell of burnt tobacco. "I'll be right there!"

2

Scobbs's good hand clutched a long, tight roll of paper while his right arm, useless since a stroke, dangled at his side. "Got another . . . poster for you to . . . put up, Mervyn. Say . . . ," the manager added, sniffing at the air, "you haven't been . . . smoking in here . . . have you?"

"No, sir. Not me, Mr. Scobbs. Must have been one of the members." The fib chafed a bit, and Gower began to fidget. "Found a cigar still going, right there on the counter, so I tossed it into the showers to make sure it's out. I'll pick it up later, sir."

"Wanna be . . . a boxer, son?" Scobbs gasped. "Don't . . . smoke. It'll take . . . the wind right out . . . of you."

"Yes, sir." Gower nodded, hands stuffed in front pockets, canvas shoe pawing the floor.

Scobbs raised the rolled poster and began to softly tap the side of his neck with it, nodding at Gower as he did so. "This is . . . it, then," he finally said. "Today's your . . . last . . . day."

"Yes, sir. Today's the day," Gower confirmed.

There was another nervous pause. More neck tapping by Scobbs.

"By the way, Mr. Scobbs, thanks for giving me—" Gower started to say.

"Mervyn, are you . . . familiar with . . . Quakers?" Scobbs interrupted.

"The oatmeal, sir?"

"The church."

Displaying more emotion than Gower remembered ever seeing, Scobbs waved the tip of the poster roll above their heads, as if summoning divine intervention. "They can help you . . . avoid combat. But only if you've got . . . *conviction.* If you . . . sincerely feel . . . you cannot bear arms . . . in good conscience . . . Only then . . . can they help you . . . avoid it."

"*Conviction,* Mr. Scobbs?" Gower puzzled briefly over the idea. He knew he wasn't anxious to die but had decided he was more or less ready to serve. "No, sir, I can't say that I have *conviction*—one way or the other."

There was more floor-pawing with the toe of Gower's shoe. He thought briefly about bringing up the Welsh thing—that they have a long history of faithful military service and, as his English father never tired of reminding him, of not coming back from the battlefield. Since he was only half-Welsh, though, he decided to skip it.

"Anyway, my brother, Wendell, is already in, sir. So . . . well, I guess that's it. I'm going in, too." He looked his manager in the eye. "Thanks for thinking of me, though."

"I . . . understand," Scobbs said, nodding. More silence. "On your way . . . home, though . . . if you don't mind . . ." He passed Gower the paper baton.

"You bet, Mr. Scobbs," Gower said. "Anything for you."

"I'm sure . . . you'll do well . . . in the Army, Mervyn. You've done . . . a fine job for us . . . here at the Y . . . You're a . . . fine young . . . man. We'll miss you." Scobbs extended his good hand in farewell. They shook long and warmly.

Gower found it hard to hold back a tear. Maybe there

was a tear in Scobbs's eye, too, by the time he at last let go. "Goodbye . . . and good . . . luck." Scobbs's raspy voice managed to work its way through the sentimental moment. "I . . . gotta go . . . and . . . lock up." He turned and left for the lobby.

Gower wondered if he was indeed "a fine young man." Or just a larger version of "Little Mervie," the quiet, well-mannered British boy, still trying to fit in. *Whatever I am, I sure don't want to end up with paper-thin lungs, like Mr. Scobbs did—or worse.* "Mr. Scobbs . . . ?" The manager was already out the door. Gower sighed. *Shoulda thanked him again for suggesting a way to get out of fighting . . . And maybe I shouldn't have been so hasty.*

Gower's eyes wandered around the room one more time before settling on the clock. *Jeez! Going to miss my trolley!* He set the poster on the load of used towels, ducked around the corner, made sure the cigar was out, and tossed it in the trash. He wheeled the hamper into the boiler room and went to his locker. *"To remember me by,"* Mugsy had said before giving Gower a five-dollar gold piece and some brass knuckles earlier that afternoon. The now ex–boxing protégé stood staring at the farewell gifts for a moment before shoving them into his pockets. "Pretty hard guy to forget," he muttered while pulling on his Franklin High letterman sweater against the late April evening.

He was nearly out the locker room door when he remembered the poster and dashed back to get it. Returning to the hallway, he collared a couple of fingers with the rubber band, pinned the poster to the bulletin board with a thumbtack at each corner as the War Department recommended, and stepped back to admire the job. "Ka-pow!" He fired the rubber band at the squinty-eyed, vaguely simian face of the Imperial Japanese soldier portrayed on the broadside. The sort of "monkey man" drawn with fangs and a dagger, posed as if about to pounce on a scantily clad white woman standing helplessly alone on a darkened street corner. "This Is the Enemy!" it read.

"I hear you're leaving us, Mervyn," Hey-Gee Nakamura said from behind him. He was standing beside a trash bin on wheels, leaning on a push broom.

"Hee-yah!" Gower yelled, spinning into the *crouching tiger* pose before releasing awkwardly out of it when he couldn't remember how to finish, and so shook his friend's hand instead. "That's right, Hey-Gee. Going to miss you and the *jujitsu* moves you've been teaching me. Who knows? They might come in handy on the battlefield. . . . Today's my last day."

Nakamura eyed the new poster warily and sighed. "Mine, too."

"Really?" Gower said, surprised not only by the news but the tinge of sadness in his coworker's voice. During the months he'd come to know Hey-Gee, there had never been much to read in the way of emotion. "Where are *you* off to?"

Wagging his head slowly, Nakamura bit his lip. "No idea," he said. "No idea at all."

3

Gower was glad to get a chance to say goodbye to Scobbs and Hey-Gee Nakamura but missed his regular Red Car because of it. The next trolley heading for downtown LA was crowded, forcing him to stand. He was strap-hanging, staring blankly out the window into the twilight, when he noticed a crowd of people around a storefront, some of them shouting and shaking their fists.

"Go back to Japan, you filthy monkeys!" one of them was

yelling loud enough to penetrate the trolley's closed windows. There were a few soldiers there, too, with bayoneted rifles, half-heartedly holding the crowd at bay. As Gower's streetcar rolled by, an Oriental couple was escorted from a five-and-dime on the first floor. They looked worried. They were dressed for travel, both wearing coats and hats. The man carried a pair of small suitcases.

Gower suddenly realized what was happening. *Relocation?! Holy cow! She's holding a baby!* As a soldier led the way, the woman shielded the child from hecklers with her embrace. It occurred to him that maybe that's what Hey-Gee meant when Gower asked him where he was headed. *But why would they take Hey-Gee? He's more American than* I *am!* He *was born here!*

He thought about going right back to the Y. *Maybe Mr. Scobbs can get the Quakers to help Hey-Gee out of it somehow.* As far as Gower knew, Hey-Gee had no family. At least none he ever talked about. *But who knows? Never says much about anything. A great friend, but kinda hard to figure out.* Reluctantly, the soon-to-be soldier rode on. *Sure hope the Army's not gonna make me kick people out of their homes.*

Well after making the switch to the Figueroa Line, while the trolley squealed and clanged its way toward Poppy Peak, Gower finally found a seat. To help take his mind off his own uncertain future—if not Hey-Gee Nakamura's—he dug out Mugsy's five-dollar gold piece. "E Pluribus Unum" shined up into the immigrant's face. He decided to try "walking" the coin over the back of his knuckles as he'd seen Levine do a thousand times.

Gower dropped the half eagle almost at once. *Shit!* The sound of money hitting the floor drew unwanted attention from other riders. Snatching the coin up from under watchful eyes, he was pretty sure his mom would call that a bad omen. He rode the rest of the way staring downheartedly at the spot where the coin had hit the deck. *Better not tell her.*

He got off, as always, at the foot of the modest, yet fairly steep, hill that was home. *Maybe for the very last time.* He nodded toward an elderly Norwegian he recognized from the neighborhood before starting up the slope. *Sure gonna miss this place.* Memories of an immigrant childhood nudged him irresistibly back in time. And when familiar spirits appeared in the shadows, he offered little in the way of resistance. The Bailey boys. The Van Zeulen twins. And Darla, his kindergarten puppy love, giggling and waving, laughing both *at* him—calling him her "British boyfriend"—and *with* him, referring to him as her "American sweetheart." *Well, "American," more or less.*

Rounding the corner school, not-so-happy memories rushed up against the chain-link fence, and rattled it. "Mervyn the Vermin," they called him, taunting and teasing. "That Welsher." The words were all too often the prelude to kicks and punches delivered after class. *"You sound like a girly boy, and your name is for sissies!"* Gower could afford to chuckle at the memory. It hadn't been very funny at the time. They'd threatened to beat him till he talked like an American. His parents had had little to say about the boys or the bloody noses they regularly presented their son. *Scolding* me *instead for bleeding all over that stupid smock some aunt I'll never meet sent me from England! Like it was* my *fault for getting my nose in the way of those bully boys' fists!*

"You must be American, now, Mervyn." It was his mother's answer to every bump in the immigrant road. *"We haven't a choice. You must fit in. You must."*

As Gower made his way up the slope a final time, the air, as usual, was filled with the music he'd been listening to all his life—the voices of recent arrivals to "The Land of Opportunity."

"Melodies trying their best to harmonize," was how Wendell liked to put it—boatloads of foreign tongues, everyone hoping to "fit in." He could hear every Nordic language, as well as Russian, Polish, Dutch, and French. To the growing concern of some—his parents included—German and Italian, too, were there. For every reason there could be, all the kids wanted to be thought of as "real Americans." Gower couldn't suppress a chuckle at the thought of how the Van Zeulen twins would invariably add *"And make it snappy, Mac!"* to every request. *As if to prove themselves Yankee Doodle Dandies!*

Gower smiled when he remembered the day his dad finally had enough of their youngest son getting the worst of it after school. He and Wendell taught six-year-old Gower how to box. And the next time a bloodstain soiled his "sissy" clothing, "Mervyn the Vermin" made sure the blood was somebody else's.

So, how's that for "fitting in"? Ah, but the girls . . . Gower always found it hard to compete with the boys, any boys—even other immigrants—when it came to the girls. He'd been raised to be quiet and reserved. He supposed that to American girls, he sounded and acted too boring, "*too* British."

When he saw *Gone with the Wind* as a seventeen-year-old, Gower decided he would rather be Clark Gable, the dashing American—not the mealy-mouthed Englishman, Leslie Howard, who played an overly deferring British-accented plantation owner. He'd even tried to grow a Clark Gable sort of mustache like Wendell had, but his facial hair was too thin in too many places.

And no matter what he did, or how hard he tried to disguise it, and despite having left the land of his birth when he was very small, for most of his high school classmates—but particularly the girls—Gower somehow always seemed to be of a different time and place. *"You've got a cute smile, Mervyn, but there's just something different about you I can't explain."* The tenth-grade version of puppy love, Darla, thus declined his request for a second date.

Arriving at the two-bedroom Gower bungalow, the Army draftee paused to gaze at the only home he'd known since coming to America as a three-year-old, and wondered whether he'd ever see it again. *Going to miss this place, and everything about it.*

"Hör auf so Depp zu sein!"

Shouting from the house across the street, and then a dog barking angrily in response, persuaded him otherwise. "Except for Mr. Weiss," Gower muttered to the growing darkness.

4

At least half the rant was in German. No one on the block knew whether Weiss was pro- or anti-Nazi, and nobody was brave enough to ask. It occurred to Gower that ever since Hitler's army swept through Poland, their German neighbor's outbursts had increased in frequency and in volume. *Wonder if President Roosevelt has any plans for relocating Americans of German and Italian heritage along with the Japanese he's already sent away to who-knows-where.*

Happily, the "Teutonic tantrum" subsided in time for Gower to hear the neighborhood owl. Despite the failing light, he spied the bird perched on the Edison pole across the street. And as he stared, the owl launched itself onto the back of warmer air rising from the Arroyo Seco, far below. Gliding toward, and then effortlessly over, Gower's head, it winked as it passed—or at least the young man supposed it did. *What would Mom say, if I told her that?* She was lately convinced owls were bad luck, adding the bird to her already very long and fast-growing list of things unlucky, or forbidden, or both. "Hard to keep up with all of them," Gower chuckled as he entered the house through the kitchen door off the driveway.

Though he'd been brought to America as a toddler and remembered nothing about Britain, whenever Gower entered their house on Poppy Peak, he felt as though he'd crossed an invisible border between place and time. The house was perennially dark, owing to thick curtains by day and sparse lighting after sundown. It always felt to him as if he had accidently wandered into a Dickens novel.

On this, his last evening, he found his father alone, nursing a glass of the gin he still favored making, though the end of Prohibition had turned his efforts from risky to quaint. Gower and his brother, Wendell, had long since given up scolding their dad for his drinking and the harm it had done the family over the years. And for his part, Hugh had sworn off alcohol several times—most ardently and faithfully after the most recent time their mother left home "to holiday" in Wales, toward the end of the Depression, spending two months with her family there, waiting and hoping for her husband to mend his sodden ways.

He'd not had a sip anyone knew about since then—until the Germans began bombing Britain, "Again!" as Hugh Gower put it, reminding Poppy Peak guests and neighbors of past zeppelin attacks on English soil. "The last time Fritz wanted to dance!"

When Gower hung his jacket on the back of another chair at the table, his father finally seemed to realize there was someone else in the room. "You home late, ain't ya, boy!" Hugh shouted over the barely three feet of distance. "Had us a worry, didn't we!"

Their dad was getting hard of hearing and shouted even

when he didn't intend to. Gower shrugged it off and went about his business, stepping to the stove to check on something to eat. "I'm not that late," he said as he lifted the lid on a pot of stew, long since gone cold.

"Yes, there's a beef stew," his father shouted. "Your mother thought you'd be home early, given the day's your last. So, she made a proper pot! But she gave up, then, didn't she, for the waiting. She's gone out for the Nurses Auxiliary, she said. O'er Saint Andrew's, I think it was. She'll be cross with you not telephoning and lettin' her know you'd be late, Mervyn. Eh? Since today be your last."

Gower lit the burner to reheat the stew, then got a pint of milk from the icebox. He pulled the paper tab, took a swig, and then set the bottle on the table. "Missed the usual trolley, but it only put me off by a quarter hour or so. . . . I'm home, now, aren't I? Besides, if I'd spent the money to call, I wouldn't have fare for the Red Car, then, would I?"

"They couldn't let you off a bit early on your last day?" his father asked, a little hurt. He huffed in disgust before sipping some more of the gin, and piling it on. "If you'd stayed at college, this would na happened, then, eh? Would it. None of it. The Army ain't taking students at college, I read."

"It's a little late for that now, Dad," Gower snapped.

"You needn't be short with me, Mervyn."

Gower sighed. "There's no more to be done, so there's no use discussing it any further."

"Well, tain't roight, is it. Tain't roight they ont let you out early from work. Your last day! We mayn't see you again, Mervyn!" Hugh said after draining his glass. "Tain't roight's all I'm saying. You going off to war and all. Our two boys . . . You and Wendell, you're Welsh, though, ain't ya? Eh? They don't come back, the Welsh," Hugh added with an ironic chuckle. "They don't."

CHAPTER TWO

Memento Mori

1

Gower couldn't prevent an eye roll when his dad started in again on the Welsh thing. It was the same old song Hugh Gower had sung when Wendell volunteered for the Navy.

"They'd rather doie, the Welsh. They would. . . . Your mum's lot, eh? They'd rather doie than give in. Stubborn . . . And you're one of 'em! Ay, you and Wendell! Poor Wendell. God only knows where your brother is now . . . Mervyn, you shoulda been home early to sit with your mum! They don't come back, ya know. It's all I'm saying ont. The both of you—Taffies . . . You won't be back."

Gower stood at the stove, staring into the slowly bubbling pot of stew. The thought had occurred to him of course. *Soldiers die. It's a well-known fact.* And despite the insult to half his heritage, he let it go by. *I hope to be a good, loyal soldier for my adoptive nation, fighting to the death, if I have to.*

But I really do prefer to come back—hopefully, not in a box, and if possible, all in one piece.

Satisfied the stew was ready, he spooned a good helping onto a plate, added a slice of his mother's speckled bread, and joined his father at the fold-down table. "I wish you'd stop saying that, Dad, about not coming back," Gower said through a mouthful of the stew. "You don't know me and Wendell won't come out of this OK. Not everyone's killed, you know. Being part Welsh has nothing to do with it. You sound as superstitious as Mom!" The stew had more beef than usual but, owing to the price of a pot roast, was still mostly potatoes, carrots, and gravy. He couldn't remember a tastier version, though—fitting for a last meal together. He regretted missing his mom and softened his tone toward his dad a little because of it.

"She saw something in the leaves, again, didn't she," he said.

"Well, she did," his father huffed. "And she's fairly duzzy over it, Mervyn. She is."

"This isn't the Old Country, though, is it, Dad. Even some of the people in the neighborhood, fresh off the boat, laugh at Mom over some of the things she says and does because they're so . . . I dunno. *Un-American!* You saw the group photo from the Auxiliary. She's the only one in it not looking into the camera! 'Evil eye,' she says, or some other nonsense. I don't remember the last time she took a picture facing front. Or looked at anyone straight on!"

"Well, of course it's rummin' squit she believes int! I knowt, lad. But you mayn't speak ill of your mother, boy! Won't have it." Hugh glared at his younger son. His eyes were no longer as clear Suffolk blue as Gower remembered them. *Owing to all that gin, I suppose.*

"Well, what did she see? Or anyway, what did she *say* she saw in the tea?"

"I'll let her tell you herself," Hugh said softly, gazing at the empty tumbler before him as if forgetting what it was there for.

"Ha! You don't believe it, either!" Gower wiped a final smear of gravy off his plate with the heel of fruit-dotted bread and washed it all down with the last of the milk. He stood up and took his dirty dishes to the sink.

"I'm going to pack and get ready for bed," he announced. "If I'm still awake when Mom comes home, I'll be out to chat. Otherwise, good night, Dad. I'll see you in the morning."

"Good night, then," was all Hugh would allow.

Closing the bedroom door behind him, Gower could hear his father let out a labored breath. He could also hear the clink of glass as Hugh likely poured himself another finger or two of the gin. Gower let out some air of his own. Leaving home, leaving his parents on their own now, to navigate the rough and getting-rougher edges of their marriage while both he and Wendell were away at war, was one more worry he didn't need. *Shoulda volunteered, instead of waiting around, hoping to luck out of the draft. Or, like Dad says, I shoulda stayed in college.*

He sighed again and started to undress. From the moment he had walked onto the campus at Occidental, he knew he was wasting everyone's time, including his own. The guilt he felt about Wendell volunteering while he was at college quickly depleted any enthusiasm he may have had for applying himself to academics. The dean couldn't agree more, dismissing him after not even one semester. *It just didn't* feel *right. . . . Though dying on some battlefield somewhere doesn't, either.*

He fished Mugsy's lucky coin from his pocket. Despite being dropped on the floor of the trolley—a definite no-no in his mother's book—Gower decided some luck might remain, stuck inside. He thought about taking it with him off to war. *On the other hand, five dollars is a lot of money. If Dad is right, and I'm not coming back, it might buy Mom something nice to remember me by.*

2

The Draft Board letter said a small suitcase was all anyone was allowed to bring with them. Gower packed shaving supplies, a toothbrush, and, at his mother's insistence, a change of underwear. *What else?* He stared at the dresser, trying to think of something he might like to take along. *A keepsake. Or maybe a lucky charm. I am my mother's son, after all.*

Staring right back at him was Wendell's official Navy portrait, framed and sitting on the dresser. Movie-star handsome, he grinned back at Gower with a Clark Gable gaze—including the dimples and closely trimmed mustache. From the brokenhearted evidence Gower had seen and heard about, Wendell's smile was nearly as devastating to women as the movie actor's—playful, yet somehow tantalizingly wicked. Gower, on the other hand, favored their mother, the small-town Welsh girl, in both appearance and temperament. Wendell was always somehow more American than "little Mervyn." *Smarter, more talented,* much *better-looking—ever my hero . . . But so hard to live up to.* Deciding he wouldn't be able to face even a photograph of his older brother if he didn't measure up, he decided not to take it.

Partially hidden behind Wendell's portrait was their Welsh grandmother's Bible. When Gower was little, his mother read to him from it every Sunday. He remembered her choosing mainly those passages concerned with daily prohibitions instead of religious philosophy. *Maybe because I was so young. But who cares if you wear something made of both linen and wool? And by the way, I just ate some fat. So, I guess the deal against eating it was thrown out the window—in our house, anyway—a long time ago.*

From "his" drawer, a couple below Wendell's, Gower pulled out the White Owl cigar box full of keepsakes he'd been collecting since before he could remember. He replaced it with the Bible, and pushed it all the way to the back so his mother wouldn't know he hadn't taken it with him. He then opened his little treasure chest with the sole intention of adding Mugsy's lucky coin but was unable to resist reminiscing with his other souvenirs. He sat down on the edge of the bed, placed the box on his lap, and marveled at the magic the totems within it still held.

There were his LA County Lifeguard pins, the medals he'd won for middle distance sprints at Franklin High, and a "real keeper," his ticket stub from the '32 Olympics. Nine-year-old Gower had sat with teenaged Wendell, high up, nearly to the rim of the Coliseum, watching the hundred-meter dash while waving the miniature Stars and Stripes flags their mother had made for them.

The Black American, Eddie Tolan, won that race, and everyone in the crowd cheered long and loudly, including someone a few rows below shouting, *Didjya see that n***** run!*

It wasn't the first time Gower had heard the word, and the shock he experienced at the Olympics was more about why the man said it than what it meant. He figured it was "Negro," but twisted by the speaker into something no longer merely identifying. Instead, it was vilifying and demeaning. But the way the man in the crowd had used it was confusing. It sounded as if he was praising the race's winner. Sitting there on the edge of the bed, he remembered Wendell's attempted explanation of the apparent contradiction as they got off the Red Car and headed up Poppy Peak.

"It's like this . . . At least I think it is . . . You see . . . the guy

was cheering for American *Tolan, but not for* colored *Tolan. So, although that guy might drink a toast to gold medal–winner Tolan tonight at his favorite bar, if Tolan actually did show up there, the guy might just throw him through the window. Or worse."*

It hadn't helped. Only nine and still struggling with his own identity problems, Gower didn't care if Tolan's skin was green or blue or all the colors of the rainbow. *We were so high up in the stadium, all I could tell was that he was American. And that's all that really mattered. Who cares what color he was?*

Any Blacks, and the demeaning words to describe them, remained rare in Gower's experience. There were no "colored people" in the neighborhood, none at work, and very few anywhere he generally went. He encountered them randomly on the streets downtown and sometimes saw them from the trolley window. Besides that time at the stadium, he'd heard the slur only rarely, and only at Franklin High, which, ironically, mainly only white students attended—with a very few Asians sprinkled in—but no Black ones.

Beneath his first aid certificate, Gower found Wendell's silver-plated but heavily tarnished lighter. He flipped open the Zippo and flicked the wheel. The feeble flame conjured up memories of stolen smokes, and of swigs of their father's gin—with Wendell and the Van Zeulen twins hiding under that part of the house overhanging the ravine behind it. They would sip the "borrowed" hooch from a silver-plated flask that once belonged to their dad's dad. It was the only thing they had from either grandfather. *"They're dead,"* was Hugh Gower's pat answer. *"What matter they to you then, eh?"*

And the glove. Among the cigar box treasures was Gower's infamous leather glove—tiny and stiffened with age. One of a pair, his mother explained. She said he'd lost the other one somewhere on the train in from Canada, where their ship had landed at Halifax.

"You wandered away as I napped."

She could never talk about the glove without weeping. Gower was barely three. He remembered none of it. He took a last, loving look at the memories, knowing he might never see them again. Of all the choices of things to take with him, and even though he seldom smoked, he snatched up Wendell's lighter before returning the cigar box to its place of hiding.

Despite thinking they might not be allowed, he added Mugsy's goodbye gift of brass knuckles and his brother's Zippo. He then undressed and got into bed but kept the bedside lamp on, using it to read from where he left off in a recent novel he liked. It was Hemingway's *For Whom the Bell Tolls*. It didn't take him long to get to the end. Robert's horse gets shot out from under him and falls on the American's leg. Pinned to the ground, he lies there with his rifle trained on the fascist officer responsible for beheading his Republican comrades as the *Fascistas* work their way toward Robert's position, hoping to kill him if he is not already dead. *Could I kill anyone if I had to?*

Gower heard his mother come home but pretended he hadn't. He turned off the lamp and lay in the dark, listening to the late April breeze swirling through the small stand of eucalyptus at the back of the house. They'd heard nothing from Wendell since January.

3

The morning of Gower's farewell to parents and home

threatened rain. Over breakfast, he dared ask his mother what she'd seen in the tea leaves.

"I shan't tell you, Mervyn," Elizabeth said, looking away. "It's bad luck if I do."

"It's bad luck for you to tell me about my bad luck?" Gower did his best not to sound sarcastic but realized when he saw her face fall that he'd failed.

"I won't tell," she said, still avoiding his eyes. "No, I daren't."

"Going in late to work," Hugh announced after putting down the phone, "so I can let you off there at the Center, after all."

When the dishes were cleared, they got ready to leave. At the last minute, Elizabeth decided not to go. Instead, she stood alongside her youngest on the walkway just inside the front gate, waiting for her husband to bring the car around.

A few drops of rain fell, but not enough to mind. After a moment or two of silence, Gower could hear his mother sobbing softly at his side. Not wanting to make a fuss and risk her feeling worse, he said nothing. Instead, he stared straight ahead, gripping the handle of the small piece of luggage allowed by the Draft Board. He held it so tightly he could no longer feel his fingers. *If only for her, I'll be back. I swear it.*

He remembered standing very near that same spot he now stood—perhaps he was five—dressed in a sailor suit, standing next to Darla from up the street, a ribbon around her waist. *The pair of us squinting into Dad's Brownie, thrilled at having our picture taken, annoyed by having to stop what we were doing for the sake of it . . . Or is it only seeing the photograph I recall?*

"Memories are what you make of them," he remembered reading somewhere.

"Ni ddylent angen y ddau fy meibion." His mother startled

him by suddenly speaking in Welsh. "They shouldn't have need for both my boys," she went on in English. "Isn't it well enough that Wendell joined?"

Gower thought about reaching for his mother's hand. Afraid of them both breaking down and things getting worse, he decided against it. He let his eyes wander. They found the oil-stained pavement of the driveway. *What's keeping Dad?* For some reason he thought about the deer Mr. Taylor shot beyond the end of their street when Gower was six or seven. He remembered watching him string the animal up by the neck from the eaves of his porch, overhanging the driveway the two families shared. Taylor gutted the carcass and left it to cool, swaying slowly in the late-afternoon breeze, stiff and lifeless at the end of a rope. Gower recalled his fascination with the process. Terrified, yet curious.

He remembered the blood draining from the slit in the animal's belly. First a stream, then a trickle down its legs, down the driveway, toward the street. One door up, banging against their garden fence, the Kalbergs' dog howled all the while. *Maddened, I suppose, by the smell of freshly butchered meat.* Gower's gut tightened when the memory presented him with thoughts of his own demise. *Soldiers die—often horribly. And alone . . . It's a well-known fact.* Submitting to his mother's concerns, he bent down and kissed her on the forehead. As she turned away—embarrassed, perhaps, for showing emotion—he could see a tear wander down her cheek. As Gower fought back one of his own, his dad at last brought the car around and drove his second son off to war.

Hugh said little on the way to the Draft Induction Center, downtown. As usual, Gower had no idea what his father was thinking. Tightly pursed lips offered no clue. It would have to be the man's fading blue eyes to betray him. But Hugh's eyes stuck to the road, where Gower's deep browns couldn't read them.

"A proper pot of tea," the older man muttered when they were nearly as far as Chinatown.

"What?" Gower asked, not sure he'd heard correctly.

"Brew yew a proper pot of tea," his father answered his son without turning to face him. "Tha'sa long the Jerries took for cutting down near whole of a Welsh division. . . . Four hundred dead—'twas near two of every three, lad. As split and splintered, they tell it, as the trees of Mametz Wood, those Taffies were. . . . They don't come back, Mervyn. . . . The Welsh. They just don't."

Gower chewed on his lower lip, straining to hold the words behind till they fought their way through his defenses.

"Uncle Albert made it back, though, didn't he!" he insisted, referring to his mother's brother. She'd kept Albert's official service photo—him wearing the Prince of Wales pin—and proudly displayed the portrait every Armistice Day.

"Aye. . . . Did do. But not his mind, lad," his father said, tapping the side of his head. "Not his mind."

The rest of the drive passed in silence. Twenty minutes later, Hugh pulled the car to the curb. Gower got out and leaned in to say goodbye.

"Mervyn, my son, do well," was all Hugh would allow him from behind the wheel.

"I will," Gower said to the quickly distant car as his father drove it away.

CHAPTER THREE

E Pluribus Unum

1

According to a nearby clock tower, it was quarter to nine. *Here a little early.* A chill ran down Gower's back. He convinced himself it was due to the cool of the morning and not fears of his future—shapeless, intimidating, unknown. But when his restless eyes settled on the mouth of a nearby alley, a smile sneaked across his face. *Me and Wendell and Harvey Fowler ran numbers for the Buffone brothers out of that alley! What was I? Twelve? Thirteen?* He decided it must have been a few years before the Mob sent Levine out to "supervise" what the Brooklynite called "the Mickey Mouse branch" of the gang—then still run by the Buffones. *Mainly me and Harvey, though. Didn't take 'em long to decide Wendell was too girl-crazy to be trusted with money.* Gower remembered how happy he was to be promoted to kitchen monkey at the Jungle Club, where Wendell's time was being split between bandleader and "host for the ladies." *Good thing Dad never found out.*

The gym on Figueroa wasn't far away, either. Gower trained mornings there before taking the trolley to the Y, and on weekends. Mugsy Levine sometimes showed up there with Moose Muscalino and one or two other goons, either on their way back from the ponies or after strong-arming somebody downtown. Mugsy, an amateur, too, in his teens back in Brooklyn, gave Gower his start in amateur boxing. *And got me the job at the Y.* Sitting ringside while "The Welsh Kid" sparred, or whenever he felt like it, the mobster from New York was quick on the trigger to offer "advice" on all things boxing, on all things no matter what. If he thought Gower wasn't listening, "The Welsh Kid" learned to regret it.

"Knock 'em dead, Kid," Gower remembered the unapologetic tough guy telling him during goodbyes in the Y's locker room the day before. *"Seriously, knock 'em dead,"* he repeated after handing Gower the going-away gifts of the five-dollar gold coin and the single fist of brass knuckles. Levine went on to repeat the story about how he and Countess So-and-So happened to meet both Goering and Goebbels in Italy before the war broke out. *"Maybe* nobody'd *hafta go into the Army, Kid, if I'd had those two bozos bumped off when I had the chance. That Eye-talian broad I was goin' with at the time, she had plenty of dough to get the job done, and some cousins over there, too! Woulda done the job for practly nuttin'!"*

"'Scuse me, sir." A voice in the present reeled Gower in from the memory.

A Black street sweeper was trying to finish that part of the sidewalk. A sort of janitor himself at the Beverly Hills Y until the day before, Gower apologized and backed out of the way. *Not drafting Blacks, I guess. Lucky guy. He can go on with his life without having to worry about dodging bullets.* After a sigh, Gower was reaching into his pocket to remind himself where to go when he noticed several other guys carrying small suitcases, and waving what looked like the same letter, so he followed them into the building. *Jeez! Must be a couple hundred guys!* They floundered in the crowded hallways, struggling for air, arguing over places in the figment of a "line," and complaining about all of it.

Barely above the din from the surge of bodies, Gower could hear a constant counterpoint. "We need *men,* not whiny brats"—or a variation thereof—any one of a couple dozen Army clerks could be heard shouting at recruits saying anything beyond what was required.

Apparently, what's required is "Yes, sir, no, sir" and nothing else. Guess that's how it is, and how it's going to be. Isn't that what that song—"You're in the Army Now"—is all about?

In what had maybe been a ballroom, the recruits lined up to receive a cousin of the wicker laundry basket Gower's mom used for carrying the family laundry to and from the line strung from their back porch to the nearest tree. The draftees were ordered to strip to their undershorts and to put everything—including their luggage—inside their basket. If a guy's suitcase was too big to fit, he was made to empty it in front of everyone close enough to watch. He could keep allowable contents if they fit in the basket but had to surrender the oversized baggage. Not far ahead of Gower, one guy had to unpack a framed portrait of a woman. *His grandma? Too old to be his mother.* Gower was very glad his own battered case had passed the basket test. He was pretty sure the Army wasn't going to allow him to bring Mugsy's brass knuckles along if anyone saw them and hoped that, somehow, they never would.

The recruits were then ordered to form five lines—soon very long and full of rubbernecking semi-naked young men. Gower stood there—goose pimpled, surrounded by dozens of other randomly selected potential defenders of democracy—marveling at the variety of what his parents called "pants." *Boxers, briefs, long johns, white, tight, colored, striped, baggy, saggy, stained. Hard to feel heroic in your underwear.* When he arrived at the head of his line, he was handed a form and told to hang on to it, or risk starting over. He needed to surrender the document to the next clerk or doctor—or, for that matter, anyone else wearing more than a pair of undershorts—to add the subsequent piece of required information. He was then asked some general questions about his health and his hygiene, before ordered to undergo cursory inspections of his eyes, ears, nose, and throat before being herded along with the rest of his particular mob into a different, equally large, though nearly empty, room. There, they counted off by eights and were told to stand in a circle, facing outward, but without a stated purpose.

"Must be a military secret," someone joked.

After several suspenseful minutes, and speculation as to why they were facing outward, a doctor and a clerk approached. At least Gower guessed the one guy was a doctor because of the white coat he had on. *"Might be a butcher, though, Kid,"* he could hear Mugsy Levine warning him, as usual, about jumping to conclusions. *"In my racket, you never know."*

Both men were wearing rubber gloves. The clerk held a small bucket and a box of more gloves. Since the recruits were ordered not to turn around, Gower quickly lost visual contact with the wandering pair. "Bend over," he heard someone say from inside the circle.

"Jeezuz Christ!" a co-circler yelled. "What the hell are you doing back there?"

"Rectal exam. Didn't they tell you?"

2

Well, so far, the Army's been full of surprises—none of them very pleasant. He knew his turn to "bend over" was coming, but that didn't make him feel any better, or better prepared for a rubber-gloved finger up his anal cavity. It did help reduce the shock, however, of the same doctor coming around the outside of the circle a bit later—*Jeez, I hope that's a fresh pair of gloves*—cupping Gower's testicles and asking him to turn his head and cough. When the poking and probing came to a merciful end, a clerk in another room typed "Army" in the blank after ". . . fit for service in . . ." on Gower's form, stamped it *1-A*, handed it back, and told him to get dressed.

"You mean I'm free to go?" Gower asked.

At first, the remark earned him merely a puzzled look, but the clerk's expression soon devolved into something far less congenial. "Yeah," the clerk sneered. "You're free to go—into the Army, wise guy."

"Ah." Gower nodded. "When you said, 'Get dressed,' I thought you meant I wasn't going in, after all. Otherwise, I figured I'd be getting a uniform."

"Lobby," the clerk said, still not sure Gower wasn't pulling his leg. "Give my regards to Hitler."

Dressed, and with allowable suitcase in hand, Gower reported in on the ground floor. When told his assigned bus was bound for Fort MacArthur, in nearby San Pedro, he asked around for a pay phone so he could give his parents the good news. "Search me, Mac," a soldier told him. "Anyways, you're out of time. Your bus is leaving PDQ, and if you don't hop on it right now, you'll be AWOL, and then I guess you can call your folks from the federal pen."

Rain began to fall in earnest. The recruits boarded the bus on the Main Street side of the building. They turned west on Fifth, then south on "Fig," where Gower got a fleeting glimpse of the gym from his window seat as they passed. Moose Muscalino was having a smoke out on the sidewalk, staying dry under an awning, and Gower briefly thought about lowering the window to say, "Hey!" but thought the better of it. *Maybe not such a good idea to be seen waving to a fairly well-known local hood.*

From there, "Fig" ran straight south to "Peedro," where Fort MacArthur was located, not far from the port. Owing to Gower's experience on the slower-moving trolley track paralleling their route, he guessed it would take them at least an hour to get there. *But it's Saturday. So, maybe longer.*

He was pretty sure he didn't know anyone else on the bus and thought probably no one else knew anyone else, either. *Kinda know them now, though, I guess, since we spent a couple hours together in our underwear. So . . . sort of a "Brotherhood of the Shorts," maybe?* He turned to his seatmate, a solidly built guy with an impressive forehead. "Gower . . . From Poppy Peak," he said, extending a hand in greeting. "Sure glad we'll be stationed at Fort MacArthur. I'll be close enough to see my parents more often. They're alone now that my brother's in the Navy."

"McCleary . . . Nuts."

"Nuts?"

"Almonds. We grow 'em. . . . In trees. Near Bakersfield. So, we got a 'dozer for digging ditches. It's sorta like a tank, but we use it like a tractor. Knocked over dead trees with it. Pulled 'em out by the roots. Fun as hell. That's why I like tanks. . . . Pretty sure we're not gonna stay long at MacArthur, though. It's only where we get issued our uniforms and stuff. Then we get sworn in and assigned to somewhere else. . . . Wherever it is, I hope they got tanks. I like tanks."

"Hope they feed us, too, before we go," a kid chimed in from across the aisle. He had a fresh crop of acne ripening on his cheeks and forehead. "Kelso . . . Lincoln Heights. Or, really Echo Park, originally, but my parents split, you know, so it's just me and my mom, and I told them that, but they drafted me anyway." His voice trailed off, and the thread of that particular conversation did, too.

McCleary picked up where he left off. "My brother said that was the deal. Went in, in January. Started out at MacArthur. What he couldn't tell me is where he ended up."

"Does your brother like tanks, too?" Gower asked.

"Naw. He likes girls."

Gower nodded and turned again toward the rain-spattered window, somewhat disappointed in the results of his first attempt at friend-making in the Army. *Conversation would help pass the time. Unless somebody drops a truckload of fish or something, the ride down Fig is never very interesting. Shops, houses, schools, a few plots of empty land . . .*

"Jeez, will you look at that!" someone suddenly yelled. "We must've rode this bus all the way to Africa!" A few others laughed when they realized what he meant. "There's n*****s *everywhere*!"

Gower wiped at the fogged-over glass. *Colored people going about their business. Not sure what Africa's like, except for what's in Dad's* National Geographics. *And this isn't anything like it. Guess maybe I know more about Africans than about American Blacks.*

"Might have to start drafting coloreds, too," McCleary said. "Who knows? Maybe they already started. President Roosevelt says we don't have enough soldiers. Not even close."

"There didn't seem to be any colored recruits with us this morning," Gower offered. *Come to think of it, didn't seem to be anyone there who wasn't white.*

"Mighta been Blacks in there somewhere," the tank lover said. "Just kept 'em separate."

Why would they keep them separate if we're all supposed to be doing the same thing?

"Oh, the Army's gonna draft coloreds, all right. . . ." It was pimply-faced Kelso. "Unless someone stops 'em. . . . She's colored, too, you know. That's why they're gonna do it."

"*Who's* colored?" McCleary asked.

"Mrs. Roosevelt!"

3

Gower exchanged a puzzled look with McCleary.

Kelso stuck to his guns. "That's why she's so ugly!"

Is he joking? Or just an idiot? Betting on the latter, Gower decided to play dumb. "Maybe Kelso's right, McCleary," he said with a wink and nudge to the almond farmer's arm. "Why not draft colored men, too? From what I've seen, seems like the Army will take just about *anybody*."

McCleary answered with a nod toward his seatmate. "Yeah, why not?"

The remainder of the ride passed the same way—a busload of small talk, hearsay, misgivings, and bravado. They reached Fort MacArthur as the rain was letting up, and parked near a few earlier-arriving, now-empty buses. The sun pried open a crease in the clouds, so when Gower took his first step onto Army property, he searched the sky for a rainbow.

"Maybe there's a silver lining," someone said.

"The silver lining is," another guy answered, "nothing here's gonna be worse than a finger up your butt."

Gower's group was added to a couple of others, and everyone was ushered into a hall significantly larger than the ballroom downtown. There were soup lines and sandwiches.

First meal courtesy of Uncle Sam! Not bad! Aside from that, the routine was pretty much the same. A sense of familiarity made Gower and the others feel more comfortable, if not a little cocky.

Soon, they were lined up alphabetically and issued their first piece of official Army gear—a large canvas duffel bag with their last name and initials on it. They were told to strip completely down this time, stow their clothes and their luggage in the duffel, and carry it slung over their shoulder by the strap. As he shuffled along in close quarters with dozens of other, nearly identical, naked young men lugging shoulder bags, Gower couldn't help thinking he'd joined a parade of nudist golfers. And when there was no longer a duffel-toting naked guy blocking his view, it was his turn to have a different body part measured—head, chest, arm, waist, leg, foot—at a succession of stations where the corresponding item of his first uniform was provided—cap, sleeveless undershirt, or "vest" as they called it, "blouse" and tie, jacket, boxers, trousers, socks, shoes. All were added to his growing hand-carried pile of "Government Issue" before being told to move nakedly on.

Like an assembly line! The process reminded Gower of some of the newsreels they'd been showing down at the York in recent weeks. They featured factories in Detroit, mainly. But, instead of cars, they were shown making tanks and airplanes and other machines needed to defeat what the papers were calling "the Axis Powers." *Henry Ford, or Alfred Sloan, or some other rich guy always shows up for a few silent seconds, grinning from ear to ear into the camera. War or peace, it doesn't matter. They still make piles of dough. Guess the Army's a sorta factory, too. Turning out the human machines needed for fighting this war.*

Having received every piece of their regular khaki "service uniforms," the recruits were ordered to get dressed and "report for assembly." Looking more like school kids donning costumes for a pageant, they marveled at the mirror images of themselves they saw in each other—helping straighten a tie, righting a wayward cap.

Simply putting on the uniform made Gower feel instantly *more American.* And then, a bit later, inside the fort's cavernous assembly hall, as he and the others stood at attention, massed in formation, one thought came shining through—*E pluribus unum.*

"As the country's motto states," the presiding officer said, reminding them of the Latin phrase's meaning, "we are many, but together we become as one."

No matter how we got here, no matter what we look like, or who we pray to—out of many peoples, one nation.

"I, Mervyn Gower, do solemnly swear that I will support and defend the Constitution of the United States against all enemies, foreign or . . . *domestic. . . .*" *Wow! Never thought about enemies coming from within! Maybe the reason they're sending Japanese to those camps. But why aren't they sending Germans and Italians?*

Gower and the other recruits ended by asking for God's help. Then he saluted—for the first time as a soldier. It gave him a feeling of unusual power—a feeling, he was sure, which they all shared in that moment—born of an aggregate energy, forged into one body, for one honorable purpose—*to fight evil.*

"I read where our Army is seventeenth-largest in the world," McCleary announced for the benefit of anybody bothering to listen. "I think that puts us right behind Portugal. . . . Or maybe it's Belgium." Gower didn't know how many soldiers that was, but he was pretty sure *seventeenth* wasn't big enough to win.

"Now what?" pimply Kelso asked. "Do I get a gun?"

On the way out of the building, they were issued helmets, canteens, leggings, first aid pouches, "entrenching tools," field bags, suspenders—*suspenders? Only Dad wears suspenders, but calls 'em "braces"*—and footlockers to put it all in.

"Hurry up and stow your gear! We ain't got all day, girls!" a decidedly different soldier yelled at them. He was wearing a Mountie-style tall hat. There were three stripes on each sleeve. *A sergeant.* Though taller and straighter, the sergeant looked much older than any of the other soldiers Gower had seen so far that day.

"Get your miserable behinds to that train at the other end of the parade grounds—on the double! We got a war to win!" When the sergeant turned to walk away, the much-shorter Gower could see gray stubble under the guy's lid. The frost on his bean had Gower wondering whether the old soldier was really still an active sergeant, or just a veteran of the First War wearing his old uniform, and come down to help out.

"Heard the other soldiers calling him 'Grandpa,'" a fellow recruit said when he noticed Gower staring. "But only out of earshot. They say he fought with Pershing in France." Gower nodded as he watched "Grandpa" disappear into the throng of dozens, if not hundreds, of his newly minted twins heading for the train.

4

It started to rain again, but only a drizzle. Gower fished Mugsy's knuckles out of his suitcase and stuffed them into his jacket pocket before slinging the duffel's strap over his shoulder. He reached for the handle of his footlocker full of gear and joined the other recruits in the slog across the rain-soaked parade grounds. "Now I know why they call it '*luggage*,'" someone said.

Arriving at the railroad siding, shoes covered in mud, Gower hoisted his gear to handlers at the door of a freight car for that purpose, then waited till it was his turn to pull himself awkwardly into the nearest passenger coach a couple of cars farther up the line. He didn't recognize anyone inside. The car was already nearly full.

He found a seat near the center, on the aisle, and sat down to wait for whatever the Army had in store. Every so often, he could hear the engine releasing steam and supposed the train was as anxious to get going as he decided he was—no matter where they were headed. *There's no choice in the matter now, anyway.* He looked down, marveling at his sleeves, his pant legs—all covered in Army brown. *I'm a soldier now, headed for . . .* where? The thought occurred to him that he might finally get to see a lot more of the America he only knew from books and the movies down at the York.

I guess anywhere would be just fine. Several minutes passed. *Anywhere would certainly beat just sitting here in this packed train car with the windows shut and long ago fogged over—even though it's not that cold outside. Anywhere would beat sitting here in a damp cotton uniform with, I dunno, about a hundred other guys, huffing and puffing in their seats, filling the coach with steam—after dragging our deadweight lockers and duffels over what must have been a hundred yards of mud!*

But they sat. And they sat some more. Gower guessed they sat for nearly an hour before the train made any sound he could associate with locomotion. Finally, the outer carriage doors were slammed shut. The whistle blew. The train moved. Or at least it tried to. Gower wasn't convinced it actually had. And if it had, he was willing to bet that it went at least a few inches backward.

"I heard 'em say it's too heavy," someone said after a few minutes.

"It's because of the mud," someone else added. "We're sinking into the mud!"

They sat. They waited. They got hotter and damper. No one was brave enough to open a window without being ordered to do so. To his great relief, Gower heard the Pullman's outer doors being reopened. Someone was shouting in a familiar voice, quickly outflanking an anticipated rush of fresh air, and entered their carriage ahead of it.

"All right, ladies! Can't keep Hitler waiting, now, can we!" Gower turned to see the gray-haired "Sergeant Grandpa" striding down the aisle. "Don't just sit there!" His rather large, piggish jowls—saddlebags astride a pug nose bent at the bridge from being broken once or twice—shook with rage.

Maybe he was a boxer. Gower felt himself warming up to the guy a little because of the possible kinship.

"Get up off your asses, get out there, and *push* your way to Berlin!" he shouted at them before passing on into the next car full of recruits.

At first nobody moved. The kid seated across from Gower leaned over and whispered. "Is he *serious*?" The Haffa-Taffy from Poppy Peak had to admit it was hard to believe that humans could actually push a train—even this many humans.

In a minute, "Grandpa" was back—furious that no one had budged. "Don't just sit there grinning at me like a bunch of lazy n*****s!" he screamed. The veins up and down the sergeant's face swelled, and he turned red. "I gave you an order!" Gower watched, amazed, as the sergeant yanked the nearest boy-soldier clear up out of his seat, dragged him into the vestibule, and launched him out of the car and onto the muddy gravel several feet below.

"Grandpa" soon popped back into the aisle. "OK. Who's

next?" he said, grinning at them like a rather well-fed skull. No one waited to find out, and Gower jumped up to join them as they scrambled out of their seats before squeezing their way through the doors of the Pullman. After his own forced exit, he turned to look—consistent brown plops forced from carriage rectums, collected in the railbed, waiting for further orders. He guessed their number at well over two hundred.

In the drizzle, "Grandpa" and some other Mountie hat–wearing GIs organized groups of recruits behind each car of the train. Along with all the others, Gower braced his boots against ooze-covered crossties before pressing arms and shoulders to the back of the nearest iron elephant. The beast was cold, hard, wet, and oblivious to his individual existence. He could hear the train's locomotive being forced into gear, if not motion. "On my signal!" Gower could hear the pig-faced sergeant shout and turned his head to look. With a whistle stuffed in his mouth and a hand raised high overhead, "Grandpa" dropped his arm and blew, puff-cheeked, into the pipe.

After only a few dozen seconds of strain, Gower felt himself reach the bursting point. *Impossible!* he decided, and abruptly slipped and dropped to one knee, scraping it on the edge of a timber. But then he had to scramble out of the way. He could hardly believe it. The train was no longer where it had been. Thanks to the boost, it gained momentum. And under its own power, the line of carriages rumbled slowly down the tracks. *We did it.*

"Three cheers for 'Grandpa'!" someone shouted from directly behind Gower's ear. Other recruits joined in.

"Hurray for Sergeant Grandpa! Hurray for Sergeant Grandpa!"

The son of immigrants took up the call. "Hip-hip-hurrah!" Gower shouted, punctuating the cheer with a punch to the air above his head, British-style, as his father had taught him. "Hurrah for Sergeant Grandpa! Hip-hip-hurrah!" He was about to add another chorus when the cheering abruptly died. Another recruit discreetly signaled for him to turn around. At first, all Gower could see was a close-up view of another soldier's necktie. Lifting his head, he locked onto two brown, burning buttons, bursting with rage and about to pop from the old gray-haired sergeant's face. Avoiding the glare, Gower's eyes fell to a lurid pink scar. It was in the shape of the letter "L" carved into one of the man's jowls.

"Gonna make you wish you hadn't done that, boot," the sergeant snarled before turning to walk away.

CHAPTER FOUR

All Aboard!

1

Done what . . . ? Gower stood there, rain running down his face, staring after the veteran sergeant, wondering why the guy was so upset. *Wherever we're going, I sure hope Sergeant Pigface isn't going with us.* Someone nudged him forward.

To avoid another stall, the band of young GIs were ordered to keep pace with the slowly moving train, but not to reboard it till after the last car had cleared the switch to the main line. Because he was one of the last to get on, Gower got stuck in the middle of the carriage, and on the aisle again. "Hope we're going to Texas," the chunky kid next to him said offhandedly, "'cause my uncle lives there." The guy offered over a meat hook of a hand to shake. "Name's Hayton. . . . Santa Monica . . . Some of the guys call me that, Santa Monica, 'cause that's where I'm from. But I sure as hell ain't no saint!" he laughed.

The victim of schoolyard bullies thought briefly about

bringing up the pitfalls of having a female saint for a nickname. He supposed being called "Santa Monica" might be a shade better than "Mervyn the Vermin" but wasn't completely sure. The guy looked like he could handle himself in a scrap, so he decided to forget it.

"Gower. Poppy Peak."

"Hey! Guys!" someone yelled.

Gower looked up to see a two-striper in the aisle at the front of the car, a hand on the back of one of the benches to steady himself against the lean of the train as it navigated another bend in the line, snaking its way north—apparently back toward Los Angeles.

"I'm Corporal Miller," the noncom shouted at them over the sound of *click-clacking* iron wheels. "I'm the duty officer for this car and the next two up ahead."

Like Sergeant Grandpa, Miller seemed older than most of the other soldiers Gower had seen that day. *Though not nearly as old as Pigface.*

"Can't tell you where we're headed. To be honest, I don't have a clue. And that's the way the Army wants it. But I can tell you this—based on the provisions we loaded up, we're going to be on this train for quite a while, so listen up. We ain't traveling first class, that's for sure. No showers on this train—least not for you lugs—and we're not letting you off long enough to take one. A few days on this rattle trap, you're going to be sore and restless and start stinking like stray dogs. So, get comfortable in your seat. You're going to get to know it real well. You'll be sleeping—and for the most part, you'll be eating—with your butt parked at that same location." He advised them to stretch as much as possible, but to resist the urge to get up and walk around—especially while the train was moving. "Uncle Sam needs you to kill Japs and Germans. You can't do that with your ass in a sling. There's a john between each set of cars. Go when it's safe, but don't block the aisles. Do as you're told, no matter what, and we'll all get along just fine. Any questions?"

"When do we eat?" Santa Monica sang out.

Gower smiled. *Mom would have called this guy "well fed."*

"When you see it in front of you," Miller said with a grin. "You're in the Army now, boys! Wherever it is we're going, enjoy the ride. You got no other choice!" With that, he headed on to the next car.

"I know why they won't say where we're going," some kid on the other side of the Pullman said. "'Cause Jap spies might be listening." The comment was met with more than a couple of snickers, making it hard for Gower to tell whether the guy was joking or not.

"Ah, blow it out your butt, Waverly," another recruit yelled from a few rows back. "What do the Japs care where we're going?"

One of the posters Gower remembered putting up for Mr. Scobbs at the Y was about "Loose Lips" being a danger. He never took the warning very seriously. He found himself wondering whether he should start. Meanwhile, the guy named Waverly persisted. "If there's no problem with spies, then how come they're rounding up all the Japanese?"

2

Gower thought Waverly's question was a pretty good one but wasn't completely sold on the government's answer. *Armed soldiers rousting the five-and-dime couple and their baby? Probably losing their business in the bargain. Doesn't seem much different from Jews in Germany getting kicked out of their homes and forced to live somewhere else. Only because of who they are, not because of anything they did, or would ever even think of doing. Hey-Gee's no spy, and neither are they.* He tried to think about something else besides relocated Japanese. *Gonna be a long train ride, like Miller said. . . . This seat is lumpy, and this Santa Monica guy's hogging most of it. . . . Already uncomfortable and the trip's barely begun!*

Gower's first in-person look at his adoptive nation beyond LA got off to a slower start than he would have liked. For the first hour or so, all he could see beyond seatmate Santa Monica's ear was the "backside" of the city. Things got appreciably better when they passed through the freight yards, and started heading east—into and through smaller towns, through orange groves, and past family farms, picking up speed.

"Woooo-woooo!" someone mimicked the engine's whistle. A few other recruits echoed the sentiment. But the feeling quickly faded when the train began to slow.

"Hey!" Gower sang out. "This is Santa Anita!" He recognized the track from photos on the racing forms Moose Muscalino and Mugsy's other boys always seemed to have on them during the season. "Mugsy Levine plays the ponies here!"

"Not anymore, he don't," someone said. "They closed it down."

It certainly looked that way. There didn't seem to be anything going on, at least not related to racing. The parking lot was full of Army trucks and soldiers, some of them armed with rifles and bayonets. And like Sergeant Grandpa, they were all wearing broad-brimmed Mountie-style hats. As Gower rubbernecked to see anything past Santa Monica's imposing melon, Corporal Miller reappeared. "Listen up! We got some official business we gotta take care of here. So, sit tight. It's gonna be a while. If you need to use the john, you know the drill. Otherwise, no one leaves their seats."

When Miller left the car, there was a sudden crush toward the windows. Those lucky recruits already there pressed noses to the glass, straining to see what Miller might be on about. The side away from Gower apparently held more promise. The Welsh Kid joined the aisle jockeys, bobbing and weaving behind more fortunate fellows, trying to get an eyeful. He was pretty sure one of the guys farther back was McCleary, the almond farmer from Bakersfield. He thought about crossing over, if only to catch up with his new friend, but wasn't able to shoehorn his way any closer.

"*I* know why we're here," someone shouted. "It's because of the Japs! They're putting them on the train. They're going with us!"

Suddenly, Gower's interest in finding a better vantage point took on a personal urgency. Hey-Gee Nakamura's parting words—*"No idea"*—still haunted him. *Was Hey-Gee being relocated? Could he be here?!* Gower leaned as far into the gang of gawkers as he could, straining to catch a glimpse of anything going on or anyone he knew. *If not Hey-Gee, maybe Corinne Okamoto from Franklin High. Maybe the shoemaker and his wife from that shop down on York, near the theater.* At the same time, he hoped he wouldn't. Wearing the same uniform as their keepers, he'd be too ashamed to face them.

"Hey, Gower, you wanna see something funny?"

3

Gower turned to look. Santa Monica handed him a large metal button like people wear during political campaigns. In the center of a bull's-eye was a grotesquely distorted face meant to represent a Japanese man.

"California Jap Hunting License; Open Season; No Limit," the button read.

"Pretty funny, hunh?" Santa Monica chuckled.

Gower didn't know what to say. He slumped down in his seat and handed it back. Since Pearl Harbor, he knew he was supposed to hate "the Japs." He knew he was supposed to think of them as subhuman, as monsters—like the ones in the posters he put up for Mr. Scobbs. *Everyone says you can't trust 'em—any Jap—because of what they did to us in Hawaii.*

"They're sneaky and shifty," he remembered a classmate saying. *"They squint like that on purpose so you can't tell what they're thinking!"*

Gower didn't feel at all threatened by Hey-Gee Nakamura. *Jeez, the guy introduces himself as "Herb" half the time—just so he seems more "American."* Gower couldn't imagine anything fishy going on with the Japanese couple running the shoe repair store, either. *Always laughing and joking—poking fun at themselves for their poor English. And Corinne was the only Japanese kid in our class—just another girl, trying not to stand out. Trying to fit in.*

Even before Pearl Harbor, there was some anti-Japanese feeling in school because of what the Japanese army was doing in China. He didn't remember kids calling Corinne Okamoto a "Jap," but he didn't hang around with her, so he really didn't know if they called her anything at all. There was a Korean kid named Sammy that Gower did hang around with. Everyone thought Sammy was Japanese until Gower vouched for him not being one, and they stopped calling him names after that. *Or anyway, they stopped calling him "Jap."*

If Wales bombed Pearl Harbor instead of Japan, would soldiers with bayonets be coming for my mother? And Wendell and me, too, because we're half-Welsh? Or would they only be half-interested? And, anyway, how would they be able to tell us Welsh from other "white" people?

As he sat in the idled train with the other recruits at the racetrack, Gower tried to imagine how it would feel to be herded off like so many head of cattle after being forced to sell, or maybe simply give away, all their property and any belongings that wouldn't fit into the single suitcase that the newspapers said they were allowed. *If Hey-Gee, or Corinne, or the shoe repair shop people are here, I'd vouch for them, too, if anyone asked. They aren't the enemy. They couldn't be. It just isn't possible.*

Bang-clang!

Gower was launched into the back of the seat in front of him. He looked up to see Corporal Miller practically flying into their carriage from the car ahead as the Pullman lurched a few feet backward.

"Jeezuz!" Miller said. "That's just what I came in here to warn you boots about! Some cars have been added to our train."

"Has to be Japs," Santa Monica whispered. "I can smell 'em a mile away. If I meet up with any Japs on this train, Gower, I swear I'm going to strangle 'em with my bare hands."

Gower thought about two possible responses—punching Santa Monica in the nose, or calling him out on it. He decided silence was golden, at least for the time being. *If this train ride is going to be as long and as torturous as Miller says it is, I don't wanna make it any worse.*

4

Another thing Miller came to tell them about was chow. They ate it at their seats. Gower was amazed by both the meal's instant availability and its decidedly unsavory nature. When he finished eating "US ARMY FIELD RATION M-1 UNIT (or M-2 or M-3) MEAT & BEANS (or MEAT & VEGETABLE HASH or MEAT & VEGETABLE STEW)," he still wasn't entirely sure what it was he'd just shoveled into his mouth.

Better than nothing.

"Says you!" he could hear nightclubbing Mugsy Levine setting him straight.

Not long after the dinner debris had all been collected, the Pullman carriage convulsed without warning once again. Gower and some of the others went through a quick and alarming combination of "attention" and "fall out" when the locomotive's energy took them by surprise. His partially digested M-1 unit nearly made a curtain call. The train proceeded to churn and chug a bit before lunging ahead—with, or without, any Japanese on board. Corporal Miller denied knowing.

An hour or so down the line, Gower was pretty sure Santa Monica had fallen asleep. His doll-faced seatmate bobbed gently up and down on their shared upholstered bench, like some giant, khaki-covered baby. With his large, round head propped against the window, he fogged and then defrosted the glass with every breath. But the "saint" wasn't the only recruit sawing logs. Gower could hear snoring from up and down the aisle. His own lids had grown heavy with fatigue, twitching open only when light shot in from the windows and bounced around the coach, splashing onto sleeping soldiers, making them seem to writhe and wriggle. *As if rising from the grave.* And as he watched the silent picture horror show, a truth stole into the carriage, leaned over, and whispered into Gower's ear.

"Some will see neither home, nor family, again."

In a Pullman full of strangers, he felt ever more lost and alone. *Maybe how it was when I wandered away from Mom, on the train down from Canada. . . . Or when she left us for*

Wales. I was only five. "Your mum's gone home to relations, boys," he remembered Mrs. Bailey telling them. *Dad couldn't handle his drink, his real estate agency, and his two boys by himself, so me and Wendell were sent to live with the Baileys down the block.*

"Your dad needs time alone to sort himself out, lads. So, make your peace with it," Sid Bailey told them. *"Jump and tumble. Oi, jump and tumble,"* he advised. *"Be brave on't, now, my lads, you must be brave. You must."*

"Peacock. Poppycock." Wendell would whisper the words at night to console me. His victory cry during games of hide-and-seek. Him and me and the Van Zeulen twins sneaking over the wall, into the garden of that huge house on the other side of Poppy Peak. Full of mazes, and guarded by peacocks! Who would have guessed? Scared the you-know-what outta me the first time I heard them. "Peacock! Poppycock!" became our code phrase for "all is well," even though maybe things really weren't. Gower managed to smile at that part of the memories, but not the next. *Mom stayed away a couple months that first time. I thought she was never coming back. Pretty sure Wendell thought so, too, but he was probably trying not to scare me, so he didn't show it.*

"You knowt's why?" Gower remembered Sid Bailey asking to silence and head shakes. *"'Tis 'cause of his brothers, tha' your dad's tippin' a glass, eh. The lot of 'em, in the Great War, they was—all, save your dad, eh? He left for America before all that, then, dint he? 'E's the regret, then, eh? Got your dad on the wonk, that. . . . But you darn't say squit about it, lads. Jump and tumble on't. Jump and tumble, says I."*

Sure hope Dad stops drinking again—and this time for good! Not sure working in the college lab helps or hurts. Doesn't have to worry about customers anymore—unless the professors count—but it puts him awfully close to some of the stuff he'd need to make more booze. As he had on the train in from Canada, Gower rode on into an unknown land, as a stranger.

5

Despite droopy lids, doubts and regrets separated Gower from slumber. One question kept popping to the top of his list. *Could I kill a man?*

"It's either him or you, Kid," Mugsy offered up more than once from ringside. *"What's it gonna be?"*

Gower's eyes drifted aimlessly around the coach, seeking solace if not answers. They settled on those of a fellow recruit. He thought maybe it was the guy they called Waverly. The other soldier offered Gower an unconvincing grin and a nod of recognition.

But his doubts about fulfilling his soldierly duties were all that came to Gower's mind. And, as if on cue, he and Waverly looked elsewhere. Out the windows, there was nothing to attract or distract him. *No towns. No lights at all. Maybe passing through a desert—empty, endless, brooding. A perfect match.*

He thought about his parents and their delicately balanced marriage. *Even if me and Wendell survive the war, we'll be away for months, maybe years. Without at least one of us there between them, how will they manage?*

"Jump and tumble . . . Be strong."

Assuring himself that Santa Monica was actually sleeping, Gower dug Mugsy's brass knuckles from his coat pocket. Keeping his boxing mentor's strange, but somehow appropriate, going-away gift partially hidden in his lap, he marveled at it. *"Knock 'em dead, Kid."* Somehow, gazing at the symbol of violence provided the draftee with a moment of peace, reminding him of his love of boxing and of home, and of friends he wouldn't be seeing again soon, if ever. *Maybe Mugsy's not the best person to look up to, but he's sure been good to me. "Taught me all I know about boxing in the ring, and about how to get to where you wanna go," isn't much of a stretch.* At the oddly comforting thought, he felt a bit of relief. And before long, he could feel himself surrender to the gentle, soothing sway of the carriage. *Like a cradle. Like a mother's arms.* He gripped the gifted "knuckle dusters" between his own joints of flesh and blood before folding them over his midsection. A few minutes gone, he drifted off to sleep.

There, he found himself toddling down the aisle of a different train, wearing a coat, a too-big cloth cap, and the leather gloves of his mother's eternal regret. All around him were sleeping people he didn't recognize.

A stranger lunged for his tiny, leather glove–covered hand.

No!

Jerked alert by a rush of thunder, Gower recoiled against a sudden crush of air. Pounding by was another train. *Much faster!* With it, insistent, throbbing, garish lights forced themselves inside the Pullman, fired and faded, reignited in staccato bursts of brilliance as he blinked back each succeeding fusillade of reborn versions, variations of the scene around him—as if inside a kaleidoscope of sleeping soldier brothers, palsied, then slumped in any possible posture, seemingly dead, fallen on a flickering field of battle, pocked and barren, completely gleaned of living things—save one.

One being, neither dead nor sleeping, stood by, adjacent, but pulsing in and out of sight, in sync with the passing train. It stared at Gower and grinned, as if in kinship, as if in friendly recognition.

Gower's eyes fought against the flashing, blinding lights,

to see, to rationalize this spirit, too small to be a fellow warrior. The apparition lingered, but a few more syncopated frames of fleeting chiaroscuro before it vanished—as if kidnapped by the passing express.

A boy . . . A Japanese boy?

CHAPTER FIVE

Getting to the Heart of It

1

Later, much later, Gower was awakened by a neck-whipping jolt. Instead of lights from a passing express, filling most of his field of vision toward the window was a large, slumbering man, covered in light brown clothing. Beyond the man was an impressive stretch of wavy beige, horizontal streaks. *Desert. No wonder I'm sweating.* The sky above it had been daubed in colors he most usually identified with dawn. A rude series of bucks and jerks followed, before one final, metallic screech abruptly ended the discovery process, and his presence was accounted for. *Still on a train, heading into the sunrise.* He looked down at his own lap. He was also covered in light brown clothing. *I'm a soldier, in a train car full of them. . . . And Mugsy's brass knuckles are gone. Shit! The Japanese boy! He musta stole them!*

Frantic fingers felt for the going-away gift—on his lap, in his uniform, everywhere on the sparely upholstered bench seat he shared with the overripe fellow private. *Santa Monica?! If anyone figures out those brass knuckles are mine . . . ! Kicked out of the Army after not even twenty-four hours? That's* not *going to sit well with Mom and Dad. Sheezuz! Worse for them than sending their youngest son off to war would be having him sent right back in disgrace a day later!*

"What?" Santa Monica huffed when he noticed Gower giving him the bug eye.

OK. Probably not him. Suspicion fell to others close at hand. *Can't ask for help or let on I might be desperate. Someone could get the idea I'd be willing to pay to get them back. I know what that game is all about. I used to work for the Buffone brothers—and I got no intention of playing!*

After a few minutes of trying to read the faces of the closest recruits, while nonchalantly leaning in different directions to peer into corners without leaving his seat, Gower gave up the hunt. Instead, he sat there thinking about the last time he saw Mugsy's knuckles and what had happened since then. *The guy a few rows back. That Waverly guy. And . . . a Japanese boy. Was the kid even real? And if he was real, did he ever come near enough to steal the brass knuckles?*

"A-tennn-*hut*!" Before Gower could come up with an answer, Corporal Miller burst into the carriage. Pig-faced, gray-haired Sergeant Grandpa from Fort MacArthur was right behind him.

"Jeezuz!" Santa Monica said under his breath. "Thought we left that geezer standin' in the rain back in Peedro!" Gower endorsed the sentiment with a grim-faced nod.

"Good morning, ladies!" Pigface grinned from underneath his high hat, now stained with sweat salts above the brim. Apparently, he was going to be with them till the bitter end of the train ride, if not beyond.

"Let's get a few things straight, right off the bat." The sergeant's eyes suddenly flared. "You miserable bastards are what we call *boots.* We call you "boots" 'cause there ain't nothing lower than a boot but the belly of a snake." He swept the recruits with a sneer fit for a matinee villain. "We don't call you *snakes,* 'cause *they* got our respect! On Corporal Miller's command, you boots will detrain and stretch your legs. Morning chow's out on the platform."

"Now we're talking!" Santa Monica whispered. "A decent meal!"

The sergeant wasn't finished. "You will *not* leave the platform. You *will* address everyone above you in rank—which, as of now, means pretty much anything that moves—with 'yes, sir' or 'no, sir,' including 'specially any snakes you happen to come across. You got it?"

The question was greeted with random mumbles and a nodding of heads. "I can't *hear you*!" the sergeant screamed. "Boots got no brains. But they got tongues. Use 'em!"

"Yes, sir!" Gower joined the chorus of voices.

"The platform is on the *north* side of this train," the sergeant went on. "If you don't know your compass points from dick, and you exit on the *south* side of this train, you *will* fall on your shit-sucking face. We will leave you there, your scrawny behind stuck in the air for the vultures, and you *will* become a permanent part of this goddamned desert. Is *that* clear?"

"Yes, sir!" came the unanimous answer.

"Do *not* fraternize with anyone not in uniform," the sergeant continued. "For you lowlifes who don't know what 'fraternize' means, it means 'shoot the shit.' Is that clear?"

The second-day soldiers again shouted affirmation as the old sergeant calmly strode to the middle of the car, stopping adjacent to Gower's bench. Even with his head lowered, the recruit from Poppy Peak couldn't help noticing one of the man's fists methodically pounding the palm of the other. *Holy cow! The guy's a southpaw!* When Gower dared look a little higher, one corner of the sergeant's mouth had forced the rest of it into a full-on snarl, aimed right at Gower's broken nose. The unpolished "boot" blinked. He could feel cold sweat trickling down the nape of his neck.

"At least *one* of you knuckleheads has figured out there are others on this train not wearing uniforms. And maybe that stupid boot even *fraternized* with one of them. . . . If *any* of you ladies are caught fraternizing with *anyone* on this train not wearing a uniform, I will personally make you wish you hadn't." The sergeant then nodded down at Gower and winked before turning to pass on to the next carriage.

"How 'bout that! The guy's a lefty," Gower could hear Mugsy saying at his ear. *"So, do us both a favor, this time, will ya, Kid, and don't walk into one. Got a sawbuck riding on you."*

The ex-boxer chewed nervously on his lower lip. *So, the Japanese boy is real. And maybe stole Mugsy's knuckles.*

"Dis-s-s-s-s . . . *missed*!" Corporal Miller shouted. "Forty-five minutes for chow!"

2

The Pullman came to life. Gower couldn't move. It was as if all his strings had been cut. *The kid took Mugsy's brass knuckles, and if Sergeant Grandpa finds out they're mine, this is gonna be my first and last full day in the Army.* He didn't snap out of it till Santa Monica tapped him on the arm with the back of a beefy hand. Gower immediately gave way. *Anywhere between this guy and food is an undefendable position.*

Out on the platform, a blinding sun and withering heat didn't help sweeten Gower's mood much. But spotting brainy

McCleary at the end of one of several chow lines sure helped. He joined him for what turned out to be a much less mysterious first Army breakfast of "US ARMY FIELD RATION C, B UNIT, BISCUIT, CONFECTION, BEVERAGE."

"Level with me, Gower," the almond farmer started in. "How'd you get on the wrong side of Hogjaw Thornton so fast? Gotta be some kinda record."

"'Hogjaw'? Is that what they call him? Been thinking 'Pigface' was a pretty good name for that guy. Glad to know I was close. You riding in the same car?"

McCleary nodded. "The kid with pimples—Kelso—I saw him in there, too."

Now certain Hogjaw's reprimand had something to do with the Japanese boy or Mugsy's knuckles, or both, Gower wasn't sure McCleary could be trusted with all the details. He decided to play it close to the vest till he got to know him better. "Don't know why Hogjaw's taken such a liking to me, McCleary. Just lucky, I guess. Maybe it's because I called him 'Grandpa.'"

"'Grandpa!'" McCleary laughed. "That's right! I remember some guy calling him that after we pushed the train. Was that *you*?!" He took a pack of cigarettes out of his blouse pocket and tore open the wrapper. "Smoke?"

"Thanks." Gower reached for one. "But I wasn't the only one calling him that—despite what he thinks." Happy for the chance to use it, he pulled out Wendell's lighter. It sputtered a bit but was up to the task.

McCleary took a long draw before letting it out slowly. "Thanks. Hogjaw probably coulda called it quits years ago and collected a pension. But like I been saying, the Army's kinda desperate. Needs all the help it can get. Even a guy like that."

Instead of lighting up, Gower sat staring at the gifted

cigarette. He wasn't much of a smoker. Part of the reason was the price of tobacco. *Maybe save it for later.*

"They say he was with Pershing when they chased Villa back into Mexico. Hey," he added when he noticed Gower abstaining, "along with the chow, we get a ration of these, free, ya know."

"Really? Well, in that case . . ." Gower was lighting up when he heard an approaching train. It was speeding toward them, also heading east. "Why can't we go that fast? Get us wherever we're going sooner, and leave Sergeant Hogjaw behind."

"Ain't that the prettiest thing you ever saw?!" McCleary gushed.

"The train?" It was a freight, made up mainly of flatcars. They were loaded with tarp-covered crates and brown-painted Army vehicles, including trucks and a few of those strange-looking things Gower heard some other guys calling "jeeps."

"Naw! The tanks!"

There were at least eight of them, two to a car. Behind the cargo came a few passenger coaches. *Uniformed men at the windows.* Some waved. Some nodded. Some just stared at the new recruits as they rushed past them. *Black soldiers!*

Kelso wandered over and inserted himself into the conversation. "Hey! Were *all* those guys n*****s?"

The train full of colored soldiers soon vanished farther into the desert. "Told ya, Kelso, we're going to need 'em," McCleary said.

Even if all of them weren't Black, that was certainly a lot more Black men than I've ever seen outside of Dad's National Geographics*!*

"Hope they're not going where we're going. . . . Hey, will ya look at that!" Pimply-faced Kelso nodded toward something going on farther down the platform. "The Pigeon's kissing Hogjaw's butt!"

Several boots within earshot turned to look. Leading a half dozen recruits in calisthenics was the guy Gower recognized from the night before. *Maybe he saw the Japanese kid, too!*

"Waverly," McCleary explained, fingering the go-getting leader of the workout. "They call him 'The Pigeon' 'cause they think he's a snitch. You know, 'Stool Pigeon.' Always sucking up to Hogjaw."

Maybe that's how Hogjaw found out about the boy. Waverly ratted on me! So, maybe he's the one who swiped Mugsy's knuckles! Why would the kid want 'em, anyway? Even if he knows what they're for, they're way too big for his hand!

A few minutes later, Miller said they'd be stuck at the siding for another half hour or so. He ordered them back on the train, "Where you can cool your heels."

"Is he joking?" someone asked. "About as hot inside that damned train as it is out here!"

Before mounting the steps of the Pullman, Gower turned to see a dozen or so armed GIs spilling out from a carriage up ahead. They took up positions on the perimeter of the far end of the platform, and then turned to face the three or four coaches at the front of the train, rifles angled across their chests. The desert sun glanced off the blades of bayonets fixed to the muzzles. *Japanese internees are definitely on this train—lots of 'em. Who knows. Maybe Hey-Gee's on it, too. "No idea," he told me. No idea where he'd be after that. Never saw him look so concerned. Like he was just waiting to be hunted, rounded up, and sent off to God-knows-where.*

3

Back inside the coach, Gower was happy to find that Kelso had commandeered his old seat. While Kelso was in the middle of sharing a laugh over the "Jap hunting license" with Santa Monica, Gower slipped into the goofy kid's vacated spot across the aisle, and back a couple of rows, nodding an apology to his new neighbor as he did so. That seat put him closer to McCleary. *A much more interesting guy to talk with. Got a lot on the ball. Seems to know the score.*

". . . based on how long we've been gone," McCleary was explaining to anyone who cared to listen. "So, I figure we're somewhere between Yuma and Tucson—on our way to El Paso."

El Paso. Merely the name "*El Paso*" conjured up Western novels Gower had read, and shoot-'em-up matinees he'd seen down at the York. "Wonder if there's going to be any cowboys or maybe an Indian or two where we're headed," he said offhandedly to the recruit sitting next to him. "Not that it matters where we're going, I guess, 'cause we're going to go there just the same."

"Bucoda," his seatmate said, offering a hand to shake. "Anywhere's better than where I was. But wherever it is, I hope it ain't this hot."

Gower completed his half of the greeting. "Gower. Poppy Peak."

"Me, I'm from Boyle Heights. You know, just this side of Little Tokyo. Where all the Japs lived before we kicked 'em out."

"I know some Japanese who don't live there," Gower offered.

"You mean you *knew* some who didn't live there. None of those sneaky bastards are left anywhere in LA, last I heard.

Least, I hope not. You know what, though? The bad thing about getting rid of those yellow sons of bitches is the n*****s and greasers moving in there instead. Now they're calling it '*Bronzeville*'! Get it?!" Bucoda laughed at his own joke. Gower didn't bite. "Don't know about the rest of these guys," Bucoda went on, "but I can't wait to get out there and kill me a bunch of those slant-eyed little bastards."

"I'll go up against anyone they tell me," Gower said. "But I hear it's the Marines and the Navy fighting the Japanese now, not the Army. Not since MacArthur left the Philippines." Bucoda cocked his head in disbelief. Gower aimed for the almond farmer. "The Army's not fighting the Japs anymore—ain't that right, McCleary? It's the Navy and the Marines."

McCleary nodded. "Pretty much."

"Might send us to Africa to fight the Germans, though," Gower went on.

"We're gonna be fighting the Krauts in *Africa*?" Bucoda asked, seemingly stunned by the prospect.

"Not yet," McCleary told him. "But that's what people say."

"Come *on*," Bucoda said, convinced they were pulling his leg. "You mean *Africa*, with lions and tigers? And those . . . whatchacallems? You-*bang*-ees? With spears and stuff?"

Gower winked over at McCleary. "Yep."

Bucoda turned away, staring out the window. "Africa," he muttered. "Don't that beat all."

"Where is Africa, anyway?" Gower heard Kelso asking Santa Monica.

"It's where all the n*****s came from, dummy," Santa Monica said. "Whaddya think?"

Gower sighed. He leaned back in his seat. He couldn't believe he'd been in the Army only a day. He pulled his cap down over his eyes and tried unsuccessfully to nap. There was simply too much rolling around in his head to allow it. He was dying to tell someone about the Japanese boy—ask them if they'd seen anything and if they knew what happened to Mugsy's brass knuckles. He wondered if Waverly took them and told the sergeant. *They don't call him "The Pigeon" for nothing, I guess. And how am I gonna explain why I had the knuckles in the first place? "A well-known gangster gave 'em to me"?*

4

Before Gower could get too worked up, the train was yanking him and the other boots deeper into the America he had always wanted to see with his own eyes. Mile after mile, staring out the window past Bucoda, or toward the view on the other side of the car, he watched and waited for something he could write home about. After convincing himself they must be in Texas, he heard McCleary announce they were likely still in New Mexico.

"I think Lordsburg's around here somewhere," the almond farmer offered. "You know . . . *Stagecoach* . . . Andy Devine . . . 'The *vaqueros*! They ran off!'" he added, doing his best imitation of the portly actor's famously whiny voice from the John Wayne film. No matter where their train actually was, the view beyond Bucoda's ear was mainly desert, stretching in all directions—impressive to the point of overwhelming. There wasn't anything specific to catch and hold his attention—certainly no cowboys or Indians. *No John Wayne riding by.*

"A whole lotta nothing, that's for sure," Bucoda said, breaking the silence. "A welcome change from the city, though, dontcha think? Except for the heat—and drowning in my own sweat. I don't know about you, Gower, but I'm damned glad to get away. Pop ran out on us, you know—Mom and me and my sisters. He was a drinker. And then, a few years ago, she goes and ties up with this new guy, a real jerk. Getting drafted was a great excuse for leaving. Shoulda volunteered a long time ago, ya know, but I was worried about leaving them with that bum still living there. . . ."

Gower could relate to a parent's drinking but wasn't interested in discussing it with more or less a stranger. Despite growing up in Los Angeles, it was still a bit of a shock whenever he heard Americans he'd just met serve up unrequested tidbits about their private lives. *By comparison, my family are monks, sworn to silence!*

Despite being told some agonizingly personal details, Gower took a liking to Bucoda for his honesty and liked him even more when the guy offered to switch places so he could at last see the scenery without someone's head in the way. Gower happily accepted. His joy was short lived when the train slowed to a crawl. The unobstructed landscape on both sides of them vanished behind lines of idled freight cars. *A railyard!*

"Will ya look at that!" Santa Monica suddenly shouted. "Mexicans! Sneaking in like rats, looking for a handout!"

In the dwindling light, Gower could see small groups of figures darting out from under nearby freight cars as they rolled past.

"If you believe the papers," the almond farmer added, "they're spies, working for Germany!"

"Naw, I heard it's the Boyle Heights wetbacks in their zoot suits!" somebody else offered up. "They're the ones!"

Gower had to suppress a laugh. *Zoot suits! I used to wear that style. Wendell and Harvey Fowler, too! Wonder if anyone ever supposed I was a wetback. Probably not. A German spy? Maybe. Some people'll believe anything!*

Miller popped in to confirm they'd reached El Paso. "We're about to be dragged through some bone-jarring switches, boots, so you're gonna have to wait till afterward for evening chow. A different railroad company's locomotive is coming to hitch us up in the morning. So, we're gonna be sleeping somewhere in this freight yard tonight." To everyone's added disappointment, "M-1 UNIT (or M-2 or M-3) MEAT & BEANS (or MEAT & VEGETABLE HASH or MEAT & VEGETABLE STEW)" was again the only thing on the menu.

"Hope they make the Japs on this train eat the same stuff as us," Bucoda said as he picked at the prepackaged meal. "And they choke on it."

Gower tried to imagine what it was like for the Japanese families huddled in the carriages up ahead. All he could think of were the desperate refugees he'd seen so many times in the newsreels down at the York. *Hard to imagine the level of hatred it would take to do them harm, much less kill them.*

"I hope they let them starve," Santa Monica added, mid-mouthful.

Later, well past sundown, and despite open windows, Gower was convinced the railcar full of men without showers or a change of underwear had taken on the aroma of very old cheese. The heat seemed to cling to him like a shrunken skunk sweater. Quite a few of the bugs arriving with darkness apparently decided he smelled delicious. He was soon scratching at the results on his bare neck and hands. Meanwhile, the bench he was sharing with Bucoda was no more comfortable than the one he'd shared with Santa Monica. He could no longer feel his butt and wondered if he'd worn it off completely. All of it made sleep hard to come by and provided the young soldier with plenty of idle time to come up with what he decided was "Gower's Law"—*The only thing worse than trying to sleep in your seat on a train moving through the desert, is trying to sleep in your seat on a train* not *moving through the desert.*

5

In the morning, they again dined on "B UNIT, BISCUIT, CONFECTION, BEVERAGE" where they sat. If that disappointment wasn't enough to shake them, Miller announced that Waverly, The Pigeon, had been made duty officer for their carriage. There was an *"I told you so!"* wink from Kelso across the aisle, and more than a few eye rolls at the news, as the train headed out of the freight yard. "Shut the windows and keep them shut till after we've left the yard," Miller added. "On the way outta here, we're gonna be so close to other trains you could lose your nose if you stick it in other people's business. Duty Officer Waverly will let you know when it's OK to open them back up again." Reluctantly, Gower complied. But when he closed his precious window, he discovered it was caked on the outside with reddish grime. It was more like a stucco panel than a pane of glass. He waited impatiently to pass through the last of the yard's hip-twisting switches and for DO Waverly's OK to drop the sash so he could feast his eyes on the Lone Star State of his fantasies.

After several minutes of straight track beyond the railyard, Gower turned to look for Waverly, the DO. The Pigeon had flown the coop. There was no one around to give him window-opening permission. The train was picking up speed. Through a clear streak in the grime, Gower could see they'd left El Paso behind. *Don't wanna press my luck with Hogjaw. Already on thin ice as it is. If Kelso and McCleary have the straight dope on this Waverly guy, he won't hesitate to rat me out. Maybe he already spilled the beans about the Japanese kid! Certainly don't want to make things any worse. But I sure as shootin' want to see if Texas is anything like the rootin', tootin', pistol-packin', bad guy–smackin' place in the books and movies!* He sat up as tall as he could and searched again for Waverly. The DO was definitely missing in action. He turned and looked to Bucoda for support.

"Why not?" Bucoda told him, as if he'd read his seatmate's mind.

"Where the buffalo roam!" Gower exclaimed before standing up and literally throwing caution to the wind.

"Hey, you!" The Pigeon shouted from somewhere down the aisle. "I didn't say you could open that window!"

"Relax, Waverly," Bucoda told him. "Gower's only taking the initiative. Like the Army wants him to do. You're the DO, aren'tcha? You oughta know that. Says so in the handbook!"

"Uhhh? Well, yeah . . . I suppose. . . ." When it was clear that Waverly didn't have an answer, everyone else in the coach who wanted to see Texas followed Gower's lead. They opened their windows and waited for Rex, Tex, Buck—or even Gabby—to come galloping by. The first hour or so disappointed, but they did at least get a hint about where they were headed. While rolling through a curve, gawkers inside the "bend" of the train learned at least the name of their new hosting railroad. "*Missouri Pacific*" was printed on the engine's coal tender, big and bold. None of the boots was willing to lay odds they were headed back toward the Pacific. All bets were on Missouri.

"Northeast of here," McCleary told them. "With a whole lotta Texas in between."

The hours rolled by. Lunch came and went. The "range" Gower had heard Bing Crosby singing about a million times on the radio, the "range" he'd been dreaming and reading about—not to mention all the other singularly *American* stuff from the Saturday matinees down at the York—never showed up. No buffalo roamed. No deer nor antelope played. A few scrawny cows dotted an astonishing expanse of slightly rolling, and mostly very empty, plains. A few possibly endless fences. One or two rivers. That was about it. *On this particular range, at least, seems like nobody's home.*

"Actually, the same river," the almond farmer clarified. "We already crossed it once." No one bothered to ask McCleary how he knew.

Much later that afternoon, hope was briefly renewed. "A cattle drive!" someone shouted.

The almond farmer quickly set them straight. It was a stockyard on the outskirts of a city, the largest they'd seen since leaving LA. "It's just little dogies destined for the slaughterhouse, boys—same as some of us, I guess you could say." McCleary's realistic, but rather discouraging, words put a bullet in the head of Gower's expectations for the Lone Star State—by then already very low. Only one Texas legend remained intact. The place was huge. They were getting close to dinner and hadn't finished with it yet.

During that third restless night, trying to sleep in his seat on a moving train, Gower thought he heard voices—two men talking. He woke bathed in sweat but shivering slightly, scratching at his arms and legs. He wondered if he'd caught something or was simply reacting to bug bites. To his surprise, cool air instead of warm was pouring in through the window. He leaned over and closed it before deciding he had to piss. He pulled himself up by the back of the bench in front of them and stepped carefully over his seatmate, Bucoda, who was sawing some serious logs. He decided the voices were coming in through the vestibule, from the car ahead of them, so he went the other way for the toilet.

Inside the john, the boot braced himself against the train's rock and sway with one hand while directing his stream with the other. As he stood waiting to finish, a flicker in the otherwise lightless nightscape caught his eye. Something big was burning near the top of a hill. The train rounded a bend, bringing the fire closer. A chill shook Gower through. *A burning cross.* The flames conjured up newspaper photos of Black men, beaten and burned, hanging from a tree, hanging from a lamppost. "Ku Klux Klan," he told himself and realized he was peeing on the floor.

CHAPTER SIX

Face to Face

1

Screeching steel wheels roused Gower from sleep the next morning. A final *jerk* from the brakes did the job for Bucoda and the others. Gower sat there for a moment scratching absently at bug bites on his wrists and neck, staring out the window without focusing on anything in particular. *Wonder if any of the other guys saw the burning cross last night. Maybe I ought to tell someone. But tell 'em what? Guess I'll just add it to the list of mysteries already stuffed under my hat—the Japanese boy, Mugsy's missing brass knuckles, and whether Waverly's in Hogjaw's pocket or not.*

The train rolled slowly to rest in the bow of a shallow curve, exhaling as it did so. "What's cooking out there, Gower?" Bucoda asked. "Anything worth a look?"

Usually, at a bend in the track, anything on that side of the train, fore and aft, was clearly visible. "Nothing," he told his seatmate, surprising himself with the truth of it.

"Fog!" Kelso exclaimed. "We're at the ocean!"

"We've been heading north since we left El Paso, genius," Bucoda said and smirked. "The only ocean up ahead's the one at the North Pole. You don't see any penguins out there, do you?"

"On a northeast heading," McCleary corrected. "We're no farther than Arkansas. Likely in a river valley. Same as the Tule fogs we get back home. And by the way, no penguins at the North Pole. Only found in the Southern Hemisphere—except for the Galápagos variety."

Unlike all the other mornings, no one outranking the recruits showed up to roust them awake. Not Miller, not Hogjaw, not even the brand-spanking-new duty officer, Waverly the Pigeon. A few of the boots got tired of waiting for permission and headed for the can. Not knowing what else to do, and waiting to be told to do it, they mostly just sat there, stretching and gabbing. "Maybe this is it," Santa Monica said. "Where we're going to be training."

"OK, fine. But where the hell are we?" Bucoda asked on behalf of anyone who cared.

To end Pullman-seat torture, and because he thought he was coming down with something, what Gower wanted was to get off the train. *And stay off. My uniform, my skin, my hair—everything smells like the Kalbergs' dog after tangling with a skunk! Wherever the hell this is, it'll do just fine.*

"I think I see buildings!" someone shouted.

Gower opened the window and stuck his head out for a better look. He confirmed buildings ahead—shadowy outlines, but definitely buildings. "Sentries on the platform!" someone else shouted. Gower could see them, too. *A detail in front of what might be a station, bayonets fixed. Like I saw in the desert, near Yuma.*

"Look out! It's Miller!"

Recruits not at their seats dashed to refill them. Miller

entered with DO Waverly close behind. "Listen up, boots! Us two-stripers got stuff we gotta do here. Waverly's been briefed. You got questions, he's your man." Miller nodded once, then passed on to the next carriage.

"Listen up!" The Pigeon shouted, voice cracking on the "*up*." Derisive chuckles drew the sternest scowl angel-faced Waverly could muster, resulting in even more laughter.

It was hard to take the guy seriously, but Gower did. He was afraid Hogjaw could come down pretty hard on anybody giving Waverly guff during what appeared to be some serious business at the depot. Opening a grimy window without permission was one thing. Whatever was happening farther up the tracks was definitely something else. *I, for one, ain't willing to risk it.*

"Breakfast is coming soon," Waverly told them when things settled down. "And we're gonna be here for a while, so when you're finished eating, you're free to get out and stretch your legs in the railbed. But *only* adjacent to this carriage, and only on the west side of the train."

Gower imagined the compass-challenged boots stewing over where west was on a foggy day. "*Adjacent*?" Bucoda chuckled. "Listen to The Pigeon, will ya! Using big-boy words now."

"Do *not* approach the depot platform up ahead. If you *do* approach the platform, the guard detail there has orders to detain you—or worse!"

Trying to be dramatic, but lets his voice trail off at the end. Needs to watch more movies!

"Come on, Waverly, let us in on it!" one of the boots called him out from behind Gower's row. "Are the Japs getting off here, or what?"

Waverly snapped to, trying to catch the culprit in the act. "Who said that . . . ? What we're doing here is secret information. I can have you arrested."

Gower watched as the same guy tried to disguise his voice by speaking into his sleeve, an octave lower. "Have that guy shot! I'll bet he's one of 'em. I'll bet he's a spy!" As if on cue, several recruits gave Waverly the raspberry, or similar sounds of gastric distress, and The Pigeon's face turned a brilliant red.

"Grub!" Santa Monica sang out. A private working for Miller appeared with a cart piled high with the same infamous tins they'd been served each morning. Between the bobbing heads of his fellows, Gower watched Waverly get jostled out of the way by the delivery guy and briefly deposited on another boot's lap. "Fall out!" Waverly shouted after scrambling to his feet.

The Pullman soon filled with a mix of laughter and grumbling about the food while "canned heartbreak" was distributed down the aisle one more time. "Not *that* garbage again!" someone hollered. "I swear I will never complain about Army food again, as long as it's *cooked*—and not in a can," the same boot continued. "I'd rather face enemy fire!"

There came the crack of hickory on leather from behind them. "I can arrange that, boot."

2

Gower turned to see Hogjaw Thornton standing at the door of their coach, tapping methodically on the side of his leg with what Gower guessed was a riding crop like he'd seen in the movies. Miller hung back, peering out from behind him. "Ten . . . *hut*!" Waverly shouted unnecessarily. Hogjaw already had their attention.

"Unlike the boots in the other cars, *you* ladies seem to

be a little out of sorts with the Army right now," Hogjaw said as he reached the center of the carriage. Miller and The Pigeon remained at opposite ends. "Or are you just a little *peeved*?" The noncom stopped in front of the soldier who jokingly asked to be sent to the front. "Which is it for you, boot? Are you out of sorts? Or are you just *peeved*?" When no answer came, Thornton dismissed the offender with a derisive snort and moved on. "I can see how barely three days on Uncle Sam's payroll could make you all experts on Army procedure," Hogjaw sneered. "I *believe* Private Waverly already told you girls everything you need to know about why we're parked at this manure pile, and what you're supposed to do while we're here. But since we need you morons to cooperate while we're stopped at this shithole, I guess I'm going to have to go against my better judgment and let you in on a few things. Though watching a couple of you dickheads get shot by the sentries for stepping out of line might provide us a little entertainment, eh, Miller?"

Gower couldn't hear or see the corporal's response, if there was one. He kept his eyes trained on Hogjaw and hoped he wasn't next in the sergeant's line of fire.

"We're stopped here to unload some . . . *people*," Thornton told them. "This won't be easy. . . . You see, *these* people are even *more* unhappy to be here than *you* are. So let *that* sink in for a minute. . . . This action will require respect for command—and *discipline* in the face of it. So far, you Nancys haven't shown me much in the way of either one! A lack of discipline is what gets you killed . . . *Dead! Do you understand what I'm saying?!*"

"Yes, sir!" Gower and his fellows put some muscle behind it.

Hogjaw shook his head. He suddenly whirled, striking the nearest seatback with the riding crop. Gower flinched involuntarily at the sound.

"I'm not sure that you *do*. In fact, I'll bet most of you boots ain't never even seen a dead body before—except maybe your grandma," he added with unmistakable disdain. "And she probably died in bed with a smile on her face." Thornton proceeded to ape what Gower supposed was the sergeant's idea of a smiling dead grandma.

"Well, let me tell ya something. That ain't how it is out on the line. . . . I've seen good men die with their guts spilling out. Blood running all over the place!" Gower remembered Mr. Taylor's butchered deer, hanging from the eaves next door.

"I wiped a buddy's brains off the side of my face! It ain't pretty. . . . *Discipline!* That's the key to being a good soldier! To *surviving*!" Hogjaw paused to look around. "Except for their armed escort, the *people* getting off here shouldn't have *any* contact with *anyone* else on this train, including and especially *you* jackasses!" he added, staring right at Gower.

Despite his fatigue, despite his ardent wish this was somehow all just a bad dream, Gower found the fire needed to meet Hogjaw's glare with one of his own. *I know I didn't have any contact with the Japanese boy, and I certainly didn't speak to him. And if having a set of brass knuckles was wrong, then OK, I can accept the consequences. But they were a gift. I've got no intention of using them as a weapon.*

The corners of Thornton's mouth yanked his face into a particularly ghoulish grin before he turned away and moved on. "Seems to me you ladies have the wrong idea about what it's like in the Army. . . . Well, I'm gonna let you in on a little something—this ain't a *cotillion*! You weren't invited here for *tea*! The Army *owns* you! *I* own you!" He struck an armrest with his stick, barely missing the shoulder of one of the men. "And if I decide, I can *make* you, or I can *break* you," he snarled, suddenly grabbing the hickory swagger with both hands and snapping it in two with a loud *crack*.

"Is *that* clear?"

"Yessir!" came the unanimous answer.

"For your sakes, I hope so." Thornton shook his head slowly again and then headed for the next car. "Or there'll be hell to pay."

3

"As you were," Miller told the carload of recruits before following Hogjaw up the aisle. "Private Waverly's in charge."

Dismissal couldn't come soon enough for Gower. The sergeant's additional dose of venom left a bitter taste. This latest serving of C ration didn't improve it. When he and Bucoda were finished eating, they stood up and joined several others already heading for the doors. "Hold on! Hold on, you men!" Waverly shouted as they pushed past him down the aisle. "Wait till I give the order!" No one paid the DO any heed.

"Fall out!" Gower heard The Pigeon yell from inside the Pullman as he and the others hopped from the bottom step of the coach's stairs. The gravel roadbed rapidly filled with recruits eager to stretch their aching limbs and grab a smoke. They stayed close to the train, as they were told. The fog lifted a bit, but not completely. What there might be to the rear of the train and to the west was left to their imaginations. They had a clear view of the platform up ahead, though, and of the sentry detail standing by.

"Guess they can't all be spies," Bucoda admitted. Gower was touched by the apparent change of heart. They sought out some of the other guys they knew. Cigarettes were offered around. With Wendell's old Zippo, Gower lit up a Lucky for Bucoda and one for himself. The one part of Army life coming easily to the kid from Poppy Peak was killing time. He puffed unenthusiastically on his cigarette while half listening to some of the others talk up their hometowns. All seemed eager to impress, and to practice cussing like veterans.

Santa Monica wandered over. "Still nothing going on, I guess," he said, motioning toward the depot. "Nobody coming off the train yet."

"A dollar says it's the Japs," Kelso offered.

"You ain't got a dollar, Kelso," Bucoda called him out. "And anyway, that's a fool's bet. Can't be nobody else."

"Hey, maybe it's starting," another boot said.

As if on cue, the escort detail formed a sort of gauntlet between the train and the station buildings. Gower spotted Hogjaw Thornton and Corporal Miller coming off the train. A couple of officers and a few other noncoms were there, as well.

"Here they come!" Kelso shouted. Other boots in the railbed stopped whatever they were doing and turned to look.

Clusters of Japanese men and women—some holding babies—emerged reluctantly from the train. Soon, there was a steady, if slow-moving, parade of adults, small children, and teens. A few elders—white hair and bent backs—were sprinkled in. All shuffled along, bewildered, working their way between parallel lines of bayonet-wielding GIs, eventually crowding up against those ahead of them in line. All craned their necks toward an uncertain future. Gower couldn't help but sympathize. *Wherever this is, it's a hell of a place to be starting life over. Thousands of miles from the only home most of them have ever known. I'd say that's pretty rough punishment for just being who you are.* Gower sighed. *And Hey-Gee could be one of them.*

Most of the soon-to-be internees clutched cloth-covered bundles of belongings. A few had suitcases. *About the same size we were allowed.* Gower took several steps cautiously closer. He thought he could hear motors running. *Trucks? Buses? Maybe waiting to take them to some kind of camp.* He couldn't help but compare the scene in front of him to the scenes of refugees on the screen down at the York. *The narrator says pretty much the same thing every time—"Fleeing for their lives, innocent civilians, driven from their homes into the horrors of war, misery etched on their faces as the sobering realization sinks in. They have lost everything but whatever they can carry on their backs."*

"Just like in a newsreel," Gower muttered.

"What's *that*?" Kelso asked from behind him.

"What's a *newsreel*?" Gower asked, surprised by the question.

"No. *That*," Kelso said, referring to something else. "Sounds like marching. And I hear singing . . . from over there."

He pointed to the left of the train, straight into the remaining fog. Beyond three other sets of idle rails and a couple of additional sidings, they couldn't see a thing. Soon, Gower could hear it, too—marching and singing, coming toward them from beyond the lingering curtain of mist.

"That ain't English," Bucoda declared.

"No . . . it's not. Sounds more like . . . ," Gower said, when McCleary and a couple others beat him to it.

"Germans!" they cried.

A small formation of uniformed men, singing and marching smartly, came out of the fog, heading straight for the American recruits with what looked like rifles on their shoulders.

"Krauts!" Kelso shouted as he stepped deftly behind the relative safety of Santa Monica, his much stouter comrade.

"Gotta be prisoners," McCleary offered.

"Better be," Bucoda whispered. "We ain't got any guns!"

4

Gower and the others stood and stared across the forty-odd yards at the advancing Nazi soldiers. *Face to face with the enemy in the middle of the US!* He glanced left and right. Except for the boots from his car and maybe the closest couple of others, nobody seemed to notice the advancing Germans, including the guards up ahead at the station.

"It's a work detail," McCleary decided. "They're carrying tools, not guns."

A lone American GI strode out of the mist behind the formation, a rifle slung over a shoulder. "Halt!" he shouted when they reached the first set of idle tracks. "Detail . . . fall out!"

The American leaned his weapon against a pile of wooden ties, then lit up a smoke. The denim-clad prisoners broke ranks, milling around before some of them started picking and poking at the gravel in the roadbed with rakes and shovels without being told. They wore headgear similar to the flat-folding garrison caps Gower and his buddies were issued, but with a short bill in the front. The sleeves and legs of their gray uniforms featured large black and white "P"s and "W"s, marking them as prisoners of war. *Missed that little detail at first.*

"OK, *meine schöne Männer*," the detail guard said after a bit, tossing them a little German while he was at it. "You know the drill. *Sie wissen was zu tun ist, ja,* dontcha."

"Jawohl, mein Korporal!" A few laughed in agreement to whatever the GI just told them.

"Ja, ja!"

"Ja, ja?" the guard responded in mocking tones. "Well, then, quit screwing around! *Dann los!"* he said. "Get to it!" The prisoners laughed again before going about their work.

The playful back-and-forth in German caught Gower by surprise. With nothing much else to look at, he and a few of his buddies watched POWs toss shovelfuls of displaced gravel back toward the rails, pull weeds, or relevel some of the ties with pry bars.

It wasn't long until one of the Germans looked up from what he was doing, and glanced over at the American recruits standing around eyeing him and his POW buddies. "Hallo, Joe!" the German called out with a wave and a smile. "Whaddya know?!"

"Look at that damned Nazi," Santa Monica huffed. "Without a care in the world."

"How come they let 'em just be walking around free like that, anyway?" Kelso demanded to know, feeling a lot braver than when the Germans first showed up.

"Some people might ask the same question about you, Kelso." Bucoda smiled. "Does the Griffith Park Zoo know you're absent without leave?"

"Murderers!" Santa Monica suddenly screamed at the prisoner contingent.

The Germans looked over in alarm. Some turned to their chaperone for guidance. Suddenly serious, the guard tossed his cigarette, scrambled to his feet, and grabbed his rifle. "You mess with my work detail, boots," he shouted, "and I'll have you on report! You get me?"

Santa Monica's chest heaved, then he looked away. "It ain't right, is all I'm sayin'." To seem less interested in what the Germans were up to, the recruits gave a little ground.

"Pretty happy out on work detail," Bucoda said. "Should lock 'em up, instead. Throw away the key."

"'Course they're happy," McCleary decided. "For them, the war's over."

"And well fed," Gower added, a little envious given what

he and the other recruits had been given to eat since being sworn in.

No question the German prisoners of war looked in better shape—tanned, muscular, and obviously enjoying the food—than Gower and his fellow recruits did. He couldn't help but notice that, with the possible exception of Santa Monica, he and his generally scrawny fellow GIs had some room to grow into their "Government Issue." The Germans filled out their uniforms nearly to the point of button-popping strain. "Like fat Nazi sausages," Bucoda offered. "Could you shoot one?" he added, turning to Santa Monica.

"I dunno," Santa Monica replied. "Gimme a gun, and let's find out!"

"You couldn't do it," McCleary scoffed. "Not while they're just standing there. It's not like shooting squirrels or rabbits. They're people."

"Germans look like us," Kelso added, as if surprised. "Thought they'd look different."

"Like how?" Bucoda asked.

"Dunno. More like Hitler, or something. . . . Anyways, *different*. But they look like *us*!"

"Not like the Japs, though, do they?" Santa Monica said, indicating the detraining Japanese with a dismissive flick of his head. "I could shoot Japs," he insisted. "They're animals. Slant-eyed little bastards! What they did to us at Pearl. And Bataan!" Some of the others nodded in agreement.

Gower thought about adding *But* they're *more American than I am!* until he thought better of it. *Who knows how many more butt-busting hours after this I'm going to be in a cramped train with the dumb apes who think Hey-Gee Nakamura must be some kind of monkey?* Instead, he drifted away from the group and a little closer to the platform, fascinated by what he saw going on there.

The crowd of Japanese moving slowly from the train toward the depot had thinned out considerably. A few more armed GIs brought up the rear, urging the stragglers along, occasionally by means of a gentle nudge with the flat of a rifle butt. *They're not animals, but the way those poor people are being treated . . . Forced out of the train, herded like cattle through a sort of chute, off to a crowded holding pen, anxious, dreading the possible outcomes.*

The scene reminded Gower of his one-and-only trip to the huge processing and packing operations southeast of LA, with Moose and Luca. The Buffone brothers had offered the owners "protection" from government inspectors in exchange for beef and other meat for their clubs. *Harvey came, too, but lost his lunch over some of the things we saw there.*

Standing there, staring up the tracks, he remembered something from history class. *Indians driven from their homes in the East, force-marched under guard all the way to Oklahoma. . . . Here we go again,* he thought, shaking his head.

He was about to turn away and rejoin his buddies when a splash of gravel near the depot caught his attention. One of the Japanese—a young boy—had jumped down onto the railbed. *Making a break for it! The kid from the other night! And he's heading right for me!*

5

"Stop him!" a sentry yelled from the station.

"Hap!" the kid was screaming. "I needa *hap*! Mistah Mabum! *Puhreeza!* I needa hap!"

"Help"? Is he shouting for help? Is that Japanese? Gower took a few tentative steps in the fugitive's direction.

One of the guards jumped down in pursuit but crumpled immediately to his knees, writhing and moaning, as if he'd twisted his ankle. The misstep gained the boy some distance before another, much older GI jumped down, slung his rifle over a shoulder, and joined the chase, losing his broad-brimmed high hat in the process.

"Puhreeza! Hap, ojisan! Fowah me!"

Gower froze. He looked from the boy to the guard in pursuit, kicking up gravel as he tried to run the kid down. Another sentry stepped to the edge of the platform and shoved home the bolt of his rifle with an ominous *click-chuck*. The older GI running toward them in the railbed was closing in. "Stop . . . that . . . kid!" he shouted between gasps for air.

"Shoot him!" Gower heard Santa Monica say from behind. "Shoot that little Jap bastard!"

Unmistakable terror filled the boy's eyes. Beyond him, Gower could see the trooper on the platform kneel and take aim. The sentry on the ground was steadily gaining. Gower dashed toward the onrushing pair. He grabbed the kid, pulled him close, and then turned his back to the pursuit and the depot.

"I needa *hap*!" the boy pleaded, staring up into his savior's eyes. "*Puhreeza!* Mistah Mabum! *Hap!*"

Gower studied the kid's face. Growing anger stopped him in mid-read—anger about what happened on the train, anger that Hogjaw had it in for him because of it. "You've caused me a lot of trouble, kid! You know that?!" The boy began to squirm. Gower tightened his grip. "Was it you?" he shouted. "Did you take them?" He patted down the kid's pockets. "Where's my brass knuckles?!" he demanded to know. "That's my good luck charm!"

Confusion clouded the boy's face. "Heh?! *Nan-da?!* No! No! I needa *hap!* Fowah *me*!"

"Good . . . work . . . boot," the approaching sentry panted. The sprint down the tracks took all he had in him. He'd slowed to a labored walk and was still several yards away.

Gower straightened and turned as if to offer the refugee over. The Japanese boy twisted in his captor's grip, struggling to get away. "Hap, fowah me, *puhreeza*!" the runaway shouted one more time before biting down hard on Gower's wrist just below the sleeve. For good measure, he kicked his captor in the shin, forcing him to release his grip when he backed off in pain. The kid dashed for the nearest Pullman, dove onto the gravel beside the track, and made as if to scramble under the train, to the other side of the line where a tentative freedom awaited.

Gower hobbled, then crab-crawled after the boy, grabbing him by the ankles just before he wriggled away. He stood the kid up and held him with a firmer grip this time, despite the pain in both his wrist and shin.

"I'll take it . . . from here," the graying sentry said, coming alongside, still breathing heavily. He grabbed the kid by the back of the collar and turned to go. "Thanks."

As he watched the kid being yanked back toward the station, head and shoulders sagging in defeat, Gower stood there wondering whether he'd done the right thing. *He ran right at me. Counting on me for help for some reason. . . . Where would he go on his own, in the middle of . . . wherever the hell we are? He's just a kid. I did him a favor. Too many people hate the Japanese. Probably safer in a camp. Anyway, what was I supposed to do? I'm a soldier, too, now.*

"That's more like it, Gower," an all-too-familiar voice said from behind him.

Shit.

CHAPTER SEVEN

Layers of Skin

1

Gower took a last look toward the depot. He locked on to the boy, wild-eyed, squirming—wriggling against the older soldier's grip as he was passed up to other sentries on the platform. *Jeez! Still trying to escape! What's with that kid, anyway?!*

As he expected when he turned away, Hogjaw was standing there, grinning approval, Waverly at his side. *Double shit.* A few other recruits stood a bit farther off, with what looked like smiles of pride on their faces.

"Might be hope for you, yet, Gower." Hogjaw grinned. "You're the new DO for your coach. Waverly, you're relieved. Give Gower your armband." The Pigeon's face fell. Gower watched him slowly, carefully peel the big, bold "DO" from his arm before surrendering the badge to Hogjaw. *As if that scrap of cloth was a layer of his skin.*

Hogjaw snatched it rudely away from The Pigeon and

jerked it up Gower's arm into place. Gower twitched and grimaced as he tried but failed to fight off the pain he'd been dealt from the Japanese kid's incisors. "What's the matter, Nancy?" the sergeant snarled. "Did I hurt you?" He lifted Gower's arm and noticed the underside of his sleeve was soaked in blood. "You let that little Jap bastard cut you?" he chided. "Well, shake it off, Gower. That don't rate you no Purple Heart. No, sir. You gonna have to earn it somewhere else besides the nursery!"

With that, Hogjaw gripped and twisted Gower's wounded wrist, then laughed before letting go. "*Now* you got something to moan about!" The sergeant turned on his heel and strolled up the railbed toward the head of the train. "You got a lot to learn, Gower," he said, casually tossing the advice over his shoulder. "You got a lot to learn."

Waverly opened his mouth as if to say something. Nothing came out. He looked from Gower to Hogjaw, then back to Gower before drifting back to their carriage.

"Good work, Gower!" Santa Monica said, stepping forward to pat him on the back. "I was all set to jump in there and help you catch that little Jap bastard, if you needed it," he added before he, too, headed for the train.

"Didn't know you had it in you, Gower," Bucoda added in passing. "Congratulations."

Gower reflexively nodded acknowledgement. "Thanks." *Not sure what that "it" is, and not sure I'm all that happy about it being "in me," either.* Some of the other guys he'd been palling around with, including McCleary, seemed none too pleased that their new friend had apparently joined the "high hats" as the car's new duty officer and gave him the silent treatment while reboarding.

Standing there, half-heartedly encouraging others to board, Gower stroked the wound beneath his bloodied sleeve as his eyes wandered up to the white-on-black armband perched above his elbow.

As new duty officer for their car, Gower took a last look around for stragglers before reboarding his rolling responsibility. He could still see and hear the German prisoners laughing and joking as they continued working on the railbeds. In the opposite direction, the platform stood silent and deserted—as if the Japanese families passing through minutes earlier had never existed. Teeth marks on his throbbing wrist were his only proof. *Many if not most of them born in the US, more American than I am, forced into a kind of personal oblivion.* With a heave of his barrel chest, Gower reached for the handhold with his uninjured arm and pulled himself up and into the coach before latching the door behind him.

He didn't feel much like joining the others right away and instead stood at an open window between the cars, to let the breeze help clear his head. "That kid has some choppers," he muttered, rolling up the sleeve of his blouse to examine the wound. It was a nasty gash. Slices of flesh hung from the edges. *I guess I deserved it.* It was only his third day in uniform. Already brimming with hate for Hogjaw, he loathed himself now, too, for what he'd done to the boy.

With a blast of the whistle and a belch of steam, the train bucked once before yanking Gower and the other young soldiers onward. Coming into, and then quickly out of, view was a sign with the name of the station on it. "Hope," it read, where the Japanese had been ushered into irony. Gaining speed, the train-bound recruits headed deeper into the country they had sworn to defend. *Against all enemies, foreign and domestic.*

2

Despite the day growing brighter by the moment, all Gower could manage in response was a particularly pathetic sigh. His Army career wasn't off to the best of beginnings. He couldn't decide whether he felt sorrier for himself or the Japanese boy. The bite wound burned and throbbed more than he thought it should have. *Maybe worse than it looks. At least the bleeding has slowed.* He stared out the window without actually taking in the details, rubbing his wrist as the train gathered speed, rushing them ever closer to war.

When the passing scenery took on an impressively emerald brilliance—*worthy of Oz!*—Gower was coaxed at least somewhat out of himself and into his practiced curiosity about distant peoples and places. *Dad's fault, I suppose—never discarding an issue of his precious* National Geographics*, sitting in the garage, driving Mom crazy with the clutter the probably couple hundred back copies presented, if not the "too many" photos of native peoples "displaying a lack of propriety but too much of everything else!"*

The train wound through rolling hills, then across flatter land and farm fields—all of it in shades of green. It was a palette unfamiliar and unnatural to him, more accustomed to the yellows, browns, and beiges common much of the year back home. Inside the Pullman, the air was moist and palpable, nearly to annoyance. *Nothing like LA.*

He was shaken from the interlude when the train rattled over and then along a still-water, jade-colored creek. *A lot more rain here.* Across another bridge and into more farmland. *And Blacks . . . Lots of them.* Suddenly he was looking down on a scene instantly reminding him of *Gone with the Wind*—dozens of what looked like an exodus of farmhands walking along a dirt road, or riding in wagons pulled by one or a pair of what the city-boy soldier guessed were mules, *if they aren't the ugliest horses I've ever seen!* Some of the men rested hoes or rakes on their shoulders. A few looked up and waved at the passing train. Not knowing what else to do, Gower waved back.

"Gower!"

Corporal Miller popped through the door leading from the carriage for which Gower was supposedly responsible. "Why aren't you with your men?! You're this car's duty officer now, son! You need to be in there with them!" Gower lowered his head. He assumed he was about to be demoted—making his tenure as DO likely the shortest in Army lore.

"You've got to stick with your men, son, if you expect them to stick with you. You ought to be damned glad I found you out here before Sergeant Thornton did."

For that, Gower was genuinely thankful and nodded somber agreement. "Yes, sir. I'm sorry, sir."

"I would advise you not to get on his bad side, Gower," Miller went on.

The private assumed he already was on Hogjaw Thornton's bad side. That things could somehow get even worse between him and the sergeant sent his already sinking feelings straight to the bottom. "Yes, sir."

"Tell your men," Miller went on, "we're a little less than an hour outside of Little Rock. We'll be detraining at the station there and then boarding buses for Camp Forrest, our final stop. Show your men what you're made of, Gower. Don't let the Army down."

"Yes, sir." Not really sure, yet, what exactly he *was* made of, but hoping to find out sooner than later, Gower snapped to attention and saluted.

"Oh, and Gower, Waverly said something about a cut on your arm, or something. You OK?" Miller asked.

"Yes, sir," the private lied. "Just a scratch."

Miller gently tilted the private's arm, exposing the discolored wound. "You oughta have that looked at when we get to camp," he said before moving on. "Better yet, have Waverly or someone apply a field dressing when you get back to your seat. He knows where the first aid stuff is. The Army needs you healthy, Gower."

When he entered the coach and told the men what was up about stopping in Little Rock, there were a few nods in response to Gower fulfilling his DO responsibility, but no one said much of anything. He figured they either already knew where they were going or, like him, didn't really care anymore, as long as they didn't have to sleep one more night sitting in the damned train.

"As you were," he said, realizing how stupid it sounded, since the men had hardly moved since he showed up. Few bothered to acknowledge his presence as he made his way down the aisle—except Santa Monica. Beaming as if at his new hero, he stood up, shooed Kelso back to the other side of the aisle into the vacancy next to a scowling Bucoda, then remained standing to let Gower slide in and over to the cherished window end of the bench.

Gower thought for a minute about asking Waverly or Santa Monica or someone to go get a bandage or something for the wound, till Mugsy's voice stole into his head—*"Don't let anyone see you soft, Kid."*

Very tired and not feeling that great, the new duty officer fell asleep at his seat.

3

Gower didn't stir till the train began to brake. They were in a city, coasting to a crawl, approaching an impressive brown-brick station with a four-sided clock tower rising high above. It was well after noon. Miller stuck his head in and called Gower out to the gangway, where he explained that the deal at Hope had made them a little late and it didn't look like they'd be eating for another hour or so. Gower returned to tell the men they'd be having noon mess late, but it wouldn't be rations and would be at Camp Forrest, their home for at least the next several months.

A raucous cheer for a decent meal erupted but was immediately matched and then quickly surpassed by celebratory applause and voices emanating from the same platform they were slowly rolling past. Gower bent over low enough to see out the windows. A small group of flag-waving civilians stood arrayed below a "Welcome to Little Rock!" banner, cheering and waving. The soldiers in "his" carriage cheered and waved right back. Two or three mothers presented their bewildered infants. *As if in offering to the Gods of War.*

Just beyond the civilians, an Army band struck up "Don't Sit Under the Apple Tree," the Andrews Sisters' big hit. Instead of three women harmonizing, a solo female voice boogie-woogied the lead. And for the moment at least, despite pain and discomfort, despite Hogjaw and everything else, Gower felt like a hero. Or at least like a warrior, and welcome.

"Will you get a load of *that*!" Bucoda shouted, practically jumping out of his seat. "There's a GI Jane here to serenade us! And man, is she stacked!"

Suddenly, everyone wanted a gander. The viewpoint-challenged got up and joined the crush against the windows on the more favorable side. "Hubba hubba! A *blonde*!" someone shouted.

"Hubba hubba!" Kelso yelled between attempted wolf whistles.

"What a doll!" another boot chimed in.

Gower heartily agreed. After the train ride through hell, the WAC was indeed a vision of heaven. An angel in khaki. *Who knew a soldier could be that good-looking?*

To the frustration of the carload of rubbernecking GIs, instead of stopping, the train kept right on going—past the band, past the blonde, past the station, and on to a siding, where, instead of music, exhaust from waiting trucks and buses provided their only greeting. As grandly as the multistory depot had stood, where the coaches full of recruited Californians came to rest was a seldom-used platform, shoddy and spare, hunkered down and deserted. Across from the end point of their nearly four-day railway journey was a shamble of tiny, ill-defined buildings appearing to lean against the foot of the grand station edifice they only moments ago had passed. Over the door of one of the smaller, shabbier structures was a hand-painted sign that briefly held a suddenly more solemn Gower in a state of wonder—"Colored Only Toilet"—until he remembered overhearing a member at the Y saying he wished they had them at Alameda Station downtown.

"Welcome to Little Rock, indeed," McCleary muttered.

They sat at the siding for what seemed like the better part of an hour. When the Army was good and ready, DO Private Gower received and then passed along the order to his charges to fall out and detrain. Feeling a little light-headed after stepping off, he passed on Santa Monica's offer of a smoke, then felt even worse when jostling for position among the dozens of uniformed Californians flooding the previously deserted siding. He stood with his buddies, waiting to be told what to do next until he noticed a man emerge from beneath the "Colored Only Toilet" sign. Despite the man's bright, white hair, Gower was struck by how straight he stood. Walking parallel to them on another platform, the civilian paid the soldiers no mind.

"Will ya look at that!" Kelso carped. "Down here, I guess n*****s get their own johns to crap in!"

"They don't prefer it that way, dumbass," McCleary corrected. "They're forced to. It's the law—Jim Crow law, it's called. And it ain't right. We gotta fix that someday."

Mention of Jim Crow reminded Gower how little he knew about the South. *Never thought I'd get sent* here*! What do I know about this part of the country except for what I read in* Uncle Tom's Cabin *and* The Adventures of Huckleberry Finn*? Movies like* Gone with the Wind*?*

He hadn't much considered the reality of separation, or "segregation" as the papers sometimes called it, and he found it hard to believe there could be a different set of laws, depending on what someone looked like. *Kinda like when I lifeguarded at Brookside. Only whites allowed to swim, most days. Coloreds—including Orientals, like Sammy, and Mexicans, too, I guess—on Wednesdays, and only in the afternoon. And afterward, the water was drained. And if the maintenance guys were running late the next morning, I'd help scrub the pool's walls and decks with bleach! Never thought much about it before. Don't remember Sammy ever complaining. Just the way things were—maybe still are. And down here, it's the law!*

Gower noticed that the Black man on the other platform had stopped to stare. *Sizing us up, maybe, wondering what we're made of. . . . As if we have any clue!* For a moment, Gower supposed the man's eyes settled directly on his own. And in that instant, in those eyes, there was something unsettling Gower couldn't quite put his finger on. *Not disdain, not distrust . . . but a sort of distance . . . not allowing me in. As if he and I could not possibly have anything in common. As if there is nothing of his experience that a young white soldier from California could possibly relate to. . . . He'd definitely have a point.* Gower turned away, feeling somehow guilty and ashamed. When he dared look back again, the man was gone.

"Guess we're gonna see a whole lot more n*****s here than in California," Bucoda announced, apparently also having noticed the man. "We better get used to it."

"*You* get used to it if you wanna," Santa Monica told him. "I won't ever."

CHAPTER EIGHT

Welcome to The Forrest

1

The business of getting themselves and their baggage from the train to the trucks and buses went quickly if not smoothly. Squabbles over seating for the last leg of the trip erupted here and there, but Miller and the other noncoms kept things from getting out of hand. Since they were no longer on a train, Gower unilaterally relieved himself of his command. He handed Miller his DO armband and boarded one of the buses for the ride to Camp Forrest. According to the corporal, it was still the better part of an hour away.

At first, no one chose to sit with Gower, which was fine, because he didn't feel much like talking. He was very tired and looking forward to a little shut-eye before they got to where they were going. But just before their bus pulled away, Waverly the Pigeon slid in to fill the bench.

"How's the wrist?" he asked his DO successor.

"'S OK," Gower said, to be polite. And before anyone

could accuse him of being The Pigeon's new buddy, he turned his face to the glass. Leaning against the window, he pretended to doze and didn't pay much attention to Waverly or anyone else for most of the way. Sometime during the trip, reality overcame pretense. The exhausted soldier slept until Waverly shouted something too close to his ear for comfort.

"How *about* that! We started at *Fort* MacArthur, but we've ended up at *Camp* Forrest."

Gower blinked a few times and took a look. Their bus was passing under an arch that read "Welcome to Camp Forrest."

"What's the difference, I wonder," Waverly went on, "between a *fort* and a *camp*? Do you suppose we'll be sleeping in tents? Maybe sleeping under the stars! Whaddya think, Gower? Back home, we used to camp outside. It was a lotta fun!"

As Gower sat wondering why Waverly thought that question was important enough to wake him, their bus joined with others lined up to pass through the gates of their new home. After an MP waved them through, they drove across a surprisingly long stretch of open ground before they came to another, more heavily guarded gate. *Afraid of spies way out here?* A few minutes after that, they rolled by row after row of nearly identical bone-white buildings, finally stopping in front of a half dozen more. Before they were ordered off the bus, some guy popped his head through the door to warn them that the flu was going around. Gower collected his gear from one of the trucks and stood around awaiting further orders.

"I told you, Kelso."

Gower recognized Bucoda's voice. They, too, had been on the same bus. "We ain't going to be camping in a *forest.* There's two 'r's in this 'Forrest.' Probably some general's name . . . Oh, wait, I forgot . . . You can't read."

"I can so *read,*" Kelso protested. "I just don't always know what it says."

Gower sat on his footlocker and took a break. Waverly sidled up to him with some follow-up to what Bucoda was on about with Kelso. "I already asked McCleary, Gower, in case you're interested. Even *he* doesn't know who this Forrest guy was. But he says they'll tell us sooner than later, and maybe we'll even have to pass a test about him or something."

Gower shrugged. *Who cares?* He was tired and hungry and not feeling that great—in fact, kind of feverish, kind of woozy.

It was another half hour or so before the boots were told anything. *In other words, standard procedure.* Five or six sergeants wandered over and organized the Californians into box formation. They stood in the early afternoon sun, twelve wide, and Gower guessed about double that number deep, their belongings at their feet. Sergeant Thornton stepped out in front of the other three-stripers and gave a welcome speech. From that clue Gower guessed Camp Forrest was Hogjaw's home base. *Sheez! Am I ever gonna see the last of this guy?*

"On behalf of General Flagg . . . ," Thornton started in.

Gower almost immediately tuned it out. He couldn't help it. Something was making him feel pretty punk. If not the flu, he supposed it might be the humidity. He couldn't remember anywhere being so steamy, except maybe the showers at the Y. The climate didn't seem to be bothering anyone else, though, so he did his best to ignore both it and the souvenir wound courtesy of the Japanese kid. *Really should have that looked at.*

". . . welcome to hell," he heard Thornton saying at one point. "It's all up to you. Depending on what you show us in Basic Training, we're gonna put you in *Infantry* Replacement School, or *Medical* Replacement School."

"Infantry for the real men. Med Corps for the sissies," Gower heard someone whisper.

Wobbly, weaving, drowning in sweat, Gower wondered whether real men were allowed to faint.

2

Though still a little shaky on his feet, Gower somehow managed to remain vertical till Hogjaw Thornton was done. "All right then, ladies. I'm only going to say this once, so listen up. Despite how some of you performed during the train ride, I'm going to go out on a limb and assume you can all count to six. You see these six buildings behind me?" he said. "The one to my extreme right is Number One. When I give the order, count off by six from the right file. Number Ones, grab your gear and go to building Number One. I'll let you numbskulls figure out the rest of this plan on your own. Anyone who screws this up is spending the night right where he stands. You got it?"

"Yes, sir!" they all shouted.

"Then count off and get to it!"

Gower was a "two." Along with his fellow "deuces," he slung his duffel over his shoulder and dragged his locker across the grass, across a gravel road, and into his new home—the second of the six identical barracks buildings. "My name is Pierce," a corporal announced as the Californians crowded around him.

Like Corporal Miller and Sergeant Thornton, Pierce was a lot older than the boots. *Guess McCleary's right. Don't have enough soldiers to win this war. Still using guys from the last one.*

Pierce told them to pick out a bed that wasn't already made up or had a locker in front of it. "Then fall in at the foot of it." All the beds, vacant and occupied, had a rifle standing by.

"Now we're talking!" Bucoda exclaimed, rushing for the nearest empty bunk and picking up the weapon. "A gun!"

"That's your *rifle*, son," Corporal Pierce corrected. "It's for fighting. Your *gun*—and I assume you brought yours with you—is for fun. Which reminds me—tomorrow we're going to start teaching you monkeys how to keep both of them clean—the clap is going around Little Rock, and we aim to keep it out of Camp Forrest as much as we can."

There were about two dozen empty spots around the room. Gower chose the first unclaimed bunk he came to. He gladly dropped the duffel from his shoulder to the mattress, set his locker down at the foot, and then stood in front of it, waiting for further orders. *Sure hope they have something to do with sleep.* While he was standing there, he spotted McCleary and a couple of others he recognized from the train ride. He didn't see Santa Monica or Kelso, which was just fine. Less comforting was the sight of Waverly the Pigeon, on the other side of the aisle and down five or six beds. About a dozen other men he didn't recognize set their gear down in front of vacant bunks. Counting the lockers already in place, Gower tallied a total of forty privates assigned to that barracks.

"The toilets and showers are communal," Pierce announced. "That means you're gonna learn a lot more about each other than you ever wanted to know. They're in separate huts from here, accessible only from the outside. You can walk over there in your skivvies, if you want, but I'd advise you to have your towel handy to cover up in case a nurse happens by. Or else, who knows, you might get lucky and she won't laugh at the gun you packed along with you." Pierce winked at Bucoda.

As they stood there laughing, Corporal Pierce suddenly snapped to. "A-tennn-*hut*!" he shouted.

Even staring straight ahead, Gower could see someone stepping into the room from a door at the rear. He assumed it was their sergeant. *Please don't let it be Hogjaw.*

3

"Welcome to Camp Forrest, boots," the noncom said. "I'm Sergeant King. It was your dumb luck that brought you to my platoon, but dumb luck can make you look a lot smarter if you turn it into something positive. Tomorrow morning, your chance to do that begins. Don't screw it up." He nodded toward his second, standing to the side. "This is Corporal Pierce. Pierce, what do we think of boots who screw up?"

"We shun them, sir," Pierce said.

Sergeant King grinned. "You'll find that Corporal Pierce is way more polite than me and has a real way with words. We *hate* screw-ups. . . . Sure, we might cut you a little slack during Basic. But if you screw up on the battlefield, it could mean someone gets killed. If you've got an excuse for screwing up, it better be a good one. And if you think you've got a legitimate beef, then you let Corporal Pierce know about it. If you've got questions, concerns, or problems, you go to him. It's called 'chain of command.' If for some reason you think Corporal Pierce is your problem, and you want to go around him? Forget it. He's top notch."

The platoon commander proceeded to stroll down the aisle between the recruits from California. He stopped and turned. "Right now, the country's in a helluva jam. You don't need me to tell you that. That's what the papers are for. So to come out on top, we've got to make you tougher, stronger, and smarter than the enemy. If not, we're going to keep losing. It's that simple." King paused in the center of the formation of beds, slightly beyond where Gower was standing. The private was surprised to feel ever more trickles of sweat running down his temples and under his arms. He didn't think it was that hot inside the barracks. He stole a glance at some of the others but didn't see any evidence they were feeling it, too.

"There'll be days when you think you can't take it anymore," the sergeant went on. "Days when you're so tired you think you're gonna puke your guts out right there on the spot. Well, let me tell you something. If you *don't* have days like that, then *shame* on you. You're not working hard enough. You're not worthy of wearing this uniform!" He jabbed at his own chest. "The uniform so many brave men have worn before you—fighting and dying for this country."

He scanned their faces, up and down the lines. "But, if you do your best, and if you're square with us, me and Corporal Pierce will treat you square in return. If not—if you think you can just waltz your way through here and the Army is just some kind of lark, just a way for you to impress your girl back home—you got another think coming. If that's the way you're going to handle this, we'll be making it hard on you. *Very* hard. My advice is not to try it. Toe the line. That's what I say. We'll all be the better for it." He paused and set his jaw.

"Take a look around," he added. "It's just you California greenhorns in here right now. The other men in this platoon have been here a couple of weeks or more already. They've got a head start—and a shorter train ride, so, maybe their butts aren't as sore." Sergeant King allowed himself the briefest of smiles. "They've been training hard all this time. Matter of fact, they're out on the obstacle course right now. Tomorrow's your chance to show them what Californians are made of. You get me?"

At first there was no response. Gower could see Pierce rabbit-punch the closest man to him on the sly. “Yes, sir!” the boot shouted. The others joined the chorus, albeit a syllable late.

“Now, report to the mess for chow,” King told them. “Then get a good night’s sleep. You’re gonna need it. Starting tomorrow, me and Pierce are gonna ride you pretty hard.”

4

It was already mid-afternoon. *Feels more like teatime with Mom and Dad than lunch. Oh well, “feed a cold, starve a fever.”* Though still on the drowsy side, Gower decided to head out with newfound buddies Bucoda and McCleary. Waverly brought up the rear. They asked around and followed their noses to the nearest mess hall. Turned out it wasn’t far away but was cleverly hidden in the maze of nearly identical, unremarkable buildings that other guys were calling “The Forrest.” *Shoulda left a trail of bread crumbs.*

They joined dozens of other GIs already waiting for some grub. Mostly other Californians, Gower guessed. When it was his turn, he grabbed a nested metal tray from a stack of them. It was divided into sections. As he moved down the serving line, there were soldiers, he supposed, standing behind the counter, dressed in white, dumping food more or less on target. Besides a biscuit, there was something mushy, very likely vegetable matter—some of which he presumed was beets, by the cardinal color—mashed potatoes, and a beige, gravy-covered, semi-rigid item that could have been just about anything. Whether any of it consisted of meat was certain to be debated later.

The four found a table together. After a bite or two, Bucoda expressed a longing for "US ARMY FIELD RATION M-1, MEAT," etc., and wondered aloud if the mess hall had any on hand. "At least we knew what was in it," he said, getting a rise out of Gower and McCleary.

"I never did figure it out completely," Waverly jumped in. "And anyway, whadda you guys think of Sergeant King?"

"I'm guessing pork chop," McCleary said, holding up the beige thing. It appeared to be attached to a bone.

"King's not Hogjaw, so that's a bonus," Bucoda said, giving ground to Waverly's foray.

"Seems like he's going to treat us square enough, though, like he said," Gower offered, nudging the stuff on his tray but rapidly losing interest in even that level of activity.

"Yeah, sounds like it," Waverly agreed. "But you gotta give Sergeant Thornton a lotta credit, dontcha think?"

Gower watched McCleary's eyes nearly pop out of his head in response to the question. *Impressive. Waverly never gives up. But yes, clearly a kiss-ass.*

"He had a pretty tough job to do, you know, getting us all the way here from California. Keeping us boots in line and all," The Pigeon added. "I'd say he's been pretty hard on himself, when it comes right down to it."

"Hard on *us*, you mean," Bucoda snapped. He took a bite from something on his tray before turning to McCleary. "Oh, yeah!" he mumbled happily through his mouthful of it. "You're right! Pork chop!"

Based on the relish with which Bucoda attacked his hunk of meat, Gower tried his own. *Tough* and *full of fat. Didn't think that was possible.* He pushed it aside. He had a few forkfuls of what he determined were mashed potatoes but soon decided he was done.

"You see how the guy smiles when he lights into us?" Bucoda mimicked Thornton's grin to remind them. "No thanks! I'll take Sergeant King over that old bastard Hogjaw *any* day. And I only just met Sergeant King!"

"You know what *I* think?" Waverly went on, "I think Sergeant Thornton acts that way because he cares about us so much. He wants us to be the best soldiers we can be. That's all."

"He needs to try something else," McCleary said.

"Agreed," Gower managed to mumble. Head resting on an elbow-supported palm, he found himself in danger of dozing off.

"Miller told me Sergeant Thornton's been in the Army since he was a lot younger than we are," Waverly went on. "I'll bet he figures this is his last chance to get into combat. I heard he was all set to go to France with Pershing when he broke his hand."

"So what?" Bucoda snapped. "Why's he taking it out on us?"

"Maybe he's counting on us to help him out. You know, if *we* look good, it makes *him* look good, because he's our sergeant."

"*Was* our sergeant," McCleary corrected.

"Oh, yeah, right," The Pigeon said. "*Was* our sergeant."

Gower assumed that was that, and gave in to his eyelids, but The Pigeon couldn't leave it alone.

"I think he only wanted a chance to prove himself," he told them.

"He's already proven way too much to me," Bucoda said. "Case closed."

"Well, all I'm saying is, Sergeant Thornton got a raw deal. If he hadn't broken his hand on that other kid's face while boxing at Fort Bliss . . ."

Boxing? Suddenly interested in the conversation again, Gower perked up.

5

"How do you know all this stuff about Hogjaw, anyway?" McCleary asked.

"He told me," The Pigeon answered. He seemed pleased to have the lowdown on Hogjaw while the others had no clue. "Couldn't go to France with a busted hand."

"While boxing? *Wearing gloves?!*" Gower asked. "Didn't think that was possible. Not while wearing gloves. Not in the ring."

"What are you, anyway? A boxer?"

"Yep," Gower said, pointing to his crooked nose. "Wanna go a few with me?"

"The point is," The Pigeon huffed, "Sergeant Thornton never saw action. That's what I'm saying. He wants to get into this war something fierce. The Army says he's too old. He wants to prove them wrong."

"Can't see how tearing our heads off and spitting down the hole proves anything," Bucoda groused. "Good riddance is what I say. If I ever see that guy again, it'll be too soon."

"Ditto," Gower managed.

"This Sergeant King seems OK, though," McCleary added. "And Corporal Pierce seems OK, too. Gonna deal with us square, is what I think."

There was general agreement. Only The Pigeon took exception. "If you knew Sergeant Thornton better, you might think different."

Bucoda beat his buddies to the punch. "Yeah, well, thank God that ain't gonna happen."

When they finished eating, the others decided to take a look around. Gower excused himself. He was feeling beat, and light-headed. He made his way back to the barracks despite a couple of wrong turns. He got down to his undershirt and boxers, grabbed his towel, and asked another boot directions to the showers.

He didn't think the evening air was all that cold but felt a chill nevertheless. Once under the spray, he scrubbed out the bite wound from the kid on the train as best he could. The pain had him backing off, though, and too soon for comfort, the water turned from more or less hot, to lukewarm, and then downright cold. *Guess that means I'm done.*

Back inside, Pierce confirmed that they were off duty for the rest of the evening. "Lights out ain't till ten," the corporal told him. "You can get in as late as midnight, if you like, but I wouldn't recommend it."

Gower had no interest in going anywhere, so he hit the hay. Sleep took its sweet time showing up and was fitful at best—punctuated first by vague sounds of other soldiers laughing and joking, then buzzing mosquitoes, and later, by snoring barracks mates. He woke up once, completely soaked. Thinking the heat was to blame, he pulled off the blanket. Soon, he was shivering, so he covered up again and hoped he'd feel better in the morning. *Can't get any worse.*

Before he knew it, Corporal Pierce was beating the hell out of one of the three cast iron stoves with the butt of a broomstick and yelling, "Rise and shine!" Gower and the others were getting out of bed at various speeds till Pierce shouted, "Ahh-tennnn-*hut*!" They snapped to it and waited for orders in their khaki boxers and sleeveless cotton vests.

At least the others did. Gower found himself having difficulty maintaining a rigid stance. He was just thinking to himself that his first full day in camp might not turn out so great, when he fell, face-first, to the floor.

CHAPTER NINE

Feeling Better, Getting Wuhse

1

Gower's eyelids bumped up against something cold sitting on his face. Although he couldn't see and couldn't remember anything after Corporal Pierce beat on the stove with a broomstick, he was pretty sure he was awake. Or anyway, not dead. On preliminary exploration with his fingers, he confirmed that the thing on his face was an icepack.

"Got you *some* fever, private!" a woman's voice said from the darkness. "And a good-sized lump on your head, too," she added before walking away. *A nurse? In the hospital?* He had the urge to remove the icepack and take a look around before deciding against it. *Don't want to be recognized as the kid from California who washed out of the Army after less than a week. And most of that week was spent with my butt parked on a train.*

He had a pretty good idea what Mugsy Levine would have said about it. *"You're embarrassin' me, Kid."*

With nothing else to do but lie there and throb, Gower tried piecing together events leading up to his hospitalization. The bump-on-his-head part was easy. *Keeled over and planted my face on the barracks floor. But the nurse also said I had a fever. Felt a little faint most of the day we arrived. Was that yesterday?* He suddenly realized he wasn't sure when that was, or how long he'd been unconscious. He didn't remember eating anything since chow at the mess hall, listening to Waverly defend Hogjaw Thornton. At the same time, he didn't feel hungry, so he guessed either he hadn't been in the hospital that long or he must have been given something to eat somewhere along the line. He felt for his wounded wrist. It was wrapped in bandages and no longer as painful. Moving made him feel a bit woozy. *Maybe got me on drugs. . . . Jeez, did that Japanese kid have rabies, or something?*

A bugle sounded in the distance. "Taps." *Perfect.* It wasn't long before he drifted off and out—remaining so until he heard a different woman's voice.

"Here's your uniform," the stranger said. "Hope you're feeling better soon, recruit," she added, "'cause I think you're kinda . . ."

"Hmmm?" Gower couldn't hear the last part of what the woman said. He thought maybe it rhymed with "recruit" and was pretty sure he heard only one syllable. A *tap-tapping* of shoes on a wood plank floor was rapidly fading.

What?! What *do you think I am? "Cute"? "Zoot"? "Astute"?*

He snatched the icepack off his face, rolled over, and raised up on an elbow. Though the quick shift made him feel a bit dizzy, he could see a woman, another nurse, he supposed, heading away between two rows of beds. The blonde hairdo and the shape of her hips triggered a memory. *The GI Jane serenading us at Little Rock Station?* He watched till she disappeared out the door. It was then that his more immediate surroundings came into focus. Everyone else he could see in the room was Black. He wondered if the flu was only hitting colored troops. Pulling himself up to a sitting position caused his wrist to hurt a little and his head to start throbbing again.

"You OK, private?" the female voice from the other day asked.

Gower turned to see a Black nurse standing by a nearby bed in the other direction. "I guess so," he replied. "A little dizzy." Everywhere he looked there were Black soldiers in or on beds, and Black staff attending to them. *No other whites! Where the hell am I?*

"We gave you something for that infection and the fever," she said. "You should be feeling a lot better, soon. And if you think you're up to it, the doctor says you're free to report back to your outfit," she told him. "Just keep the dressing dry and change it before you go to bed this evening. Nurse Lane said she pinned your orders to your blouse, on that chair." She pointed. "If you don't feel up to it, you don't have to do drills for the next couple days. There's a note from the doctor in charge. I'd say you are one lucky dogface."

The nurse went back to whatever she was doing, leaving Gower to puzzle over his condition and whether being called a "dogface" was a good thing. Reaching for his uniform, he had a feeling he was being watched. He looked up. *More like being studied.* His eyes met those of several of the sick or injured Black soldiers, staring over at him from their own beds. *As if wondering what I'm going to do next, and whether it's what they would have done under the circumstances. In other words, exactly what I'm wondering about them.* A wave of self-consciousness rolled over the former lifeguard. The five fingers of one hand came out ahead of the number of Blacks he'd ever been this close to before. *Well, if I'm expected to fight and die with these guys, I guess I shouldn't mind dressing in front of 'em.*

His uniform had been laundered and pressed. His shoes were under the chair. They shone as if recently polished. He checked the blouse for blood from the bite wound. There wasn't any. He remembered a clerk at Fort MacArthur telling them that only their first uniform was free. *This uniform is new! How am I gonna pay for it? I haven't even got my first paycheck yet, and I'm already in the hole!*

He unpinned the orders and took a look. There was a handwritten note attached. "Get well soon!" it said, signed with a lipstick imprint. *That blonde's puckered kisser!*

He looked around briefly for the Black nurse to thank her. When he didn't spot her right away, he hurried for the door, hoping to catch up with the white one who thought he was something that may or may not have rhymed with "recruit."

2

Outside of the hospital, two things immediately struck him—the glaring sun and the soldiers. Everyone he saw—standing around, walking by, shooting the breeze, having a smoke—was Black. He knew from what McCleary said that the Army separated colored troops from white ones. *Is there a separate side of Camp Forrest just for them? Or have I been sent to a different Army base altogether—one for Blacks, a few miles down the road, or something?*

He was thinking about asking one of the colored GIs for directions to Camp Forrest when he spied a white man in blue fatigues and a "clamdigger" hat, casually raking at some litter along the walkway.

"Hey, Mac," Gower hailed him on approach, "how do I get to Camp Forrest from here?"

The man was clearly upset by being addressed. He took a furtive look around, as if worried someone might be watching. "Ummm," he started. "*Hee*-ya," he insisted while pointing emphatically to the ground at his feet. "*Hee*-ya Cawmp Fawst!"

"Camp Forrest is *here*?" Gower confirmed. *Sounds like maybe he's got some sort of speech problem.*

"Ja! Ja! Das ist es . . . !"

It was then Gower noticed the "PW"s stenciled on the guy's denims. *Ahhh. Mystery solved.*

"*Englisch,* no," the German added, shaking his head and waving his hands apologetically in front of his chest, apparently afraid there could be consequences for fraternizing with the former enemy.

If this is Camp Forrest, there must be two hospitals—one for whites and one for Blacks! He supposed he may have been sent to the hospital for colored troops because the one for white GIs was full. *And figured I wouldn't notice,* he sarcastically supposed. "Take it easy, pal. I'm not going to shoot you or anything," Gower tried to reassure him. The POW smiled and nodded. *Clearly clueless.*

All Gower wanted from the prisoner was a hint for getting back to the white part of camp. He searched his memory for the German word for "white." *All I got is "schwatzuh"—what Mr. Weiss uses when he's complaining about the Black people hanging around his butcher shop downtown. Don't remember if I ever heard Weiss say the German word for "white"!*

"*Hee*-ya *ist schwatzuh,*" Gower said slowly to the POW, while indicating their surroundings. "Yah?"

"Ja, sind Sie," the man said, giggling and nodding, relieved to have the GI speaking his language, if only minimally.

"So . . . *vo ist,* um . . . *white*?!" Gower quickly gave up finishing the sentence in German and simply tapped the back of his hand, then his cheek, and finally the white "PW" stenciling on the POW's denim jacket. The Nazi just wasn't getting it. "White!" Gower again blurted out in English. "Where the hell's the *white* part of this damned camp?!"

"What's the trouble, bud?" A colored soldier approached them.

3

"Are you lost?" the Black private followed up.

"Yes," a red-faced Gower admitted. "I didn't realize there were two separate hospitals here in camp. They brought me to the one over here after I passed out, so I don't know the way back to my barracks."

"They sent you over *here*?" The colored soldier couldn't completely suppress a laugh. "Well, I suppose they had their reasons," he said, once he'd more or less recovered. "Anyways, to get back to where you came from, mainly, you just keep heading in that direction." He pointed toward the west.

"Thanks," Gower said. "Much appreciated."

The other soldier nodded and started to walk away before turning to add something else. "It's the Army's way of doing things," he said. "Camp Forrest has a Black part and a white part. Fits right in, down here . . . I guess you must be new, then, hunh? To the Army *and* to the South."

"Yeah. Just arrived . . . yesterday? Maybe before that. I was out cold. I've lost track. From Los Angeles . . . Gower," he said, stepping closer and offering to shake. The Black soldier stared incredulously at the white man's extended hand for a moment before accepting it.

"Johnson . . . Chicago."

"Guess I got a lot to learn."

"Yes, you do." The other man grinned, and nodded before going about his business. "Yes, you do!"

"Schwarzer Mann . . . Weißer Mann," the POW was saying as he pointed first at Johnson walking away, and then at himself.

"Yeah. Thanks. Got it. You've been a big help, Fritz," Gower said before heading west, as Johnson had suggested.

The layout of the place soon became clear. *Like Johnson said, there's two separate camps—a Black one and a white one. . . . And maybe three, if you count the Krauts.* At one point during the search for his new home, Gower could hear multiple voices singing in what he supposed must have been German. *Mr. Weiss would be right at home.*

The colored version of Camp Forrest had meeting halls, at least a couple of chapels, and mess halls. There were rows of tents—dozens of them—with colored troops in and around them. And barracks buildings, too, he guessed, though they seemed fragile and unfinished compared to his own. The bottom half was plywood, but the top half was more like a large tent. The "windows" were square holes under roll-up canvas flaps. *Kinda slapdash and unorganized over here, if you ask me.*

He recalled what Santa Monica or someone said about Negro troops—that they were lazy and wouldn't be any good in a fight. *Maybe the guy had a point.* Most of the Black GIs Gower saw as he made his way back to his own part of The Forrest seemed to have nothing in particular to do and nowhere to go—even though it was the middle of the day. *Hey! Could it be the weekend already?!* He had no idea how many days he'd been in the hospital. A glance at his orders didn't help. There was a date on it, but he wasn't sure what day of the month he'd arrived.

It wasn't till Gower walked for what he guessed was about a half mile that he figured he was back in the white portion of the place, or very near it. The buildings looked more like his barracks. He saw few, if any, Black GIs. And in fact, he saw few soldiers at all. He could hear what he thought might be commands being shouted at soldiers-in-training and random *booms* he supposed might be artillery rounds from a range. *Must be out marching or training, or something. So,* not *the weekend . . .*

"Sah! Look out, sah!" someone shouted.

Gower turned to see an airplane bearing down on him. There was a swastika on the tail.

4

The plane veered away before crashing to the ground a few feet away. It was only a model plane, but a large, very realistic-looking one. Gower guessed the wingspan at over a yard.

"Oh, sorry, sah! Sorry! I'm *so* sorry 'bout that, sah!" A Black soldier bowed and saluted and bowed again, then bent down to inspect the damage. Gower guessed the model was supposed to represent a German fighter of some sort. The detail was impressive.

From the loving way the man inspected the decoy, Gower figured him for the builder. "Great-looking plane," he told the guy.

"Thank yah, sah. Thank yah kindly," the GI said without looking up, from his hands and knees. "Flies real good, too. Got away from me, there. . . . Bit a wind . . . Just hope it ain't too badly broke. . . . Lost a strut!" he announced before suddenly turning and scrambling around in the dirt at their feet before snatching up a small piece of the wreckage. "Ain't seed a tail flap, has yah?"

"Is that it?" Gower pointed.

"That's the one!" the soldier said, happily gathering it in. He stuffed the broken pieces into his breast pocket, carefully cradled the model, and stood up.

"Name's Gower. From California."

"Pleased to meet yah, sah. I'm Eberley. From 'round these parts."

"Eberley?"

"Yassah."

"You built that airplane?"

"Yassah. I did build this here aero plane. Well, mostly I built it—some parts for sure, I did."

"Good job. What's it for?"

"Targeting ID," Eberley said, placing a hard accent on the first letter of the acronym. "We string 'em on a wire, yonder," he said, pointing vaguely to another part of the camp, "and pass 'em by, ovah head the GIs sose they can practice aimin' and identifyin'. You gotta lead them aero planes with yo rifle faiah, they say. Jes like huntin' a duck. Else you cain't hit one, they say. 'Course, I ain't never been huntin' a duck, so I wouldn't know it for a fact. But this here's a Messerschmitt's what 'tis. One of them *Nazi* aero planes, what I built."

"By the way," Gower added, offering to shake, "you probably outrank me, Private Eberley, 'cause you've been here longer than me. So, you don't need to keep saying 'sir.'"

"Yassah," Eberley said, smiling warmly while awkwardly extending a hand from under the Messerschmitt he cradled. "Well, I got to be gettin' back now, sah. Thanks for findin' that wing flap."

"No problem," Gower told him before remembering he wasn't really sure where he was going. "Say . . . ," he quickly added, pulling out the referral from the colored hospital. He snatched off the lipstick-smooched note before handing the document to the model builder.

"Do you know where this barracks is? I'm kinda lost."

Gower watched as Eberley glanced briefly at the document, certainly without reading it.

"No, sah. I don't know nothin' about that. Nor where 'tis, neither," he said, backing away. "Sorry, sah, but my eyes is pretty bad. Can't make it out 'zactly. Anyways, I gotta get goin'. Sorry I cain't help yah, sah, but I hope yah do find it." Eberley's head bobbed slightly once or twice more before he turned and hurried off.

Gower gave the handwriting on the referral a puzzled look. The barracks "address" seemed pretty clear to him. He simply didn't know how to get there. *How can this Eberley guy be working on model planes if his eyesight's so bad?* He'd seen some men issued eyeglasses during the induction process and wondered why Eberley wasn't wearing a pair. *And before maybe deciding I wasn't going to report him, or chew him out, or something, was he doing a sort of "Stepin Fetchit" routine with all that "Yah, sah, no sah" baloney? Because I'm white? Because he was in the middle of the white part of camp?*

Gower pressed on, wandering through the maze of identical barracks buildings, trying to match the written numbers to one of them and asking passersby along the way, until finally arriving back home. He went in. There was no one else around. The walk had tired him out. *Must be the drugs.* He went to his bunk and sat down. He kicked off his shoes and leaned back for a snooze. Sleep came easily.

He dreamed about lying out in the rain. He could feel a few drops landing on his face.

"Yo! Sleeping Beauty!"

5

Gower's eyes fluttered open to a guy standing by the bed, in his underwear, a towel draped over his shoulder. His hair was wet. He was flicking drops of water in Gower's direction. "That's my bunk you're sleeping on, case you didn't know."

Gower had only been in the barracks for the one night before he fainted. He hadn't bothered to look at the name on the locker sitting in front of the bed before crashing on it. "Oh! Sorry!" he said, and dragged himself over to where he belonged. "Missed my own bunk by one."

"You're one of the new guys, so I'll cut you a break. You were gone a couple days, werentcha?"

"Yeah," Gower started, embarrassed by his debut and hasty exit. "Not sure how many. . . . Had a bit of a problem."

"Yeah! I remember you hittin' the floor pretty hawd. *Bam!*" the guy said, slapping his forehead with the palm of his hand. "Musta hurt somethin' awful." He wiped his hand on his towel before extending it. "Bet you're from Caufornia, like those other guys . . . Conroy. From Phluffia. You know. Philly." *Wow! First Eberley and now Conroy. Different ways of talking. Like Mom and Dad with their accents. But, in America—so many more! Like different songs and different music!*

"That's in Pennsavenia, case you didn't know," Conroy went on. "You been there? Probbly not. That's OK. I ain't been to Caufornia neither, so we're even."

"Gower. Los Angeles."

"Haven't been here too long myself, come to think of it," the guy said. "Whaddzit now? Maybe a mundt?" As he talked, he finished drying his hair with the towel and pulled out bits and pieces of a uniform from his locker to change into.

"Already got the KP, though. That's Kitchen Patrol, case

you didn't know. Big deal. Worked in my uncle's restaurant before the Army. For two weeks. Piece a cake. Ain't really my uncle, though. Two weeks for the KP, I mean. Worked at my uncle's place longer than that. Pretty good lasagna, if you ever go there. He's Itayan. That's why we ain't related, 'cept 'cause he married one of Mom's sisters. Probbly set a new record for FTTP . . . Me, I mean. Not my uncle. Fasdest Time to Punishment . . . For the KP. I made that up, by the way, FTTP. The fasdest. Woont surprise me. But, hey, I'm from the Sout. That's how we oberate."

Gower nodded. *Quite an accent this guy's got.* He started to explain himself, but then realized there really wasn't much to explain. *I arrived. Slept. Woke up. Fell down. Was taken to the hospital. Walked back.* "Met two colored guys," he mumbled. "Oh, and a German."

Conroy nodded and gave Gower a polite few seconds of silence before starting in again. "That's a joke, by the way. 'I'm from the Sout.' In case you didn't know. From Sout *Phluffia.* Anyway, that's why I ain't out with the other guys, marching around—on account of the KP they give me. Two weeks. Almost done, though. It's really good lasagna. At my uncle's place. Just don't call him that if you go there. 'Danny's uncle.' He don't like it. They been divorced a while, he and my aunt. She run out on him. Hates lasagna."

While Conroy got dressed, they talked some more—that is, Conroy talked. Gower mainly listened—if nothing else, fascinated by his new way of talking. "Gower" tumbled out of Conroy's mouth as "Gowah."

Gower liked Conroy right away. He liked the guy's outlook. *He's got some moxie. Reminds me of Mugsy—or anyway, Mugsy's good side. Being in the Army doesn't seem to bother him.* He decided to show Conroy the note he got. "For some reason, when I passed out the other day, they sent me to the colored hospital. I was the only white guy in the whole ward.

Took me a while to find my way back here. Got this note from the doc over there." Gower handed Conroy the referral. "At least I guess it was the doc who gave it to me. It was pinned to my blouse when I woke up. So, I figure with that paper, I can probably take it easy for a couple more days."

Conroy studied the paper before handing it back. "Wouldn't count on it."

6

Gower gave the paper in his hand a puzzled look. "Why not?"

"Number one, look at the date they took you in." Conroy leaned over and pointed to that particular space on the form. "That was Tuesday, first thing. This is Thursday. Almost ovuh. You was gone three full days. Maybe gonna give you some of that KP, too. Hey! Then *you'd* be the new FTTP champeen!"

Fastest Time to Punishment. The thought had Gower suddenly feeling sick again.

"Number two, you were in the cullert hospital, right?"

"Yeah? So?"

"So maybe you got that order from a cullert doc."

"I never saw him. What difference does it make what color he was?"

"Stuff from that side of the camp don't count for a lotta folks on this side of the camp, is whad I'm sayin'." Conroy shrugged. "That's how it is. Maybe you don't got sides or nuttin' in Caufornia, but they got 'em down here. And we got 'em in Phluffia, too. Sides, I mean."

The Brookside pool scrubbed with bleach after the colored swimmers used it. The Japanese couple led away under guard. Hatred of the "zoot suiters." Things some of the guys said on our way to Camp Forrest. "Yeah," Gower quietly admitted, "in California, we got sides."

Up until Conroy told him how many days he'd been gone and that his referral was likely no good, Gower had been feeling remarkably upbeat—the best since he left home. Returning from the hospital more or less healed and healthy and making a new friend in Conroy were two of the brighter, if not the only bright, spots in his so-far abbreviated and otherwise very gloomy military career.

"Cheer up, Gowah," Conroy told him. "It could be wuhse."

"Oh, yeah? How?"

"Whad am I? A fortune tellah or sumpin'? That's what people say. 'Could be wuhse' . . . Just tryin' to make you feel better. Usually, they're right, though, come to think of it."

Gower nodded. "I guess that's true, hunh," he admitted. "It could be worse." The now-maybe-uninitiated recruit at Camp Forrest was learning a lot of things. One of them was it was hard to stay down for very long with Conroy around. Gower and the guy from *Phluffia* sat in the otherwise empty barracks shooting the breeze for another hour or so until the other boots came back from the field, hot, sweaty, and complaining.

"Finally decided to show up, eh, Gower?" Bucoda said, giving the absentee a look. Sweat mixed liberally with dust on his face and the faces of the others. "Should we tell him?" he added, turning to McCleary.

"Not me," McCleary said, shaking his head. "I haven't got the heart."

"Bad news? What?" Gower asked.

"Gower!" Waverly said, coming over to greet him. "Great news!"

"The war's over?" Gower quipped, trying to be funny.

"While you were gone, Sergeant Thornton took over our platoon!"

"Oh, yeah," Conroy said. "Forgot to mention it. *Hogjaw* they call him. Real hard-ass . . . Guess I was right, though, hunh, Gowah? Things got wuhse."

CHAPTER TEN

Brothers in Arms

1

Except for Waverly, everyone else was pretty blue about this development. It turned out their first day with Sergeant King had also been their last. No one knew when or why King was relieved of duty.

"King never showed up that morning," McCleary explained. "After they took you away, we dressed for drills and headed for the parade ground. Corporal Pierce led us over. When we got there, we were met by Hogjaw."

"Told us Sergeant King was being relieved."

"What could we say? We're soldiers."

"But, you know, I figure it's just like Conroy tells us," The Pigeon jumped in. "It could be worse."

That night, Gower thought he heard voices. *Two men. Laughing softly.* His mouth was dry. He was drenched in sweat. *Maybe from the drugs.* He went out and over to the toilet hut to take a pee and get some water from the sink.

On the way back, he passed someone in the dark hugging the walls, heading for the showers. The guy had a towel over his shoulder. Gower thought it might have been Waverly.

Reveille sounded around seven. Since he missed the first few days, Gower had to study the others to figure out what he was supposed to be doing. Everyone else shaved, dressed, and snapped to attention in plenty of time. Gower finished out of the money.

"A-tennn-*hut*!" Pierce shouted at them.

As he saw the others do, Gower stared straight ahead. Eventually, Hogjaw Thornton came into view. He seemed to be working his way slowly down the aisle between the two rows of beds, pausing every so often to sniff or poke at something. *Some sort of inspection.*

"Corporal Pierce!" the sergeant shouted.

"Yes, sir!"

"You're from Missouri, Pierce. You know what n*****s smell like, don't you?"

"Sir?"

"You don't smell one right here in the barracks this morning, Pierce?"

"Not from here, sir. I can't say that I do, sir."

Hogjaw sniffed at the trooper opposite Conroy. "Getting closer, Pierce," the sergeant reported. He drifted over to Gower's new friend and sniffed at the Phluffian's puss.

"This one here smells like an Irish Philly whore. But not a n*****. Nope. Not quite."

Hogjaw then stepped directly in front of Gower before pressing in very close. Because of the height difference, Hogjaw's broad-brimmed high hat accommodated them both. Staring straight ahead, Gower was faced with the pink, "L"-shaped scar he'd seen on the sergeant's jowl just before they boarded the train at Fort MacArthur.

"Whaddya know, Pierce," Thornton said, turning to his

second in command. "That n***** I smelled is *right here*!" He grinned. "Welcome back, Gower! While your betters were sweating their balls off in the field, you spent the last three days on the dark side of camp jerking off with your n***** pals, didn't you?"

"I was over there, sir. Yes, sir. In the hospital, sir."

"Put this man on report, Pierce. He owes his country three days of drill. Let's call it even at two days, in full battle pack—and the eight-mile march at the end of both of 'em."

"I was hoping to rest a little longer, sir. Still not feeling too good." Gower started to reach for the referral in his blouse pocket. Hogjaw tensed, eyeing the lowly boot suspiciously. Gower froze. "With your permission, sir." Thornton's head flicked the slightest affirmative in the private's direction.

"They gave me this at the hospital, sir." Gower presented the referral to the sergeant.

Hogjaw snatched the folded document from the boot and spread it open without bothering to read it. Instead, he hocked up a throat-rattling loogie, and spat the load into the form before wadding the paper up and handing it back.

2

Thornton pressed in again. "That spit-wad you gave me was addressed to Sergeant King, Gower. He's no longer with this outfit."

"Yes, sir."

"Report to Pierce after chow, then join us on the parade ground if you're not too busy butt-fucking with your n***** friends," Hogjaw added before turning to Conroy. "Lucky you, Philly. You're off KP. Report to me with the others."

Conroy was visibly disappointed. *"Piece of cake,"* Gower remembered him saying about mess hall duty.

Hogjaw laid out the day's plan. "After morning chow, rifles, cotton vests above the belt and field dress below for the men, Pierce. Add helmets, blouses, and cartridge belts after lunch. . . . The n***** joins us in full battle dress and pack all day, on my order. Eight-mile march for him after drills, on yours."

"Yes, sir," Pierce said.

"On second thought," Hogjaw snapped. "Conroy, you're a lazy bastard, too, ain'tcha. Got a lot in common with your bunk buddy here. You know your way along the course of march. Keep him company out there on the trail. Eight-mile march for you, today, too. Mosquitoes starting to bite. Put on some of that sissy aftershave you like to wear. And on your friend while you're at it. The skeeters will love you for it. The chiggers, too. . . . Hey! Chiggers love n*****s. That rhymes! Whaddya know, Pierce," Hogjaw chortled, retreating toward his quarters at the back of the room. "I'm a poet, and I didn't know it. Dismiss the men," he said over his shoulder. "Oh, and the n*****, too."

After breakfast, they dressed for drills. Everyone fell in outside the barracks before Hogjaw quick-marched them off to wherever it was they were training—everyone except Gower and Corporal Pierce.

"Grab the field gear you were issued in California, Gower," Pierce said as he headed for the door, "then meet me out back, in front of the supply hut."

The greenest of the greenhorns opened his locker and stood staring at the contents. *Where to begin? Helmet?* Before retrieving it, he remembered the cloth "garrison cap" still on his head and took it off. Folding it over his belt, he pulled the steel "brain bucket" and its much lighter liner from the locker and set them down on the bed. *Never noticed how much heavier the helmet is than the liner!* The liner had adjustable webbing inside and a chinstrap. The helmet itself had neither. After nesting them, he set them on his head. When he leaned over to gather some other stuff, the liner remained strapped to his noggin, but the helmet hit the floor like a rock. Looking at the upside-down metal turtle shell rocking gently on the solid plank floor, Gower decided it might make a better pail than a hat. He stuffed it with his "Field Ration Type K Dinner Unit," first aid kit, suspenders, and bayonet, and then set it on the bed. He put his poncho, his half shelter, entrenching tool, canteen, and belt in his field pack, and laid it on the bed, too. He grabbed his rifle from the bunkside rack, slung it over his shoulder, strung one of the field pack straps over the barrel, grabbed his stuffed-olive helmet, and shuffled out the door to meet up with Pierce.

"Oh, yeah," the corporal said when he saw Gower approaching. "Forgot you weren't here when we went over how to strap all this stuff on."

Pierce got him squared away with the gear he brought over from the barracks—especially his helmet—and then started pulling pieces of equipment from shelves and pegs in the supply shed and handing them over. "About seventy pounds' worth of gear, all told, Gower. Hope you can handle it." Pierce proceeded to add a rifle-cleaning kit and a couple of grenades. "They're dummies, so don't worry," he chuckled. "Better to fear the butter-fingered, two-legged dummies using real ones out on the range."

It didn't take long for the accumulation of gear to outstrip Gower's ability to decide where and how to attach it to his person. A pile of unassimilated items grew rapidly at his feet. "Cartridge belt . . . ," Pierce was saying, his head buried in a locker. He turned to hand the recruit a thick canvas belt with several pouches on it. "We fill the pouches with slugs and washers, so it weighs about the same—but no cartridges."

"*Cartridges*? You mean, like, 'bullets'?" Gower asked.

Pierce cast a doubtful eye on the private. "Yeah, sure, Bronco Billy. 'Bullets,'" he said sarcastically. "Just don't ever call 'em that in front of Sergeant Thornton. He'll make you eat one." The corporal turned his attention back to the locker. "So, where was I? Gas mask and pouch, grenade pouch, and hatchet. . . . I guess that about does it."

They were heading back to the barracks when Pierce remembered something else. "Forgot to fill your canteen. You're going to need it. You're too loaded up to make it to the taps. Wait inside for me. I'll go fill it for you."

In the barracks alone, Gower gave himself the once-over in one of the full-length wall mirrors. *Certainly look like a soldier. Literally dressed to kill.* He then remembered what Sergeant King said about guys joining up simply to impress a girlfriend back home. *Not a problem for me. I don't have one.*

3

Pierce returned with a full canteen and inserted it into the pouch on Gower's utility belt. "Not bad, Private," he said, inspecting the results. "Not bad. . . . Oh, wait. One more thing."

The corporal reached over and undid Gower's tie. "You won't be needing this for a while, unless you decide you want to hang yourself with it by the end of the day. Just kidding. Uncle Sam needs to keep you alive long enough to kill at least a couple of Japs or Germans first."

"Thanks for the help with all this, Corporal Pierce. I really appreciate it. Sorry for all the trouble I caused by missing a few days."

"It happens," Pierce said. "Though come to think of it, the last guy it happened to *did* hang himself."

There was a thoughtful pause while Gower wondered whether it was possible to hang oneself with a necktie. He decided to change the subject. "Wish I could be a better boot for Sergeant Thornton. I just haven't been able to figure him out. Maybe you heard. He rode with us on the train all the way out here from Los Angeles."

"Your tough luck he replaced Sergeant King, I guess, hey, kid?" Pierce said, patting Gower on the shoulder.

"Yeah. Quite a surprise."

"Yeah, well, better get used to it, Gower," Pierce told him, checking the straps of the Californian's field pack one more time. "The Army's full of surprises. Sergeant King got reassigned. That happens, too—especially if you rub certain people the wrong way." He pulled particularly hard on the cinch.

"Excuse me, Corporal Pierce . . . but is he still around?"

"King? Oh, yeah, he's still around, all right," Pierce said, at last looking Gower in the eye. "But you and I might not be seeing him again real soon. They put him over with the coloreds. A Medical Replacement Battalion. There aren't enough colored noncoms. They'll take anyone they can get. A double whammy, if you ask me. Most colored recruits can't even read or write. What a waste of a good sergeant. Those boys're never gonna set foot on a battlefield. Kiss of death if King was ever hoping to see combat again."

"Again?" Gower was pretty sure King was nowhere near as old as Hogjaw, so he decided he couldn't have seen action during the First World War.

"Yeah. Shanghai in '38." After saying his piece, Pierce abruptly backed off. "Listen, Gower . . . you didn't hear any of this about Sergeant King from me. OK? None of it."

Gower nodded but had no idea what Pierce meant and wasn't sure what he was agreeing to do, or not do.

"And I don't know nothing about Sergeant Thornton, either, except what he orders me to do. You got it?"

Gower nodded again—now, even more confused.

"Or Captain Mennur, for that matter."

About to nod a third time, Gower asked a question instead. "Do I know Captain Mennur?"

"Forget it!" Pierce said, angry with himself for letting the name slip. "Now get out there before we both end up on the darker side of this place!" He literally spun Gower around to point him toward the door and then swatted him on the butt cheek not shielded by his canteen.

The battle-ready boot took a few unsteady steps with the added seventy pounds before performing a cautious about-face. "Excuse me, Corporal Pierce, but where am I going?"

"Head that way," Pierce said, pointing south. "Turn left at the cannonballs and the statue of General Forrest. Then right at the main road. You'll hear Hog—Sergeant Thornton's voice before you see him or the platoon. Your buddies and a couple thousand other guys'll be drilling on the parade grounds. You can't miss 'em."

4

Whether it was from the drugs, or because of the seventy-odd pounds of added, awkward weight, it took Gower a couple dozen paces to simply figure out how to walk in a more or less straight line.

"Find your center, Kid, and stick with it." A bit of ringside advice from Mugsy came in handy. *"Even southpaws can't mess with you if you find your center and stick with it."*

Enduring ten minutes of stares and one wiseacre telling

him, "Turn around, buddy! The Philippines are thataway!" Gower found the Civil War cannon and the pyramids of shot piled beneath the watchful eyes of a bronze General Forrest on horseback and turned left as instructed.

Well before arriving at the yard, Gower heard Hogjaw's booming voice. *Like Corporal Pierce said I would.* The battle-dressed private waddled onto the parade grounds and straight to the rear rank of his platoon, hoping nobody would notice. The men were in the middle of a drill. Each one was using his rifle like a barbell—thrusting it overhead, out in front, or to the side. Waverly was leading the exercise by example. He was standing on a small platform a few feet off the ground so the other boots could see what they were supposed to be doing.

Sorta like at the Y. Gower mimicked the others as best he could while carrying seventy extra pounds and being overdressed for the weather. He was doing OK but was soon drenched in sweat.

"Platoon . . . halt!" Sergeant Thornton shouted. "Gower! Fall out and fall in at the front rank! On the double!" Gower hustled to the opposite side of the formation as fast as he could, then snapped to attention.

"You're out of line, Private N*****!" Hogjaw snarled at him. "Get down and give me twenty! And keep your field pack on."

From one of Conroy's soliloquies about Army punishment, Gower knew the order meant he owed the sergeant that many push-ups. Standing around at the Beverly Hills Y, in the locker room or by the pool, waiting for guests or for Mr. Scobbs to give him something to do, Gower had done push-ups. Sit-ups. Curls. Whatever. Calisthenics and workouts in general were how he whiled away idle time.

He handed his rifle to the nearest boot and got down as ordered. To The Welsh Kid's own surprise, he was able to get to six and a half before collapsing under the added weight. He lay there, facedown, spread-eagled flat on the ground beneath seventy-plus pounds of Government Issue, hoping he could somehow disappear.

"Get up, Gower! You're a disgrace to this outfit!" Hogjaw shouted over his shoulder before turning to mount the drill leader's platform himself, shooing The Pigeon away in the process.

While Thornton wasn't looking, two or three other boots helped Gower to his feet. One of them was Bucoda, giving him a wink and a nod as he did so. With their help, Gower reachieved verticality just as the sergeant launched into rapid-fire close-order marching drills.

"Parade! Ready at my command! Shoulder . . . arms! Forward, march! Dress right . . . dress! Ready, front . . . cover!"

The way the others went about it, Gower supposed they all knew what to do. He didn't have a clue. His missteps soon caused a few near-miss collisions. After a couple more minutes of boot-on-boot chaos, even Thornton apparently had had enough. He led the platoon in more calisthenics and rifle drills instead. They went on for another hour or so before he dismissed them for noon mess.

While the others returned to the barracks to unload what they could before heading for lunch, Gower headed back alone to do the same, several minutes behind them. By the time he got as far as the statue of General Forrest, newfound friend Conroy hurried past him going the other way. "See you later, Gowah!" he called out. "Need to see a guy about a ring."

A ring. For his girl?

By the time Gower made it back to the barracks, most everyone else had either left for lunch or had already returned after eating. In the mess hall, he found Bucoda, McCleary, and Waverly still hanging around, so he parked his tray at the same table. He cleared his plate in no time and briefly considered going back for more. He decided any additional weight could only add to his problems during drills. So, instead of more food, he sat back and took in some of the table talk.

". . . old buzzard is trying to show us how tough he is," Bucoda groused. "But he's killing us in the bargain."

"We've got some catching up to do, that's for sure," McCleary added. "Three days sitting on our butts on a train didn't do us a whole lotta good. Those East Coast guys are way ahead of us."

"I led some drills a couple times during the trip," The Pigeon reminded them. "You guys coulda joined in, too, you know."

"Looked kinda fruity to me, Waverly, out there in the desert," Bucoda scoffed. "Like ballet or something. I don't know about you, but I forgot to pack my tutu."

5

After chow, the other recruits put on helmets, blouses, and weighted cartridge belts. Gower climbed back under his seventy-plus pounds of battle gear. Sergeant Thornton marched the platoon off toward the obstacle course. Gower and Corporal Pierce—now wearing a field bag over one shoulder—brought up the rear. The obstacle course was well beyond the parade grounds, on the edge of a gully, much wider than it was deep.

As was true in the morning, Gower—with Pierce alongside him—soon fell behind. For the better part of three hours, the weighted-down boot tried to copy any recruits still close enough to study. They ran through and along, then into and out of ditches, natural and manmade. They hopped back and forth over the same ditches. They charged through brush, uphill and downhill. Sometimes, the other guys were so far ahead Gower had to rely on Pierce's description and pantomime of what he was supposed to do next.

They'd been out of visual contact with the rest of the platoon for several minutes when at last Gower could see the guys up ahead helping each other over a wall at least half a foot taller than even Sergeant Thornton. Beyond it was a barrier nearly double in height. Long since finished with their drills, the other recruits had reassembled. They were standing to the side, awaiting further orders.

After trying and failing to scale the first wall, Gower was done. He stood to the side, hunched over, panting and puffing, completely soaked in sweat. *I wonder if it's actually possible to puke my own guts out like Sergeant King said.* Pierce, on the other hand, leaned against the wall, stifling a yawn. *Maybe that's why Corporal Pierce brought that shoulder bag—for me to puke in.* He scratched at his wounded wrist. The bandage had long since fallen off. The partially scabbed-over bite marks burned from the constant rubbing of his sweat-sopping cotton sleeve. He worried about reinfection. His spirits were briefly lifted when he spotted Conroy approaching at a jog, then flagged when he realized Hogjaw was with him.

"Pierce!" the sergeant shouted, though closer than shouting required. "How many kinds of rattlers we got here in Arkansas, anyhow?"

"Six, sir. Six types."

"Six? Oh, yeah. Forgot about the moccasins and the copperheads. Well, just another obstacle, right, Pierce? Eight-mile march, Gower," Hogjaw said, turning to the private. "You and Sweetie Pie better be back by sundown. Hard to see snakes in the dark. Could hear them rattle, of course, but by then, it might be a little too late." Thornton grinned at the thought. "I hear it's a long, painful death, girls. Good luck. Pierce, give the n***** and that sweet-smelling Philly whore the word while I escort the real men back to the barracks."

While Thornton jogged after the other recruits, Pierce swung the field bag around to his belly and opened the flap. He produced a wire hoop and handed it to Conroy. "Here's the token you'll need to exchange, Conroy," the corporal told him.

Gower guessed the hoop was a little more than a foot in diameter. A single brass cartridge casing was strung on it through a couple of holes.

"Bring back the one hanging at the four-mile marker. Leave this one there, and . . . Hell, you know what to do."

To prove we actually did the march?

"Yes, sir!" Conroy said, ambushing Gower with the sudden, unbridled expression of joy. "I sure do, sir!" He stuck his happily grinning face through the hoop and let it settle around his neck.

Maybe because it's got a different number of casings strung on it, or something. But why's Conroy so happy about the whole deal?

"The route is pretty well marked," Pierce went on, "but you could easily miss a sign after dark. Like Sergeant Thornton said, there's some critters out there you probably don't want to tangle with once you run out of daylight. Despite what he said about rattlers, what you better be looking out for is the pigs."

"The pigs?" Gower asked.

"Yes, sir," Conroy said, still smiling broadly. "The pigs. Yes, sir, we will, sir."

"Wild hogs, Gower," Pierce explained. "Razorbacks. Some of the boars get as big as a bear. You can usually hear 'em rustling around in the brush. If you do hear 'em, stay clear. They're as mean as . . ." He started to say something but thought the better of it. "Anyway, the best way to avoid 'em is not to be out after dark. If you can keep up a good pace, you might make it under three hours. It's a little after four now. I suggest you get moving. Good luck."

"Thank you, sir," Gower said and saluted as Pierce jogged off to catch up with Hogjaw Thornton and the "real men" of the platoon.

Despite all the work he used to do in order to last at least ten rounds in the ring, Gower's legs had turned to rubber. *No thanks to Hogjaw.* He wasn't confident of a successful eight miles, or of even remaining upright for very much longer. Conroy, on the other hand, seemed actually anxious to get going. *But he hasn't been carrying seventy pounds of added weight around all day.* He turned to go. "We better get moving." Despite worries about cramping, the ex-boxer took off at a fairly good clip.

"Hey, Hollywoot, hold on a minute, wouldya? Pierce's gone. The coast is clear."

A frustrated Gower stopped and waited impatiently for Conroy to catch up. When the Phluffian came alongside, he shed his rifle and handed it over. "Hold this, will ya?" he said, then pulled the wire token with one casing on it they got from Pierce up and over his head and offered that to Gower, too. "And this," he added, before undoing his cartridge belt and holding it out for his buddy to take. "Ditto."

"Getting late," Gower complained, but reluctantly complied. "Hey, how come your cartridge belt is so light? Is it empty?"

"Never mind that now, Gowah," Conroy said and got busy undoing his fly. "Today's your lucky day!" he announced, and let his trousers fall to his ankles.

CHAPTER ELEVEN

Rehearsal

1

"Wait a minute! Wait a *minute*! What the hell are you doing?!" Gower used his buddy's cartridge belt to cover his eyes. "Jeezuz, Conroy, I don't need any more trouble, thank you!" He leaned Conroy's rifle against a large rock and tossed the cartridge belt to the ground nearby before taking several steps farther along the trail. "You can do what you want, but *I'm* gonna do this course, even if it kills me."

"But we already *did* the course, Gowah. . . ." Conroy winked. "Dontcha remembah? And no offense, but I think it'd be pretty hard for you to have any more trouble than you already got . . ." Gower stopped and turned to say something, but then quickly faced away again when he saw Conroy digging into the crotch of his underwear. "Meanwhile, get a load of *this* pair of beauties!"

"Hey! Hold on, will ya? I'm not that kind of guy!"

"Relax! Dontcha get it? All we gotta do to prove we did

the march is bring back a hoop like what Pierce gave us—only with a different number of casings hanging on it."

Gower dared to look in Conroy's direction again as his buddy pulled two bullet shells up over the waistband of his briefs. The Philadelphian tugged a little harder. The two brass shells were strung on a metal hoop around his waist. It was identical to the hoop Corporal Pierce had given them, still parked around Conroy's neck, except Pierce's hoop only had a single bullet shell. This hoop had two.

"Tah-*dah*!"

"Where'd you get that?"

"Cigarettes," Conroy said, pulling the hoop above his underwear before letting it slide down to his trouser-covered ankles. "But I ain't paid it off totally yet. Had to scramble around to get what I got." He nodded toward the cartridge belt lying on the ground where Gower had dropped it.

Gower picked it up and looked inside. "Jeez! That's a whole lot of smokes!"

"I know a guy. Here . . . Trade ya." Conroy took the cartridge belt and handed Gower the hoop he had just dug out of his underwear before pulling his trousers back up and securing them. If Gower or anyone else had any doubts as to where the token's casings had recently been, residual warmth confirmed that, until recently, they'd been nestled next to the other private's privates.

"The guy's a tight-ass sonuvabitch, though, woontcha know it. And a Porchagee, he says. He's only a supply sergeant, but they say he's a big wheel in camp and got a lotta pull with the brass, especially some captain named Minor or Manner, or sumpin', who's cozy with General Flagg. That's how it works in The Forrest, I guess. So, when I first got here, a guy from back home said I should look up this Porchagee sergeant. So, I done that right away and was trying to get in good with him, ya know, if that's how it is, but I guess I said his name wrong or sumpin', cause he suddenly goes nuts and says to me, 'Hey, boot,' he says. 'Name's Rodrigues, not Rodriguez, 'cause I ain't no Mexican, understand?' He says, 'So, don't call me Rodriguez with a *z*. Call me Rodrigues with an *s*, if you wanna stay on my good side.' Or maybe he said it the other way around. *Rodriguez. Rodrigues.* Howdafuckdoaiknow which is which? Can *you* hear the difference?"

Gower shook his head.

"That makes two of us. Anyway, the guy doesn't *have* a good side, so whaddya gonna do?"

Indeed.

Conroy huffed a self-reprimand. "Jeez! I shouldn'ta ruined the mood, Gowah. Today's Friday!"

"Yeah. So?"

"So, as long as we're in this neck of the woots, we oughta drop by and say hello. They probbly already got started."

"Who? Doing what? Marching?" Gower glanced back down the trail, thinking Conroy might be referring to other soldiers out on the course.

"Rehearsal! Don't wanna miss the action, Jackson!"

When Gower turned to respond, Conroy was off the trail, heading into the brush, making a beeline back toward camp. The light was beginning to fade. Dusk would soon make it harder to move overland. "Your rifle!" Gower offered up Conroy's Springfield for him to reclaim. When he realized he might lose sight of the guy if he didn't get a move on, he slung his pal's piece over his other shoulder and followed as best he could.

2

Under the weight of his own gear plus Conroy's rifle, Gower was hard pressed to keep up. He nearly lost sight of his Philly friend a couple of times while extracting the barrel of one, if not both, of the Springfields from low-hanging branches.

After scrambling cross-country for several minutes, they came to a creek and crossed it by stepping on the tops of stones barely above the surface—or tried to. Gower slipped and landed with his right foot in the drink, filling his boot with water. "Shit!" he said as he joined Conroy on the other side.

"Shhhh!" his buddy warned him.

"Now what?" Gower whispered.

"We're almost there," Conroy explained. "But we gotta wait for the MP patrol to pass by first." He lifted Pierce's hoop from around his neck before undoing his cartridge belt full of cigarettes.

"Almost where? Say . . . you're not going to take off your pants again, are you?" Gower asked warily.

Conroy ignored his questions. "By the way," he said, "you owe me a carton of Luckies. . . . Oh, wait a minute. I'm supposed to be doing the eight miles, too, aren't I? Make that a half carton. Or you can pay me with a half pint of something with a kick to it. 'Sup to you."

"One more question," Gower whispered. "Before Pierce gave us the token, how did you know it only had one shell casing on it?"

"I didn't," Conroy admitted. "Just a lucky guess, I guess."

"Oh," Gower said. He nodded and then bit down on his lip as if to remind himself to keep quiet. *An MP patrol. How convenient. We'll be the easiest arrest they ever made.*

"Take a load off, Gowah," Conroy said after consulting his watch. "We still got about ten minutes."

They stayed down and silent in the creek bed for what seemed closer to half an hour. Gower heard a truck or something heading their way. Conroy stirred.

"Wait here," he whispered hoarsely, and scampered up the bank with his cartridge belt full of cigarettes and the one-cartridge hoop token Pierce gave them.

Gower could hear the vehicle slow down and then stop. It wasn't there for very long before driving off again.

"Pssst! Gowah!" Conroy soon beckoned from above. "The coast is clear! Come on!"

Gower clambered up to and then across a gravel road. He joined Conroy on the other side near a row of canvas-roofed barracks buildings like the ones he saw on his way back from the colored hospital. "Hey, what's that smell?" he asked, getting a noseful. He recognized the odor from childhood pony rides at Brookside Park. "Smells like a stable."

"This is the cullert part of camp," Conroy explained.

"The camp's got horses?"

"Naw. Not no more. Not since the Depression. Maybe they ate 'em, come to think of it. Now, they're puttin' the cullerts way over here near the old stables to keep 'em separate. The MPs didn't used to do that, by the way—patrol the cullert camp—but now they do a couple times an hour. Good thing they do. Comes in handy sometimes, like tonight for instance."

"They afraid of someone sneaking out? Or sneaking in?"

"Both," Conroy said. "Local white guys sneaking in to bust a few cullert GI heads, or sumpin'—and cullerts sneaking out widdout a pass. Gettin' the clap. Or just hanging around over in Dream Town or Nort Liddle Rock. The locals ain't so happy about all these cullert GIs being so close by.

You know. They got those signs everywhere—'Cullert Only' this and 'Whites Only' that."

"I've only seen one. Are there a lot?"

"You got a lot to learn, Gowah."

It was the same advice he remembered getting from the colored soldier named Johnson he met on the way back from the hospital. "So I've been told."

"Stow your stuff here." Conroy indicated the space between the ground and the raised floor of the nearest barracks building. The Phluffian hid his helmet and rifle as if going through a practiced routine. "Don't forget where you put it, and especially that two-bullet token I was hiding. We gotta give it to Pierce when we get back. You know, to prove we done our eight miles."

"What happened to the one he gave us?"

"Musta run off with the cigarettes, I guess. That's another thing you gotta learn about the Army, Gowah. It don't pay to ask too many questions."

Conroy put on his flat-folding garrison cap. "Hope you brought yours, too, Gowah. Didn't have time to warn you."

"Tah-dah!" Gower said, producing it from his waistband.

"Good boy!" Conroy congratulated him.

"Dumb luck," Gower admitted.

"If there's such a thing as smart luck, I woont know."

3

"Boots," Gower said, pointing to his feet. "What about our boots? And leggings?"

"No problem! For this crowd, they'll think it's a fashion

statement! After they get a load of us, they'll all be wantin' to dress this way." It occurred to Gower that he still didn't know where they were going, but decided he didn't really care. *As long as I don't actually have to do the march.*

Conroy stepped nonchalantly out from among the barracks buildings and headed farther into the colored part of Camp Forrest. Gower followed, but not as confidently. His sopping right foot made a squishing sound with every other step. He was about to ask Conroy if the noise was a problem when his friend gave out with a healthy "Yeah!" and started snapping his fingers, apparently to a beat. Soon, Gower could hear it, too—strains of band music, getting stronger as they neared a sort of hall. Another few seconds, and he could make out a woman's voice. It sounded familiar. There was a man's voice, too, a tenor, singing the harmony.

"'Body and Soul,'" Conroy announced. "Louis Armstrong recorded it first, you know. But most people only remembah the Paul Whiteman version. Woontcha know it."

They passed by several small groups of mostly colored GIs, standing around in the open area in front of the hall, gabbing and grabbing a smoke. Gower thought he saw one or two acknowledge Conroy with a nod.

Conroy reciprocated. "Hey! Howya doin'?"

"You know those guys?" Gower asked after they passed by.

"Naw, not really. But hey, they like music. I like music. We're all in this together, right? Whad the heck? Don't hurt none to be frennly."

There were a number of soldiers hanging around near the entrance of the place—all of them Black as far as Gower could tell. More were visible through the open double doorway. Despite the good music, the place wasn't full. Far from it. "This is just rehearsal," Conroy explained. "Udderwise the place'd be jumpin', Jack!"

After a few more friendly nods between Conroy and a

couple of colored GIs, Gower followed suit. And soon, the lifeguard from an all-white immigrant part of LA felt himself floating on waves of a welcome harmony—there, in a rehearsal hall within the bleeding heart of America. *Yeah. What the heck? We're all in this together. "E pluribus unum." Like the money says.*

To one side of the hall was the standard setup for a swing orchestra. *Horns, but no strings. Like at the Jungle Club—except for Wendell on violin when he wasn't tickling the ivories.* The white and Black musicians were taking a break between numbers. It was the first time Gower could remember seeing a mix of the races in a band. *Wendell took his violin with him when he volunteered. Maybe he joined a band on his ship, or wherever he ended up. Hope he's doing OK. Or at least has a friend like Conroy, who knows the score.*

The two white recruits stood out among the two or three dozen other soldiers, all Black, soaking up the scene, taking it in. The bandleader waved his baton, and the familiar guitar intro led into "I'll Never Smile Again." The female singer stepped to the mike, and for Gower, everything else suddenly vanished into the background. *The blonde from Little Rock Station! Was that really her at the colored hospital? The one who said I was something that rhymes with recruit?*

"Gonna catch flies widd your mout open like that, Gowah," Conroy told him. "Some dish though, hunh?"

Gower silently nodded. He couldn't peel his eyes away from the woman as she glided around the stage, doing more than justice to the Ink Spots' two-year-old hit. The song ended. Gower drifted back to earth, where he finally noticed the male singer, a colored GI who looked vaguely familiar.

"Johnson!" the Californian blurted out.

"Yeah," Conroy said, a bit stunned. "You know him?"

"Met him the other day. . . . Just in passing. Pretty good voice."

"*Pretty* good? Man, you ain't kiddin' it's *pretty* good. It's *great*! Johnson coulda been a pro. But, he's cullert, you know, so that's kinda tough."

"The blonde's pretty good, too."

"Lacey Lane," Conroy said. "Not only a dreamboat, she actually *is* a pro. Coulda been a movie star, if you ask me."

"'Lacey Lane,'" Gower repeated the name. Somehow it seemed to fit.

"Before the war, she sang with some band oud in your necka da woots. For some reason, she quit and joined the Army. Crazy dame."

"Maybe she's just patriotic."

"Well, she's got my flagpole saluting, that's for sure!"

Despite the musicians all being GIs, Gower was impressed with how well they played. "They do this *every* day?" he asked.

"Only Fridays. Rehearsal. Like I said. They play for dances on the weekends. And ceremonies—ya know—visiting VIPs, stuff like that."

"With everything else divided up in this place, I'm surprised to see there's Blacks and whites playing together," Gower offered.

"Woont be together usely. No Blacks allowed to dance at the white dances. And vice verses. But there's not enough good white musicians in camp, so the brass said it's OK—just for having a band for the dances and ceremonies and stuff. Like when Rosaveld comes here."

4

"*President* Roosevelt?!"

"Yeah . . . Or maybe Mrs. Rosaveld's coming, instead. Heard a rumor during the KP. It's on account of we need to eat more vegibles or sumpin' like that. . . . Whadda I know? Me and the Rosavelds ain't on speaking terms."

"Vegetables? What do they care? As long as we're willing to fight, who cares if we eat our vegetables?"

Conroy shrugged. "They told us there in the kidchen about how she's complaining to the Army how we ain't eating good. . . . I eat my vegibles. But not the beeds. Not wild about beeds, that's for sure."

"Beets? I don't mind 'em. Mom cooks 'em up pretty good."

The band broke into what Gower thought was a serviceable version of "A String of Pearls." The singers Lane and Johnson took advantage of the break afforded by the instrumental and were off to the side having a smoke. Gower edged closer. He couldn't help staring at Lacey Lane, marveling at the way she carried herself. *Conroy's right. She could be a movie star.* He thought maybe he caught the blonde's eye for a second—maybe even a glance of recognition from when she dropped his uniform off at the hospital—until reason yanked his chain.

"You're dreaming, Kid," he could hear Mugsy Levine adding his two cents. *"Face it. You're meatloaf. . . . That dame's New York prime cut. Forget you ever saw her. She's more my type, if you ask me."*

And, of course, Mugsy would be right—as he pretty much always was. *No way she could place my mug as the same one at the colored hospital. And even if she could, who'd settle for meatloaf? Though Mom's is pretty darned good.*

He turned his attention back to the music. "String of Pearls." Released just before Pearl Harbor. Glenn Miller. *Great number! The drive in that rhythm line! The trombones. The dueling saxophones—Beneke and Klink—so danceable! Man, it's got it all! And these guys are doing all right by it, too!* The soothing sounds helped wipe away at least some thoughts of Hogjaw Thornton and the Army and sent Gower right back to Los Angeles, to the dances. *Wendell, on violin at the Jungle Club. Happier times.* "Great way to end a pretty crummy day," he said aloud.

"Nod over yet," Conroy told him. "I think the next numbah's gonna be up tempo."

Sure enough, the band stepped on the gas with "It Don't Mean a Thing" the way Ellington did it. Nurse Lane and Private Johnson got the vocals going as a call and response. It was a toe-tapper, no question. A few of the Black guys couldn't help themselves. Despite the fact there were no women in the hall other than the singing nurse, they paired off, or joined up in small groups to cut a rug.

"Come on, Gower! Led's show 'em whadda coupla white guys can do!"

Conroy grabbed his friend by the hand and pulled him toward an open space on the floor. At first Gower resisted, if only because his tired legs refused to move. But resistance didn't last long, and he got into the action soon enough.

There was no way Conroy could have known it, but Gower was a pretty good dancer, even in combat boots, and he didn't mind showing off. *A credit to Mugsy's lessons on footwork.* He was pretty worn out from all he'd been through, though, and had to cut it short. After that number, Conroy decided they'd better get back to the barracks.

"Gotta show up eventchally," he said. "But, look, we're sweadin'! That'll help put it over on Pierce and Thornton. They'll think we got a good workout. And we did, too. Just not eight miles' wurt of marching with the snakes and the mosquitoes."

"And the pigs."

As they left the hall, Lacey Lane was slipping into "Don't Get Around Much Anymore." The way she stretched out the lyrics, Gower thought maybe she was taking it personal. He looked back at her one last time, trying to catch the singer's eye. He couldn't say that he had. He couldn't say that he hadn't.

CHAPTER TWELVE

Soldiers in the Dark

1

After Saturday morning drills, Gower and chaperone Pierce headed for lunch. *Day two, waltzing under seventy pounds of gear. Even my hair hurts! Probably from the goddamned helmet. Eight miles in this heat after lunch—hotter and even . . . what?* Stickier *than yesterday! And this time, without benefit of Conroy and his token-down-the-underpants trick.*

Hogjaw passed them on his way out of the mess hall. "Not so tough now, are you, Nancy?" he laughed, punctuating his opinion with a swagger stick to Gower's pack as he hurried by. "Have fun!"

"Don't know why Thornton's got it in for you, Gower," Pierce said over lunch, "but I sure wish you'd kiss and make up. Got better things to do than babysit your behind."

"Haven't a clue, Corporal Pierce," Gower lied. "If I thought kissing the sergeant would do any good, I'd certainly consider it." *Called him "Grandpa" that first day. Still not sure why that upset him so much. He's been piling it on ever since—"fraternizing" with the Japanese kid, my butt! How could I help it if the kid singled me out? Seemed to soften up when I helped capture the kid. But here I am, on his shit list again. . . . And what the hell happened to Mugsy's brass knuckles?! That's what* I'd *like to know.*

Between forkfuls, he thought about asking Corporal Pierce if he knew anything about why he was sent to the colored hospital but decided to leave it alone. They finished eating and walked out past the obstacle course toward the starting point for the eight-mile march. That is, Pierce walked. Gower sort of hobbled. *After all I've been through the past week, can I march at all—let alone for eight miles?*

"Sorry I gotta do this to you, Gower. But if I don't . . ."

"I understand, Corporal Pierce. We've all got to follow orders, like them or not."

"You can say that again. . . . By the way, *that's* not an order, so don't say, 'that again.'" He took a token hoop from his field bag and handed it over.

The one Conroy got from Rodrigues—not Rodriguez—for a carton of Luckies. He sighed, then thought of his mom. *"You must fit in, Mervyn, you must!" Gotta be an easier way than this.*

After a cautious look around, Pierce pulled out some smokes. "Still on duty, so gotta watch it." He stuck one in his mouth and lit up. The long, grateful drag reminded Gower of his dad. *With his pipe, home from cleaning up after students at the lab all day. Least he's got something—"suffen," as he'd say it. Only thing he could get was at the college, I guess, with work still so scarce.*

"Just between us, Gower," Pierce said, sending up a cloud of smoke, "why dontcha stow some gear along the trail—behind some bushes or something? Lighten your load a bit. Pick it up on the way back." He looked around again. "The

Army's got a lot invested in you, kid. Uncle Sam would much rather have you stop a German bullet than drop dead during boot camp."

"I keep hearing that," Gower said, looking at the corporal from under the brim of his helmet. "Not sure Sergeant Thornton shares that opinion."

"Give it some thought. No one needs to know." Pierce took the cigarette and stuck it into Gower's mouth. "See ya later," he added, turning to walk away, "hopefully, still kicking."

I hope so, too. His pace started out steady but slow and painful. It didn't get any better. Despite thinking everyone was off after lunch, he heard marching cadences in the distance. *Other guys being punished?* And later, he thought he saw a model plane like the one that dive-bombed him a few days earlier. *What was that guy's name . . . ? Something like "ever be."*

Eventually, the course led away, through rolling terrain with a line of low hills beyond it. After about an hour, he decided he deserved at least some water. He propped his rifle against a large, flat rock, then chased his tail a turn or two until he snagged the canteen from his hip and savored a swig. Swaying slightly with fatigue and the heat, he had another thought. *Good time to take a full-on break.* He told himself it'd only be for a minute or two and sat down on a rock about the same height as the seat of a chair.

He was enjoying the break until the sound of several sets of quick-timing boots shocked him upright, but not to his feet. They refused to budge. A half dozen soldiers rounded the bend. It was five or six Black soldiers, all dressed in T-shirts, trousers, and boots. Gower recognized Johnson, the helpful stranger from when he was lost near the colored hospital—the same guy with the wonderful voice from the night before. Recognition crossed the crooner's face. He stopped. The others did, too. "Say," the boot from Chicago said, approaching, "don't I know you? I mean, I don't know that many white guys here anyway, except the ones in the band, but you look familiar."

"Gower," he said, wincing as he tried to stand. "Sorry. My legs. Cramps, maybe."

"Got it! *Gower.* The other day. Near the hospital."

Gower nodded. "I was at your rehearsal last night. You've got a great set of pipes."

"Oh, well . . . ," Johnson started. "I try. But that Miss Lane is the real singer."

"Yeah, and a looker, too."

"Yeah, well, I suppose," Johnson said, managing a modest grin.

An awkward silence followed. Gower nodded. Johnson, too. More silence. The crooner looked up and then down the trail before eyeing his buddies—one of them shrugged. Johnson nodded and turned again to Gower. "You need any help, or anything?"

"Giving my legs a rest before I finish the course. Guess I'm about halfway through."

Johnson grinned and shook his head. "Naw, man. Sorry. But you still got a ways to go."

2

Johnson's smile quickly faded, as if something else crossed his mind. "You alone?"

Gower nodded. "Yep. Just me and seventy pounds of Army love."

"Didn't you tell me the other day you just got here?"

Gower nodded. "About a week, I guess. For a lot of that,

though, I was out cold, in the hospital. Been kinda hoping I'm still dreaming."

Johnson offered a grim nod of sympathy. "None of my business, Gower, but if you're alone out here carrying all that gear after only a week, I'm guessing somebody's got it in for you real bad. You gonna make it OK?"

"Yeah. Sure. Once my legs start working again."

Johnson looked around, then at his buddies again before stepping closer to the white GI. "Listen, Gower, I don't know what you did to deserve this, but I'm pretty sure they don't want you dead. Is that one of those hoop things I've seen you guys carrying out here?" he asked, pointing at the wire token around Gower's neck. "It's like some kind of proof you did the march or something, isn't it?"

Gower nodded.

"Well, I was just thinking . . . Maybe someone could make the exchange for you—you know, 'cause you would have done it on your own, if you could have. No one's doubting that, you understand."

"*I* am. *I'm* doubting it." Gower took off his helmet, then handed over the precious wire circle. "I need a token with anything but two cartridge shells. Thanks, Johnson. I owe you."

"Naw. You don't owe me nothing, man," Johnson said before turning to go.

"You guys don't have a token?" Gower asked, putting his helmet back on.

"Naw, man, we're just . . . out here on our own, you know. Getting in some work." The Black recruit bit his lip and looked again at his fellows before adding, "They told us they don't have enough colored sergeants or corporals in camp to tell us what to do, or nothing," he went on. "So . . . we're just out here on our own 'cause . . . well, with no one telling us what to do, I guess we're just bored, mainly." His buddies laughed and nodded.

"Sounds pretty good to me. I mean the part about no sergeants."

"We'd rather be training to fight than just sitting around, though," Johnson told him. "I mean, that's what we signed up for, right?"

"That is the idea, isn't it," Gower quietly agreed. "Well, thanks again, Johnson. Much appreciated."

"Just boots looking out for each other, that's all. Maybe you'll do the same for me someday."

"You got it." Gower gave the singer and the others a modest wave as they moved on down the trail.

Alone again, he tried unbuckling his battle pack so he could at least do a better job of stretching his aching muscles, and then maybe hide the damned thing somewhere along the course as Pierce suggested. He leaned back and lowered his chin to get a better viewing angle of the still-unfamiliar buckles. Gravity took charge instead. He reached around behind his back to prevent the better part of seventy pounds from toppling him backward off his sitting rock.

"Ahhh!" His thighs exploded in pain over the sudden change of position, agony announcing his defeat.

An upended turtle, Gower lay there on top of the pack, his arms pinned underneath it. His thighs had been wedged in close to his face by his former throne, his helmet jammed down over his face by another rock behind him. Without the use of his hands to raise the headgear, he couldn't see much beyond the rim of it.

"*Fuck!* That *hurts*!" he said to no one. There was no one there to hear him.

3

Gower had no clue how long it was after that when someone asked, "You OK, buddy?"

"Wendell?" He'd been dreaming of his Navy brother, waving from the stern of a ship. He opened his eyes. He could hear crickets and frogs. He stared at the darkness before realizing that most of it was likely the inside of his helmet.

"Wendell? Nope. Don't have a Wendell. Got a Woodrow. Did you mean Woodrow?"

From under the brim of his headgear, Gower strained to see anything beyond his own thighs. With effort, he managed to find his kneecaps. Between them was a man peering back at him through holes in what could be a bedsheet. The private blinked. The man was still there. The man blinked. *Never met anyone through holes in a hood before—including on Hallowe'en. Not a soldier. Maybe this is one of the white guys Conroy said sometimes showed up around here to beat on some colored guys. Hope Johnson and his buddies didn't meet them on the trail.*

"We call him Woody, though," the man went on. "That's short for Woodrow. I don't think Woody is short for Wendell. But I guess it could be. If we had a Wendell, we could verify. But like I said, we don't. Least not since I joined. Is your Wendell a soldier, too?"

"Uhhh."

"Say, you seem to be hurting some. Are you in pain, son?"

"Maybe," Gower said. He wondered whether he'd somehow passed beyond it. "Can't really feel anything at the moment. Just kinda numb. Could use some help getting up, though. Been pinned here for quite a while, I guess. Don't really know how long."

"Don't move!" The man's hooded head abruptly disappeared, revealing a bit of the early-evening sky between Gower's upended knees.

So it's night. And . . . looks like this guy's a Klansman. Great. Just what I needed. More problems. "I won't. . . . I can't," Gower told him.

"Boys!" he heard the guy whisper hoarsely. "This here soldier needs our help!"

After the sound of several sets of footsteps, and a flurry of rustling fabric, Gower could hear hushed voices off to the side. He couldn't pick up anything anyone was saying but "I s'pose so," at the end.

More rustling fabric preceded the feeling of being lifted—battle pack included—by multiple pairs of hands. He was placed more or less upright next to his sitting rock. During the process, something fell from his chest and *clinked* when it hit the ground.

"You dropped this here thing, son," one of the hoods said, extending a shrouded arm as Gower secured the straps of his gear, then straightened his helmet. It was a metal wire token, with one cartridge strung on it. *From Johnson! Why didn't he wake me? Maybe they'd seen these clowns hanging around and . . .* Gower reached out to claim the ring about the same time the cloth-covered men released their grips of support. Gravity dealt itself in.

"Whoa there, fella!" a stouter, much taller hood said, reaching out to grab Gower by the arm to keep him from falling. "Little early to be imbibing, don't you think? Or maybe not. It's a soldier's prerogative, I suppose," he said, chuckling at his own remark.

"Thanks," Gower said. "I am a little woozy." By the distant glow of Camp Forrest, he could see he was surrounded by five figures in hooded white robes emblazoned with the telltale cross-in-a-circle.

"You think you're going to be all right, then?" the larger man asked.

"Yep." Though hunching awkwardly under the weight of his gear, Gower nodded reassurance. "Thanks. I'll be fine. Please feel free to go." He meant it more as a plea than a pleasantry.

"We *do* have to be getting along," the larger man admitted. He took a quick look up and down the trail before turning to the others. "Boys," he told them, "I reckon we ought to skedaddle before someone comes along." Gower nodded his support for the suggestion. *An MP patrol. Hopefully, they'll catch these guys before they do any damage.* The white-robed strangers then fairly floated off into the surrounding woods.

"Owww! Damnation! That smarts!" one of them shouted a bit later when he'd apparently run afoul of a tree branch or something before they eventually disappeared.

Things do look different at night, Gower reminded himself before sizing up his own cross-country predicament. It was a race against total darkness, and a possible run-in with wild pigs. He decided to simply backtrack along the trail until it veered away from the lights of The Forrest. The strategy didn't serve as long as he would have liked, though, and it wasn't long before he was making a beeline cross-country for what he hoped included his barracks and bed.

After the better part of an hour, Gower picked up the aroma of the former cavalry corral he'd smelled the night before. *Never thought I'd appreciate the smell of old horse manure.* He found a fence and followed it till he could turn a corner. After several minutes on the new heading, there were two things of which he was certain. One, he was walking between a couple of rows of facing tents, and two, he was being watched.

4

Gower decided to ignore whoever—or whatever—it was and act as if he belonged there. A light suddenly shone in his face. *Whoa!*

"Halt! Who's there?" a voice said from behind the beam.

"Uhhh . . . Private Mervyn Gower?" *Jeez! Sounds like I can't even remember my own name!*

"Advance and be *reck*-oh-nized . . . Oh, well, never mind that. I can see you pretty plain," the sentry added and lowered his light. From the ambient glow of the down-facing lantern, Gower could tell the man wasn't white.

"You a little lost, though, ain'tchya." It wasn't a question.

"Just passing through—on my way to . . ." Gower still hadn't memorized the location of his barracks. "Over there," he said, pointing vaguely toward the more well-lighted part of camp.

"Well, you headed in the right direction, I 'spect. So, good night to ya, then."

"Good night," Gower said, "and thanks."

He had no idea why he thanked the guy, except maybe for not shooting him. *If the folks in white hoods showed up anywhere near here earlier, that sentry has good reason to be skittish. Compared to me, though, he seems pretty calm.* For some reason Gower couldn't put his finger on, being there in the dark among rows of tents in the darker part of The Forrest made him feel uneasy. *Jeez! My palms are sweating. I should be glad to see these guys. . . . Come to think of it, being with those dopes in white hoods didn't seem to bother me half as much. Why not?*

When the rows of canvas were well behind him, Gower felt better but ashamed at having been upset in the first place. He turned to have another look. *They're probably the same tents I passed on my way from the colored hospital the other day. They didn't bother me then. Why do they bother me now? Because it's dark? They're my "brothers in arms," like someone said. Why does being near them make me uneasy?*

Eventually, he worked his way back through the sprawling campus maze to a landmark more familiar though no less intimidating—General Forrest on horseback. The bronze monument stood on a concrete pedestal at the center of the camp's sort-of town square, strangely deserted on this Saturday evening until Gower remembered what Conroy said about Saturday night dances and realized he was missing another chance to see the delightful Miss Lacey Lane. *And maybe grab a dance or two with her.* He raised his head to gaze into the shadow-browed statue's face frowning down. *You're from around here, General. What was that all about back there, with me and the tents in the dark?*

"It's you!" An all-too-familiar human voice responded instead. "It's really you!"

5

Great. . . . As if this day wasn't already nothing to write home about. Reluctantly, Gower turned to face Waverly, grinning and waving from the porch of a building to one side of the bronzed general's bivouac, capped by a steeple. *Must be a church. Just what I need—someone to "save" me.* Gower waved but started walking toward the barracks. Undeterred, Waverly dashed across the quadrangle, past the PX, straight toward the camp's namesake and his barracks buddy.

"Where've you been, Gower?!" The Pigeon said when he'd come alongside.

"Hey, Waverly. How's it going?" Gower said wanly. He couldn't help but notice the guy had a book in his hand. *Probably a Bible. Bet he's gonna read me chapter and verse.* So as to cut short any conversation, Gower kept on walking. *I'm tired—especially of revelations.* Grimly amused by his own joke, he grinned on the inside. *Though it'd be nice to know for sure whether this kiss-up knows anything about Mugsy's brass knuckles.*

Waverly kept pace. "We were worried about you, Gower. You're way overdue! Corporal Pierce was going to send some of us out looking for you."

"Let me guess. Hogjaw wouldn't let him."

Waverly stopped. He looked away. "Yeah. You're right. He wouldn't. How'd you know?" When he looked up again, Gower had moved on without him. He quick-timed to catch up. "You OK?" Waverly asked when he came alongside again. "Looks like you got a limp."

"Yeah, maybe two or three. Nothing a hot shower and some sleep won't cure, I hope. What time is it, anyway? I suppose I'm too late for chow."

"Chow was a couple hours ago. But maybe you can get something at the Service Club. It's open till eleven. Only a little after eight now."

"Yeah, maybe I'll do that. Thanks. How come you're not at the dance like apparently everybody else?"

"Oh . . . well . . . I wasn't really that interested."

"What? You got a girl back home, or something?"

"Yeah . . . something like that."

Gower thought Waverly seemed kind of down. Against his better judgment, he continued the dialogue, but didn't stop walking. "I saw you coming out of the church there, just now. As far as I know today's not Sunday."

The Pigeon perked up some at Gower's question. "Chapel," he corrected.

"Church. Chapel. What's the difference?" Gower shrugged.

Waverly managed a smile despite his otherwise somber mood. "Yeah. 'Tomayto, tomahto,' right?" he said, then suddenly became serious again. "It *doesn't* matter, does it." He went quiet for several paces. "I was talking to the chaplain," he finally said.

"Yeah? What's he got to say? 'Thou shalt not kill—unless it's a Jap or a Nazi'?"

"Yeah. Maybe so, hunh," Waverly said, apparently not much in the mood for humor. "No," he said, again turning inward. "I was asking him about . . . you know . . . *things*."

Jeez. Usually, the guy won't shut up. "Yeah, well, I guess there's a lot of *things* in this world to ask about, aren't there? Especially now."

"Yeah," Waverly said sadly. "There are." More silence. "Listen, Gower," Waverly said, "as much as I'd like to shoot the breeze, I really want to be alone right now. Think I'll just take a little stroll around. Maybe see you later at the Service Club."

"Yeah, sure. Maybe," Gower told him, glad for the out. He felt bad for the guy but had enough problems of his own. They went their separate ways.

After hanging the token "proving" he did the march on Pierce's doorknob, Gower decided he was too tired to eat. He showered and went to bed debating whether or not to report the white-robed strangers he met on the trail. *What would I say? Who would believe me?* He decided not to mention the incident. According to what Conroy told him the night before about white intruders looking to cause trouble, the MPs were probably already aware of the Klan's "courtesy calls."

Later that night, Gower found himself dreaming about the hooded men. They were gathered in a circle, surrounding the Japanese boy from the train. After shouting "Hap! Hap!"

a couple of times, the boy turned to look straight at Gower, his GI Judas.

"It's your *fault,"* Gower thought he heard the kid say. The sleeping private was jerked awake when he realized the words were real, and coming from somewhere under the same roof.

Though hushed and indistinct, there was definitely a conversation going on near the far end of the building. Gower thought maybe he knew who the voices belonged to, but decided not to mention that to anyone, either.

CHAPTER THIRTEEN

SOS

1

Gower never did figure out exactly why he, in particular, found his way to the top of Hogjaw's shit list. And just as mysteriously, he soon seemed to be absolutely off of it. Not only had Thornton stopped singling him out and calling him names, but seemed to be purposely ignoring him. Though certain he was performing nearly as well as anyone else in the platoon—confirmed by Corporal Pierce—Hogjaw paid him no attention, let alone any compliments.

Instead, except for the bimonthly dances, where he spent most of his time standing near the stage listening to the music and the intoxicating voice of Nurse Lane—all the while hoping to work up the nerve to ask her to dance during those rare times she was on the floor, giving a few of "the boys" a brief fling—Gower's days took on the rhythm and routine of the average recruit—wake, shave, dress, eat, drill, eat, study, practice, eat, sleep, repeat.

"Unless someone's shooting at you, soldiering's a whole lot and length of the same ol' shit." That was the deal according to Corporal Pierce. The "same ol' shit" was seldom interrupted. This was fine with Gower, since all he wanted to do was get through Basic Training, be assigned to an Infantry company, and go fight to defend his adoptive country. *Like any American would—born here or not.*

Besides the "S-O-S"—aka their daily routine—Corporal Pierce liked to remind his boys not to keep their parents and girlfriends waiting for that first letter home. *"Let 'em know you're not dead."* So, on a quiet Sunday afternoon, Gower finally got to it. *"Dear Mom and Dad, sorry it has taken me this long to write. There hasn't been much to write about. There still isn't."* In deference to his parents, he purposely left out any mention of Sergeant Thornton, Mugsy's brass knuckles, the Japanese boy, his time in the colored hospital, and the KKK—in other words, just about everything his brother would have been keenly interested in. He mentioned "weird Waverly" at first but thought better of it and threw that draft in the trash.

"The train ride out here was long and boring," the final version continued. *"Training has been long and boring, too—as our corporal warned us it would be. But having nothing else to do allows me to drill as hard as I can and qualify for the Infantry, so I can serve the country you chose for me and Wendell, and make you both proud. Love, Mervyn. PS. I met a girl from LA who's really swell. Before the war, she sang in a band in some of the clubs downtown, so maybe she knows Wendell. By the way, have you heard from him yet? I hope he's OK. I dreamed about him the other night. He was on a ship, waving at me. M."* It occurred to Gower later that he couldn't tell whether Wendell was waving a greeting, or a farewell.

There was really only one remarkable interruption in the monotony Gower could point to. During a break in calisthenics one afternoon, he noticed dozens of other soldiers at the far edge of the parade grounds doing some of the same drills as he and his fellows. They were dressed the same, they moved the same, and they were going about everything exactly the same. The only difference was, except for the sergeant, all those other soldiers were Black. He remembered what Johnson told him about there not being enough colored noncommissioned officers to train Black troops. He thought maybe the white noncom leading the Black soldiers looked familiar. The distance made it hard to tell.

"Isn't that Sergeant King over there with those colored boys?" Bucoda spoke Gower's mind.

"Naw. Can't be," another boot offered. "Heard he lost his stripes and went home."

"Drank his way outta here. Been discharged."

"I'd rather be caught dead than be assigned to a colored unit—even if they gave me an extra stripe for it."

"Why they drafting n*****s, anyway? Waste of time. They ain't worth shit."

"I think we're going to be glad to have 'em," McCleary replied. "And the Japanese men they've been rounding up, too—if only for their language skills."

"Whaddya shit for brains looking at?" Hogjaw shouted at the gawkers. "That over there? That ain't part of Camp Forrest. Can't you tell? That's Camp *Jungle*. That's why it's full of Little Black Sambos runnin' around! Now, fall in and get back to work before I have those savages eat you for lunch!"

For the next two solid weeks, Gower and his buddies jumped, vaulted, ran, climbed, rappelled, crawled, crossed, wriggled, and scrambled over, through, on, under, between, and across ravines, beams, trenches, walls, creeks, ladders, mazes, and fences. They were training to be soldiers but had yet to fire a single shot. "Unless you're a total idiot, you'll get your chance," Pierce continually reassured them.

2

On Saturday, at the end of Gower's sixth grueling week, they had to cross a gully Tarzan-style, swinging on a rope. The return trip was via monkey bars. "Hey, Conroy, I hear this is how your parents met," Bucoda shouted just before he fell off and twisted an ankle. Luckily, it was the last drill of the afternoon. Gower was thinking Hogjaw might have Bucoda do knee bends, if only to make sure his ankle hurt all the worse. But the sergeant was apparently just as anxious to call it a day as they were. Instead of fast-timing the boots back to the barracks, Thornton dismissed them on the spot.

A little later, Gower noticed him wander over to Waverly and put his hand on the private's shoulder. He seemed to be trying to convince The Pigeon to do something. Waverly shook his head a couple of times before a reluctant nod seemed to satisfy the sergeant and the two of them walked back toward the barracks together.

Gower, McCleary, and a couple of others took turns carrying Bucoda and his gear on their backs. They returned to the barracks later than they would have liked, but it was Saturday afternoon. They were off duty. "Time to cut a few rugs, boys!"

"I hear the USO's bringing some girls over from town, Gower," Conroy warned him, "so this time, you're gonna have to find someone else to dance with. My card's gonna be full."

"You *wish* I was available," Gower told him. "I got other plans."

After evening mess, they showered and dressed while laying out their separate strategies. Conroy produced a half pint of "courage." McCleary recruited a scouting party to "reconnoiter" the dance hall. Kelso and a few others were on board. Even Bucoda limped along after them.

Not surprisingly, Waverly begged off, mumbling something about Chapel.

Once they were inside the hall, a brood of pretty young things quickly flocked to the injured Bucoda. *As if he's a wounded warrior fresh from the front!* Pretty soon, Gower could see a couple of others in the posse near the edge of the dance floor faking a limp. *Hoping to become half as popular. Hah! Conroy's having trouble deciding which leg is "injured"!*

To further his own objectives, Gower wedged his way through the guys packed tight in front of the stage—anything to get closer to Lacey Lane, "the blonde with the voice of an angel, and the body to match." As far as Gower was concerned, the description was spot on. When Lacey took a break from singing and was willing to give a few GIs a twirl, Gower had his battle plan ready, including the angle of approach. If the band played something suited to the Lindy, or the Balboa—or better yet, something slow—he was ready to cut in and grab a few turns before another guy could do the same.

"You look familiar, soldier," she said, almost as soon as he had her in his arms. "Haven't I seen you somewhere around camp?"

"Well, as a matter of fact, Miss Lane, the funny thing is—funny now, anyway—when I first got here, I wasn't feeling well, you see, and I passed out in the barracks my very first morning! But the strange part of it is—and I still haven't figured this out—instead of the regular hospital, they sent me over to the colored hospital!"

For some reason, Gower simply couldn't turn himself off, or even just down. He could tell Lacey quickly lost interest. "Time's up, bub," she said, letting another guy cut in after less than a minute.

"Whaddya doing?!" Once Gower was sidelined, it wasn't hard to imagine Mugsy Levine letting him have it. *"Dames*

don't wanna hear your life story, for crying out loud! Even if they ask you! You gotta keep 'em guessing. Let them do all the talking. Shaddup and be a man of mystery. She'll be eating out of your hand!"

Despite following Mugsy's advice, round two wasn't much better. "Back for seconds, eh?" Lacey started. Gower acted as if he had better things to do.

"So . . . did we decide if we've met before, or what?" she asked, after a moment or two, apparently tired of the silence.

"Could be. . . . I get around."

What were you thinking?! he asked himself when he'd been bumped after not even half a turn around the floor. *If I do get another chance, I'm just going to be myself.*

"Good luck with that, *Kid."*

And Mugsy would have a point. "Myself" never had much luck with the girls. "Too British."

"Weren't you just here?" Lacey asked when Gower tapped in a third time.

"Can you blame me?" he asked.

She rolled her eyes. "Listen, Mac . . . You got a name?"

"Gower, Mervyn." Nerves had him spill it out military style.

"You are kinda cute, Gower Mervyn, and I admit I'm a sucker for a busted beak, but there aren't enough gals here to go around, so . . ." But before she broke it off entirely, she decided to ask him a question. "Where'd you get that, anyway? Boxing?" Lifting her hand off Gower's shoulder, she gently stroked the twisted bridge of the soldier's nose.

He nodded. "Yeah. I was in training for a fight when I got drafted. . . ." He stopped talking. He stopped thinking. Her fingers had the touch of magic. Their eyes met for the briefest of seconds.

"Oops! Sorry, pal. Gotta go. They're calling me back for the last number! But who knows . . . ? Maybe I'll see you around, and we can talk some more about your nose." She winked at him as she turned to leave.

3

Sunday was quiet and restful—except for the restless. Gower couldn't get his mind off Lacey Lane. He hadn't had a steady girl since he got kicked out of college. *And I'm not even sure she'd wanna admit to even knowing me, now—let alone to dating me.* He didn't snap out of it until Conroy suggested they join some of the other guys granted a pass by Corporal Pierce—much more sympathetic with a barracks full of bored boots than Hogjaw—and catch the camp shuttle bus into Little Rock "for some real food and a little action." Gower jumped at the chance—anything but sitting around and moping.

"How about you, Waverly?" he asked when they were about out the door.

The Pigeon was lying faceup on his bunk, staring at the ceiling. The guy's arms were folded over his chest, resting on what looked like a Bible.

"Naw. Thanks anyway," Waverly said and sighed. "Think I'll just stick around here."

"Yeah, the flies *do* need counting," Conroy said. "I noticed that, too."

"What's *with* that guy, anyway?" Bucoda added. "First we couldn't get rid of him, and now he won't give us the time of day."

"Something's sure eating at him," Gower said. "Not sure exactly what."

"Maybe he finally realized Hogjaw's not the hero he thought he was."

"Aw, that duck's just quackers," Conroy decided.

On the way to the depot, they passed by the statue of General Forrest and the pyramids of Civil War cannonballs he seemed to be guarding. "Hey, McCleary, you ever figure out who this Forrest guy was?"

The almond farmer shrugged. "All I know is he was a Confederate general. A cavalry officer. This place used to be for the cavalry, so maybe that's the connection. Other than that, I got nothing."

When they arrived at the depot, there was a long line of colored GIs waiting for a different shuttle. *Looking all spit-and-polished. Maybe headed for town, too.* An MP with a pistol on his hip stood nearby, arms folded, eyeing them as if he expected trouble. *What's the big deal? Some horsing around—nothing unusual for a group of guys heading to town on a Sunday afternoon. Nothing worth an MP's trouble, is there?*

"Bet we get a bus before they do," McCleary said, out of the blue.

After a few minutes a bus pulled up to where Gower, his friends, and a few other white GIs were waiting. Laughing and joking, they boarded. The bus, nearly empty, took off for town, passing the Black soldiers still waiting for their own ride to show up.

"What'd I tell you?"

Once off the bus, the two pairs of friends went separate ways. Conroy ushered Gower toward a café he'd heard was pretty good for a sandwich and a Coke.

"Dyin' for a hoagie, but no one 'round here 'cept other guys from Phully know what's a hoagie."

When they got there, Gower spotted three Black soldiers waiting near the kitchen door at the rear of the building. "Why don't they just go inside?"

"Probbly won't let 'em," Conroy suggested.

"Why not?"

"'Cause they're cullert. Why else?"

Sure enough, on the front window was a sign. "We Serve Colored Carry Out Only." An arrow pointed toward the back of the place.

Inside, Gower was surprised to see a small group of Nazi POWs—officers, from the looks of their uniforms—sitting around a table in the dining room, laughing and joking in German. They didn't seem to be under any sort of supervision. Conroy headed for a table. Gower stopped in his tracks. "Let's go," he said, turning to leave.

"What? You gonna let a few Krauts get between you and a sandwich? What kinda soldier are you, anyway?"

"Lost my appetite," Gower said and wandered off to find a place less willing to exclude GIs in favor of sworn enemies.

4

June rolled right along, as did the Imperial Japanese Army—right through most of East Asia. In *Stars and Stripes*, Gower read that the Japs had taken Mandalay. The city was only remarkable in his mind because of Kipling's poem of the same name. Shortly thereafter, all of Burma had fallen. *The war's gonna be over before we even get a chance to fight in it.*

A few beds down the row, Bucoda looked up from a hand of poker. "Hey, McCleary. Didjya hear? Some boot in another platoon shot his foot off with a forty-five caliber Colt at the range."

"We aren't even going to be issued pistols," the almond farmer reminded his buddies. "They're for officers and MPs. What's the point of learning how to use one?"

Conroy formed a pistol with his fingers, pointing it just

above his ear. "Maybe he was aiming for higher up." He winked and pulled the figurative trigger. "But missed."

"Either way, I guess he failed, hunh." The tone of Waverly's voice had Gower wondering.

"I'll bet the chickenshit did it on purpose," Bucoda said, "just to get out of combat."

In addition to drills and field training, Gower and the other boots attended classes like Organization of the Army—*"The Army's organized?! Who knew?!"*—to Personal and Sex Hygiene, Chemical Warfare, and Grenades.

There was even a lecture on the importance of eating vegetables. The talk was delivered by a Captain Mennur—*"rhymes with winner,"* the captain told them—from Classification. *Mennur,* Gower wondered. *Isn't that the guy Pierce mentioned? Something to do with what happened to Sergeant King?*

During his talk, laced with what sounded to Gower like it might be French, Mennur informed the men that there was a standing order from General Flagg's office to eat more vegetables—especially beets. "That is, there *will* be a standing order, *toot sweet,* as soon as the general reads my report."

If nothing else, the "Eat Your Vegetables" campaign meant Gower and his buddies had to do more KP. "There ain't enough POWs for the kitchens no more," Pierce told them. "They've got 'em out working in the fields!"

Not long later, at evening mess, Waverly reported from the religious front. "Eating greens is being encouraged in Chapel by the chaplains, too. They've been slipping references into their sermons!" *So, not only is it unpatriotic to leave vegetables on your plate, it's also somehow a sin.*

"Heard this whole *vegetables* deal is a way to get the locals to quit complaining about the Army bringing so many soldiers in here—especially the Black ones," McCleary explained one day at lunch. "The Brass think once the locals figure out more troops means more money in their pockets, they'll be a little more hospitable. At least, that's the theory."

"But why the emphasis on beets?" Waverly asked. "Even the people I know who like them don't really like them."

"Turn my pee red," Bucoda reported.

"You sure it's the beets, Bucoda?" Santa Monica sniped from another bank of tables. "I hear the clap's been going around." Gower was anticipating a worthy comeback when everyone on Bucoda's side of the table suddenly jumped up out of their chairs and snapped to attention.

"Are you going to eat that, soldier?"

"Hmmm?" Gower turned around to see who was interested. The first thing to catch his eye was the silver bars on the guy's shoulder. He sprang to his feet, upsetting his tray and launching the load across the table. It was Captain Mennur from the vegetable lecture.

5

Gower stood staring at his wayward lunch, amazed at how far it had traveled. *Pointing me the way toward more KP.*

"As you were," Mennur told them, then proceeded to go around the table, pointing and poking at items of food with his riding crop while a sergeant with a clipboard and a pen walked a few paces behind him. "Beets," Mennur said, smiling approvingly in regard to the tray of one of the guys. "Very good. *Tray bee-an!*" He nodded. "*Very* good, indeed."

The captain seemed generally pleased with everyone else at the table, too, until he stopped behind one poor boot who looked particularly guilty. "I don't see any evidence of beets on your tray, soldier," the captain said. "Nor any manner of vegetable matter at all, for that, uh . . . matter. Did you not have any today?"

"Yes, sir. I mean, no, sir. I didn't," the boot apologized. "They give me gas, sir."

"I see. *Kell da-madge,*" the captain said. "A pity." He then turned to his pen-poised sergeant. "Fitch, put this man on report."

"Yes, sir!" The sergeant scribbled something on his clipboard.

"Bicarbonate," the inspecting officer said, turning again to the delinquent.

"Sir?"

"Of soda. For the gas. Oh, yes," the captain said, nodding. "*May wee. Say-saw.* You ought to try it. But eat your vegetables. That is an order."

"Yes, sir."

Captain Mennur beamed at the rest of the recruits. "You others, well done. I'm very proud of you. The lowliest of soldiers—raw, untested recruits—doing your duty by supporting the home front, consuming that which the host community lovingly and patriotically produces. This is as important as—well, *nearly* as important as—fighting the war itself. After all, it's a team effort. *'La victwoir ah bowcoo day pears,'* as they say. The French, I mean. They say it. 'Victory has many fathers.'" He smiled and nodded a few more times. "As you were," he said and headed for the door. "Very good. Oh, yes, very good, indeed. Come, Fitch!"

The offending recruit looked anxiously up at the trailing sergeant. Apparently satisfied his commanding officer wasn't looking, Fitch waved away the young GI's concerns. He tore off the salient page from the clipboard and handed it over to the guilty party before hurrying off to catch up with Mennur.

Out of the corner of his eye, Gower could read, *"At the PX, buy car bone it of soda."*

CHAPTER FOURTEEN

Final Exam

1

The end of Basic Training was fast approaching. Despite Captain Mennur's wishes, vegetables remained far down on the list of the boots' concerns. "Depending on where you put the accent on that captain's name, he could be full of it," McCleary told them the next time "Captain Cabbage's" name came up. Gower couldn't remember the almond farmer ever making a joke before. *Maybe all the SOS finally got to the guy who likes tanks.*

Their final days included more classes than fieldwork. Besides lectures on diet and hygiene, they attended "Why We Fight" lectures, where they were shown at least once-weekly newsreels of goose-stepping German Nazis, or pouty Italian Fascists, or banzai-charging Imperial Japanese, followed by scenes of desperate, terrified civilians fleeing the irresistible onslaught of one or the other. No matter what month, or country, or battle it was, Gower decided, the ending was always the same. *The bad guys won—mowing down anyone presenting a threat, real or imagined, because they just happened to be in the way.* Swept up in the currents of war, haunting so much of the grainy, black-and-white footage, were the broken bodies of innocents from yet another place The Welsh Kid had never heard of. *Maybe that's the one I won't be coming back from.*

One recent bit of film did make him and his buddies feel better. The Allied naval victory at Midway had them standing and cheering. *First good news since before Pearl Harbor!*

Less happy news returned soon enough. While staring at a wall map full of unpronounceable place names during biweekly "War Orientation," Gower and the other boots were told that a Russian offensive pinning down several German divisions was "critically important to the overall strategic picture, but we're not sure how long the Russians can hold on."

As Gower nodded agreement without really knowing why, the instructor reminded the class that the British had somehow managed to hold on to Malta. Later, at mess, when McCleary brought it up, no one else seemed to know or even care where or what Malta was.

"Had a girlfriend named Malta, once," Conroy announced. With his Philly accent, Gower supposed her name was really probably *Marta*.

"She had the *biggest* . . ." Conroy spread his arms apart to show his buddies exactly how big they were and inadvertently backhanded Waverly on the side of the head. The more Gower thought about it later, though, the more he doubted the thump was accidental.

Regardless of the misappropriation of the island's name, McCleary soldiered on. "Holding on to Malta should help the Allies defend North Africa."

Nobody cares, McCleary, Gower wanted to tell him but didn't. He was pretty sure most everyone around the table was too busy daydreaming about holding on to Conroy's well-endowed former girlfriend.

With very few exceptions, news from either the Pacific or European fronts was never very good, and usually depressing. Forget about the significance of "Soviet Sector Viability," none of the boots wanted to talk about the war. At the end of the day, all they wanted to do was help try and win it.

But before setting foot on a battlefield, there were a few other things to worry about, closer at hand. Besides boredom and homesickness, there was trench foot, jock itch, heat rash, poison ivy, poison oak, chiggers, mosquitoes, and no-see-ums. *"If you can't see 'em,"* Corporal Pierce unhelpfully explained, *"they're no-see-ums."* In some cases, men who should have known better, but didn't, were also battling gonorrhea.

Toward the end of boot camp, they were finally going to get a chance to overcome any fears of shooting or being shot at. After successfully disassembling and then reassembling their rifles during a timed exercise—blindfolded—they were rewarded with rounds of live ammo for target practice at the range.

Of the forty men in Hogjaw's platoon, Bucoda scored highest for marksmanship and also bayonet drills, earning citations for both. To Gower's surprise, he turned out to be a pretty good shot, too, and improved every time they practiced. He figured his success at bayonet—both fixed and free—was due to his ring-related footwork and hand-eye coordination. In hand-to-hand, he sometimes did too well for Pierce's liking.

"Gower! Wouldya quit taggin' the other guys so damned fast! They don't get any practice in if you beat 'em to it every time!" It was a request the corporal expressed fairly often.

"Who knows, Gowah?! Maybe you'd be really good at killing people!" Conroy gushed after one particularly impressive display of talent. "Woont surprise me. Got some lightning in those mitts!" He pantomimed his pal boxing. "One, two!"

Meanwhile, though previously jumping on Gower's every fault—real or imagined—Sergeant Thornton paid Gower no notice. *Probably already decided not to recommend me for Infantry School—no matter how high my combat scores are.*

The "live fire" test was still ahead of them, though, so Gower thought he might have one last chance to impress. They would be crawling seventy-five yards under low-strung barbed wire and a constant barrage of machine-gun fire aimed barely high enough to keep them from getting shot in the head.

"Final exam," Gower whispered under his breath at Lights Out.

2

Another Sunday afternoon slowly rolled around. Not much was going on until Corporal Pierce burst in through the barracks' back door and dashed down the row of bunks, shouting, "Gower! Where's Gower!" till he found him. "Gower! For some reason, you never passed gas!"

Without his Chemical Warfare certificate, Gower couldn't graduate with the rest of his class. "But today's your lucky day! Just heard about some kind of 'make-up' session this afternoon! You gotta report to the Chem War hut on the double! It's just past the motor pool!"

Begging off a trip into town with Conroy and the gang, Gower pulled his CW kit out of his locker and headed for "My Little Gas Shack." He'd been through a few drills with the other guys, taking out the mask, putting it on and all, but he'd never done it with any gas around. If he had any doubts dealing with gas could be a problem—on a battlefield, or elsewhere—he only had to think of wheezy Mr. Scobbs, his former boss at the Beverly Hills Y.

"You're one lucky guy, soldier!" the clerk told Gower when he got there.

"I know! Corporal Pierce told me. You're doing a make-up session today."

"'Make-up session . . . ?'" The clerk chuckled. "Yeah, I guess you could call it that!"

Puzzling briefly over the guy's remark, Gower made his way around to the front of the shack and fell in behind the other hopefuls. Though only five-foot-seven with his boots on, it occurred to him that all of the participants already in line were significantly shorter than he was.

"What we're using to test you with today probably won't kill you," the instructor was saying, "but if you nurses don't strap your masks on in time . . ."

Nurses! These guys are all women! Ahhh! I get it. "Make-up" session!

". . . in serious trouble—blacking out, or worse."

After the brief introduction, the instructor led the group, masks still in their pouches, through the "Enter" door of the small, windowless shack. "Breathe in that air . . . ," he told them. "Any gas? No, not yet. But when the buzzer sounds, gas will be flowing in. Above all, don't panic. Put on your mask and test it as you've been taught—without hesitation, but without rushing it. Once the mask is strapped on, breathe normally. You won't be able to see much but clouds of smoke. The drill lasts for five minutes. When the bell sounds, the door behind me will open. Since it's gonna take a while for the gas to clear out enough for you to see where you're going, place one hand on the trainee in front of you. File out calmly and orderly. And that's all there is to it!"

As the instructor left through, and then closed, the "Exit"

door behind him, someone else shut the "Enter" door. The lights went off. The trainees stood in silent anxiety till one of them joked she forgot to put lipstick on her mask. The smattering of laughter died away with the sound of the buzzer.

"I smell it!" one of the other nurses shouted, setting off a rush to put on their gear.

Feeling the need to be manly in the shed full of WACs, even though he wasn't sure they knew he was there, Gower feigned calm control while fumbling with the flap of his chemical warfare kit's pouch. Careful to avoid the proverbial deep breath to steel himself, he held it in while taking off his helmet and slinging the strap over his left wrist, as he'd practiced. He pulled out the full-face mask and strapped it on before replacing his helmet. Soon the shack was filled with noxious, blinding fumes, and the trainees stood there in the murky silence anxiously awaiting the signal to leave. *Kinda like being sucked under some of those swells north of Malibu. Longest few minutes of my life!*

When the bell sounded, the "Exit" door opened, and the trainees began filing out as instructed, one hand on the shoulder of the person in front. Gower brought up the rear. He managed only a few steps before the woman he was hanging on to stumbled and nearly went down. She'd apparently tripped over one of the other WACs, now sprawled on the floor, apparently unconscious and blocking the way. Dropping to one knee, Gower's training kicked in. He cradled the fallen woman in his arms, stood up, and rushed her outside—nearly sideswiping a couple of other WACs in the process. After laying the unconscious nurse down on the grass, he gently removed her helmet and then her mask.

Lacey Lane! She didn't seem to be breathing. While the instructor raced over with a bucket of something to rinse her eyes out, Gower turned her over and began artificial resuscitation—just as he'd done while patrolling the beaches back home. He didn't stop till Lacey suddenly, violently coughed—a welcome prelude to breathing on her own again.

"Nice work, bud!" one of the WACs said to Gower, as she and a couple of others shooed both men away and took over. "We'll take it from here."

Gower hesitated. "Lacey! It's me, 'Gower, Mervyn'! Remember? 'Busted beak'?!" he added, pointing at his nose while being shooed out of the way.

Luckily, before leaving, he remembered to press the instructor for the chit he needed to show Corporal Pierce he'd qualified for Chemical Warfare, and then headed back to the barracks. *Maybe someone'll tell her I more or less saved her life. And then maybe she'll at least consider spending more time with me at the next dance—or maybe even somewhere a little more private. "Dream on, Kid. Dream on,"* would have been Mugsy's sure-bet reaction.

When he got back to the barracks, an uncharacteristically upbeat Waverly practically ambushed him at the door. "Hey, Gower! Where've you been?" he gushed. "I was hoping you'd go with me to Chapel this afternoon."

"I was busy passing gas," Gower said without stopping. "Maybe next time."

McCleary popped in soon after and was Waverly's emotional opposite. "The Russians folded," he announced, kicking off his shoes before plopping down hard on his bed.

"To hell with the Russians, then," Bucoda carped from a hand of Lowball. "Can't do nothing about nothing sitting here on our butts, that's for sure." No one could argue with that.

3

After returning his CW kit to his footlocker, Gower noticed an envelope waiting for him on his pillow. It was a letter from home, opened and then resealed by censors. He decided to read it before the final exam—crawling seventy-five yards under live machine-gun fire—in case he "got lucky" and caught one in the head. *"It happens,"* Pierce had told them.

> *Dear Mervyn,*
>
> *We know you must be very busy, with little time to write, so we were glad to finally hear from you. Your ma is well and busy with practicing at first aid. I pretend to be wounded, and I tried to get "Herr" Weiss from across the way and his missus into the practice as well. He begged off, as I figured, but not for the reason I pegged him. A friend wrote him from Switzerland with news about his son. Weiss told me something about his boy being "with the Nazis." But as his accent's thick as black pudding, I ain't sure exactly whether it's by the boy's choice or not. Whichever it is, if that's what he's up about, then I suppose we ought allow him a blow now and again—though from the way he's been carrying on of late, he may have gone fair bonks! I suppose you can't truly know a bloke till you see the world same he seen it.*
>
> *All else is good, as we've lately heard from Wendell! He's been in Chicago, of all places for a sailor! But now has been assigned to a* "[BLACKED OUT] *headed for destinations*

> *unknown," which he's supposing will be somewhere in the* [BLACKED OUT]. *Your brother added something else to his note, which the censors didn't like and blacked out entirely. Take care, my son, and do well,*
>
> *Your dad.*
>
> *PS. The War Department have asked limits on Fourth of July crackers. And as I have volunteered for the Civil Defense, wearing helmet and armband, I will be glad of not having to scurry about, left, right, and centre when the time comes to celebrate. We're all jarred off here as it is!*

Gower mentioned the censored letter to Conroy. "Yeah, ours, too, if we send something home," his Philly friend told him. "I get around that by not writing."

In case the live-fire drill happened to go wrong for some reason, Gower decided there were too many things buzzing around inside his head he didn't want to take to the grave. He unloaded two of them on Conroy—Mugsy Levine's brass knuckles and the Japanese boy.

"Oh, and one more thing. I'm not an American. I wasn't born here."

"Tough about the Japanese kid, Gowah," Conroy told him without batting an eye. "But what could you do? What could *anyone* do, for chrissake? It's a crazy world, especially now."

"Did you hear what I said? I was born a British citizen and raised like a British kid. Well, anyway, a Welsh one."

"Yeah? Well, we all got problems, don't we. I was born and raised in Sout Phully, so whaddya gonna do? They say it ain't what, or where, you are when you come into this world. It's whatcha do wid whatcha got after what really counts. Least, that's what my Eye-talian uncle says. Started out with nuttin', but now he's got his own place and makes some pretty good lasagna, so, I guess maybe he's right. . . . Helps if you're not cullert, though, come to think of it."

4

Not a minute into Gower's turn at crawling in the mud beneath barbed wire and a deadly spray of machine-gun fire beside five other boots, the blistering stream of lead was replaced by one of profanity. Even facedown in the muck, Gower could hear Hogjaw Thornton screaming about how badly the drill was being run. After a minute or two, the sound of bullets whizzing overhead resumed—alarmingly closer.

It wasn't long before Gower's head snapped to the side when one of the slugs *pinged* off the top of his helmet. He was pretty sure that wasn't how things were supposed to go, and soon once again, the firing mysteriously, but thankfully, stopped. After a lull during which he could hear several angry voices—including Hogjaw's—the stream of lead started up again, resuming its earlier, safer altitude, and Gower finished his turn without any more thirty-caliber love taps.

Later, at mess, Waverly told Gower what happened. "I couldn't believe it! Sergeant Thornton shoved aside the regular gunner! And even though the training officer tried to stop him, he released the barrel lock, lowered the Stinger's line of sight, got down behind the gun himself, and pulled the trigger!" Bucoda confirmed it with a single grim nod from the next table.

"Never seen him like that before," The Pigeon went on. "The way his eyes looked . . . Just firing away. I'm worried about him, Gower, I really am." Gower wondered why

Waverly wasn't a little more worried about the guy whose brain bucket got kissed by one of Hogjaw's angrier slugs but let it lie.

That night, thoughts of the dent at the top of his helmet and the sound of the round glancing off it kept Gower unsettled and wide awake. He couldn't dismiss the possibility that Hogjaw had meant to kill him. And later, above the ambient cricket chorus, Gower again heard the voices, the same ones from several times before. They started out calm and quiet but gradually grew more intense. One of them for sure was Hogjaw—angry and barely contained.

"That's what *you* think," he was saying, "but it ain't gonna fly!"

Gower turned to look. Through the partially open door of the sergeant's quarters, there appeared a sliver of the angry man himself, stripped to his briefs. Thornton was staring menacingly at another near-naked figure in the shadows. Gower recognized the other soldier, too, and feared for the private's sanity if not his future safety.

CHAPTER FIFTEEN

Independence Day

1

Infantry or Medical Replacement? Out on the parade grounds, Gower and the several hundred others of his graduating class stood in formation, unit by unit, waiting for General Flagg to show up and begin the ceremony. Meanwhile, a band marched around and in front of the soon-to-be *ex*-boots, playing a medley of Sousa favorites. The reviewing stands had been hung with red-white-and-blue bunting. *The Fourth of July, but without fireworks. Hopefully, for Dad's sake, there weren't any on Poppy Peak, either.*

As he stood there, he could picture his dad wearing his Civil Defense armband and white "bedpan" helmet, hoping the phone wouldn't be ringing with reports of neighborhood kids blowing their fingers off or sparking fires in the scrub brush on the hill behind houses up the street. *Mom and Dad . . . they think of themselves as more or less Americans now, and proud of it.* Gower smiled. *Given their accents, I'd say it's a pretty tough sell. But as long as they feel and believe it . . .* He thought of his father's ready answer for preferring the US over Britain. *"No bloody king."*

The music stopped. "Testing . . . Testing . . . Good morning!" someone said over the new PA system. According to an article in *The Camp Forrest Call,* the reason for the improvements was the increasing numbers of troops now stationed there—somewhere near fifteen thousand GIs, and still growing.

"Mostly white, of course," McCleary reminded them at breakfast that morning. "But with a few thousand Blacks thrown in, too. Come to think of it," the brainy almond farmer added over poached eggs, "they've been moving Japanese civilians away from the West Coast because they don't trust them, right? So, why not Japanese GIs here, too? You can't get much farther away from either coast than Arkansas."

Glancing to his far right, Gower could see several platoons of Black recruits included in his graduating class. They, too, were standing at parade rest, waiting for the ceremony to begin, but with at least a couple dozen yards separating them from the white formations. *General Flagg and the VIPs won't be able to see colored troops without turning their heads. Maybe that was the plan. And if McCleary's right about Japanese GIs eventually joining the party, where're they gonna put* them *so no one will notice? Over on the obstacle course?*

A half dozen staff officers stood waiting on the dais, but the podium remained empty. With nothing else to look at, Gower watched the last of the VIPs settle into their seats. A few sat shading their eyes or fanning themselves against the rising heat and the early afternoon glare. The same PA voice returned with greetings for some Little Rock city officials and clergy before listing the names of groups represented. "The USO, the DAR, the United Daughters of the Confederacy, and our nearly three hundred prisoners of war."

Though Gower remembered Captain Mennur or someone telling them that POW officers were allowed to do it, it didn't dull the shock of seeing Nazis stand attentively in full dress uniform and acknowledge the honor paid them by saluting—*German style!* He could hear McCleary whispering from somewhere close behind. "Interesting choices for Independence Day, those last two groups, don't you think?"

A staff officer approached the podium. "A-tennn-*hut*!" he shouted into the mike before striking a salute and holding it. All soldiers in attendance followed suit, including the Germans, again using the method they preferred. General Flagg shuffled out from somewhere behind the dais. The civilian VIPs rose in respect. *Wow! He's* old*! Walking kinda gimpy, too. War wounds, maybe?*

As Flagg made his way toward the podium, he gave particular civilians a brief nod of recognition—a courtesy he afforded also to the German officers, and some members of his staff—including, especially, Gower noticed, Captain Mennur of Eat-Your-Vegetables fame. Finally arriving at the podium, Flagg lowered his arm and nodded solemn approval toward the ramrod-straight ranks of GI graduates while slowly scanning them, from his right to his left.

Before doing or saying anything else, the general leaned awkwardly toward a nearby aide. "Holy smokes, Prescott!" Flagg's off-mike comment burst through the new and improved speakers. "If they can't even read or write, then how come we're graduating so many n*****s?!" Somehow Flagg's last word echoed as it bounced around that firecracker of an Independence Day, and, with the possible exceptions of the stone-faced Nazi officers, Gower was pretty sure the remark came across loud and clear to everyone else in attendance.

The general mumbled an apology for not being used to the new equipment before fishing for his glasses and launching into some prepared remarks. He began by thanking everyone he apparently ever met during his long career, and many of those present, including rather effusively, Gower thought, Captain Mennur, "for his brilliant work, tirelessly sorting thorough . . . *through* the backgrounds and, uh, abilities of new recruits, so as to . . . place them where they will be able to do the most good and . . . have the biggest impact."

After the intros, he went on for nearly an hour about duty and honor, sprinkled with anecdotes about his own experiences, and concluded his remarks by mentioning the need for "unity" and "a willingness to defend liberty and justice for all—except troublemaking Bolshevik outsiders like we had right here in Arkansas a few years back."

At the end of the proceedings, feet still apart, hands behind his back, but now more at parade *restless*, Gower stood worrying about his soon-to-be-revealed future. *Infantry? Or Bedpan Battalion?* The Civil War cannon guarding General Forrest's statue had been brought over for the traditional salvo of twenty-one. To a tune Gower remembered from elementary school—*What* is *a* caisson *anyway?*—his turn came at the head of the line. He saluted the staff officer handing out orders and stoically accepted his fate.

2

Dear Mom and Dad,

Sorry I didn't write again any sooner than today. I am fine, but there hasn't been much in the way of good news to write about. There has been better news, lately, but it's still a mix. I guess I'm learning that's what life is—a bit of everything—hopefully more good than bad.

Maybe realizing this shows I'm growing up. We've definitely grown up pretty fast here at Camp Forrest. We needed to be "fit and ready to fight" as soon as possible. After two months of hard training, I believe we are.

Camp Forrest is what they call a "Repple Depple." That's GI talk for "Replacement Depot." Training till now has been general. But from now on, we learn to be either combat, or medical "replacements." That is, we are assigned to a regular outfit somewhere when it needs someone to replace soldiers who are . . .

Gower thought about writing "dead or wounded" but decided on "no longer able to serve" instead.

I hope you won't be disappointed in me and my new classification. I tried my best to qualify for the Infantry but didn't make it. Even though I had high scores in combat training, they assigned me to the Medical Replacement Battalion instead. Perhaps, Mom, you will like that, as I suppose we are to be sort of field nurses, and so I guess we are less likely to engage the enemy directly. We could fight if needed, of course, but our first duty is to provide aid to the wounded on the battlefield and at field hospitals. I'm sure my training and experience as a lifeguard will come in handy. Up until now, anything related to lifeguarding was kind of a joke around here, since the nearest ocean is the Gulf of Mexico, four hundred miles away! At least that's how far away McCleary, my friend from Bakersfield, says it is. (I did put some life-saving skills to good use on dry land recently, though, which I will explain below.)

McCleary was *the "brains" of our platoon. And a bit "off" as you might say, Dad, but in a good way. All he can think about is tanks. But there aren't any deployed at this camp for him to play with, so he's hoping to get sent to Tank School. When he graduates, we like to joke he'll get a Tank U Certificate! Unfortunately, I guess I won't be seeing much of McCleary anymore, though. Unlike me, he qualified for the Infantry. Same for a guy named Bucoda—a real character I also liked a lot. They're good men and good soldiers. I'll miss seeing them. And that's another thing about the Army. Guys you pal around with may not be here for long. Our corporal warned us from the beginning not to get too chummy with anyone because he might be the next to go.*

Despite the corporal's advice, I made friends with a soldier named Aidan Conroy, from Philadelphia. (He's Irish!) Calls himself Danny for short. He's a real "live wire" with an accent that's sometimes hard to understand, even though he's a third-generation American! Luckily (for me), Conroy was also "demoted" to the Medical Battalion, even though his combat scores were pretty good, too. I say "demoted" because I think the reason we're in the "Bedpan Battalion" (as the Medical unit is sarcastically called) is because we somehow got on the wrong side of our former sergeant. Everyone calls him "Hogjaw." He's a real "hard case" if there ever was one. (Ask Wendell the next time you see him. He'll know what I mean.)

It's not just us, either. Here's a particular example. A few weeks ago, during aircraft ID training, "Hogjaw" didn't like the way the referee's assistant was handling the model German airplane we were supposed to identify and pretend to shoot down, so he grabbed someone's rifle and used it like a cricket bat to smash the plane to bits. As it happens, I know the assistant, a Black soldier named Eberley. It was a model plane he built himself. And when he tried to grab it away from the sergeant, he was led away under guard! I hope they don't punish him too severely. He really didn't do anything I wouldn't have done in his shoes. That's the best thing about my new assignment, not seeing Sergeant Hogjaw ever again!

Now, for some better news. That girl I mentioned before. The singer? She's a nurse, also in medical training. We were both in a group practicing how to survive a chemical attack not long ago. She passed out so I carried her outside, and then gave her some artificial resuscitation. Lifeguard training saves the day! Her name is Lacey. I hope to go dancing with her next Saturday night! Can't wait!

Love, Your Medical Replacement Son, Mervyn

Before sticking the letter in an envelope, Gower added a PS.

> *Almost forgot—maybe because in some ways I'd like to forget about it, but I can't. A guy in my outfit, I should say my former outfit, hanged himself a few days ago. There's a memorial service for him here tomorrow. His name was Waverly. We called him "The Pigeon," and I admit we picked on him a bit. I know what you're thinking. I should be the last person to bully anyone, and of course I'm sorry for what happened, and for what we did and said to him, but I doubt that's why he killed himself. I don't know what it was, exactly, but I think there was something going on between him and our former sergeant. Life is precious but sometimes gets wasted. I'm doing my best not to let anything happen to me. Hopefully, after I've done my duty, I will return home to you eventually, and hopefully in one piece. M.*

"Probbly going to black out the parts about Hogjaw and The Pigeon, though," Conroy said when Gower mentioned what he wrote. "Hey, and you know what? Heard the censor guy here's that Captain Cabbage. You know, the guy inspecting our vegibles."

By the time news about Waverly hanging himself had found its way over to the medical trainees' new barracks, The Pigeon had already been packed in ice and put on a train heading home to California for burial in Fantasy Springs. The service at The Forrest's chapel was nice enough, but a little odd, reminding Gower of "poor Waverly" himself.

3

On the appointed day, Gower and Conroy went over to the chapel, where they met up with some other guys from Hogjaw's former platoon who knew Waverly as well as anyone—including Bucoda and McCleary. Corporal Pierce was there, too, but not Sergeant Thornton. A few guys Gower didn't know from other units showed up. Most said they knew Waverly from Chapel services and Bible study.

To get things started, the chaplain mentioned a few memories he had of the deceased. He even tried to add some humor into the mix by imitating the guy's voice when it cracked. Nobody laughed. The one word Gower heard the pastor use most often while eulogizing The Pigeon was "troubled." The whole thing was bracketed by a couple of prayers Gower knew by heart from childhood, but in the Episcopal versions preferred by his mother.

When it was over, Gower thought about asking Pierce what he knew about the connection between Waverly and Thornton, but the corporal excused himself after some brief *goodbyes* and *good lucks* before Gower could figure out a way to bring it up, and Bucoda suggested the former platoon buddies all go for beers at the Service Club.

Talk about The Pigeon generally followed two common threads: "He seemed kinda squirrely" and "I didn't really know the guy that well." Somewhere around the third or fourth beer, Gower found himself floundering around in regret for brushing Waverly off whenever he got the chance. *He was only trying to be friendly—be one of the guys!* The admission pressed all the harder on his already-slumping shoulders. The mourning party broke up when they'd had all the alcohol they could handle—probably more.

Since Bucoda and McCleary made Infantry, they'd been

assigned a barracks in a different part of The Forrest from the two new "Nurse Nancys," Gower and Conroy. *Won't be seeing much of either one of those guys from now on, I guess—except by chance.* The respective pairs of friends offered heartfelt *farewells* before staggering off in different directions.

Gower and the Phluffian passed unsteadily by row after row of the nearly identical, bone-colored buildings, full of randomly selected young men from the forty-eight states. *Shoulda tried harder to help Waverly get through whatever it was that sent him over the edge—or at least show him a little sympathy. . . . Shoulda said something to somebody about what I saw and heard between him and Sergeant Thornton all those times after hours—on the train and in the barracks. But who? And what would I tell them—that a couple guys were shooting the breeze late at night?*

Every few minutes, either he or Conroy or both would have to stop, lean against something conveniently located, and stare at the surroundings to get his bearings—or simply try to keep from falling over. Occasional laughter and swearing wafted out of open doors and windows from unseen fellow soldiers, likely also far from home for the very first time. *Wondering who they really are. Wondering if they could kill another human if they had to—hoping they get out of this alive . . . "Dogfaces." It fits! Down-in-the-dumps dogfaces, with nowhere else to go on a Sunday afternoon, hanging around the barracks—open doors and windows . . . trying to beat the heat . . . Ha! That's the easy part. It's yourself you sometimes can't seem to live with.*

Voices from the past piled it on. *"You must fit in! You must!"*

"Mervyn the Vermin!"

"You're just too British."

Gower turned to his buddy. "We didn't do right by the guy, Danny. We coulda done more."

Conroy shrugged. “Like what, frinstance?” He hung back to light up a smoke after offering one to Gower. Gower turned it down and walked along without him. *There was just something about the guy that rubbed everyone the wrong way. No one else defended Hogjaw the way Waverly did—not even Corporal Pierce.* If only for that reason, Gower supposed, no one liked the kid from Fantasy Springs all that much.

Conroy eventually caught up. “Whaddya gonna do?” he said, dropping his spent Lucky to the pavement and crushing it under a heel. “The Pigeon was an odd duck. Sooner or later that sorta thing happens to guys like that, I guess.”

Gower abruptly swung around, grabbing Conroy by the front of his blouse and slamming him against the nearest wall. While pinning him there with his left hand, he drew back his right to deliver a blow. “*That* sorta thing?!” Gower shouted, inches from Conroy’s face. “What’s that supposed to mean?! *Hunh?!* I’m sick of all your *what-do-I-care* bullshit, Danny!”

“Big mistake, Kid,” he could hear Mugsy warning him. *“You’d probably kill the guy. Take it from me. . . . Real friends are hard to come by.”*

Another few seconds and Gower released his grip. “The guy’s *dead*!” He stepped away. “Waverly was a better soldier than *any* of us. Don’t ever talk about him that way again!”

“Jeez! I was only trying to help,” Conroy told him, struggling to straighten out the new kink his friend’s treatment had wrenched into his neck.

Gower wagged his head before looking away, waving Conroy off a few times as he did so. “Don’t. . . . Just don’t.” He turned and wandered off in a different direction—across the parade grounds, then nearly as far as the abandoned stables. Not knowing what to do or where to go, he lay down on the grass, staring up at the fading sky until he decided to try looking for answers somewhere else. He found his way back to the statue of General Forrest and sat down on a bench in front of the chapel, thinking about going inside. *To find God. To find Waverly. To find that Welsh kid far from home.* He thought about all those Taffies who never came back, and in that moment, envied them their release, and then he passed out.

At about curfew, Gower was roused by the chapel's bell and made his way back to the barracks. By the lights from the walkway outside, he could see that Conroy's bunk was empty.

4

They didn't cross paths again till the next morning. Despite Conroy's attempts at conversation—getting dressed, at mess, during training classes—Gower refused to respond. He didn't talk to Conroy all that day, or the next couple after that. He decided he didn't hate the guy and blamed himself for how blind he'd been about Waverly.

At one point, he thought about tracking down any chaplains Waverly may have confided in. *Maybe find out what made the guy tick.*

But when he couldn't see how talking with anyone could help, one way or the other, he let the whole thing go. Or tried to. He felt helpless. Worse than that, he felt useless. Being in the Bedpan Battalion didn't make it any easier. *If I was training for combat instead of changing someone's bandages, I'd be that much closer to doing something to make a difference—and maybe that much closer to making someone else hurt as much as I do.* Anything *to feel better.*

Gower didn't buck up till Saturday rolled around. That evening's dance was his first chance with Lacey Lane after what happened during the Chem War drill. He ran his fingers over his face and decided to shave again. *In case I luck out with Lacey, cheek to cheek.*

Tying his tie, he fumbled the Windsor for the first time he could remember. *Am I that nervous? Maybe nobody told her it was me who carried her out of the Gas Shack—maybe saved her life. Would she remember me even if they did? Maybe she'd rather forget. Maybe Mugsy has it right. Lacey's prime cut . . .* Staring back at him was a guy he hardly recognized. *Now I look like an actual dogface. Does a smile help?* He gave it a shot. *Sorta does but looks kinda phony.* "And I'm meatloaf."

Gower headed for the dance hall early. He wanted to avoid running into Conroy but also get a read on whether Lacey knew anything about what he'd done after she passed out. The musicians were warming up when he arrived. Lacey and Private Johnson were going over some sheet music on stage with the bandleader. The place was rapidly filling up with small groups of anxious, lovelorn puppy-mugs, sniffing around, alternating between bravado and the awkward silence of the inexperienced. The USO volunteers arrived to set up the refreshment table and to chaperone the group of local gals they'd invited to help serve and to dance with "the boys." Gower folded his garrison cap over his belt and waded in.

When he'd threaded his way up to the stage, Lacey noticed him immediately. "*There's* my hero!" She winked. Johnson recognized him, too, grinned broadly, and nodded toward Gower when he realized what Lacey was on about.

To Gower's great surprise, she excused herself and came down to join him on the dance floor. He felt an honest smile eclipse the facade he'd brought with him.

"Well?!" she gushed, holding out her arms in anticipation. As if on cue, the band struck up the evening's first number—"Stompin' at the Savoy," one of Gower's favorites. The tempo was upbeat and jive enough for doing the Balboa, something Gower really knew how to hoof. Later, after stepping through the Lindy—or anyway, a less "hoppy" version, during "Back Bay Shuffle," they nodded and smiled through gasps for air over how well it worked out. Assuming Lacey would break it off to dance with other GIs, Gower released her hand and lowered his head, unable to face the end of the dream.

"Got some pretty good moves, Gower, for a soldier boy."

Hearing the words, he looked up into her eyes and smiled. *She's sticking with me!* "Told ya, didn't I?" He grinned. "Was training in the ring to be a pro, till I got drafted."

"I'm impressed." The glow on her face lit up the room. At least Gower's corner of it.

With Private Johnson at the mike, the band struck up "Perfidia." Gower couldn't resist stepping Lacey through a simplified rumba. *No strings, but man! Johnson's spinning out enough silk to cover for 'em!* Next up, they glided around to Johnson's rendition of "I'm Glad There Is You."

The lyrics hit Gower like never before, and the more comfortably chitchatting Angelino proceeded to drop the names of some of the LA clubs he knew and the handful of bands he'd heard there, but omitted any mention it was mainly while washing dishes and bussing tables. He went on to tell Lacey about Wendell and his violin and was about to tell her about the night Momo's boys shot Johnny Three-Cheeks, but decided better of it. "My brother used to front for the Buffone brothers' band at the Jungle Club before he joined the Navy."

"*No!* The *Buffone* brothers?!" Lacey gushed. "You're kidding! They helped me get my start! Maybe your brother and I've even been on stage together somewhere along the line!"

When Gower realized mention of Wendell left him with his guard down, he tried to parry Lacey's roundhouse with a counter. "I got *my* start with them, too!"

"Small world!"

"Yes! Isn't it? 'Course, I wasn't in the band. . . . I ran errands—*important* errands." *Jeez, that sounds so dopey.*

"Next thing you're gonna tell me your brother knows Mugsy Levine!" She laughed.

"My brother?"

"Yeah! You know," she said with a wink. "If your brother knows the Buffones, he *must* know Mugsy!"

Gower felt his knees buckle "No! Not my brother! *Me! I'm* the one!"

"How about it, Lacey?" Anxious voices began to call her out from the sidelines.

"Yeah! How 'bout the rest of us?"

"It's been fun, Gower, but I guess our time is up," she told him, flicking her head toward the growing group of impatient GIs.

"Not my brother!" Gower repeated, raising his voice when he realized one of the other guys was about to pounce. He tried to twirl Lacey in the opposite direction from the circling wolf but failed to prevent her from being swept away. *"Me!"* Gower pleaded with the empty space lately occupied by the singing nurse. "*I* know Mugsy Levine!" He couldn't help notice more than a few heads turn his way at the mention of the well-known gangster. "*Not* Wendell," he mumbled. "Wendell knows *the violin.*"

"Next time!" Lacey Lane called out. "Just you and me, Mervie! It's a date!"

CHAPTER SIXTEEN

Liberties, Classified

1

Lacey's sudden interest in Wendell's nonexistent friendship with Mugsy Levine shot to the top of Gower's growing playlist of blues. Not Making Infantry had been leading the way, with Waverly's Suicide, and Lingering Remorse over the Japanese Kid coming in at Place and Show, respectively. Ignoring the harm that drinking had done to his dad, he piled up the empties that night and all the next day. Not only beers at the Service Club, but some of the harder stuff that was now irrigating The Forrest with increasing regularity.

"This ain't what you came here for, Gowah." Conroy's words found their way through the fog of something not quite resembling sleep, inspiring the down and nearly out Welsh Kid's eyelids to flutter during an unreasonable facsimile of sleep, while his peepers searched for the source of the reminder.

"You can't do nobody no good like this. Believe me, it's

only gonna get wuhse unless you snap out of it. Besides, who am I gonna dance with?"

Gower locked in on his buddy, and stared in semi-wonder. *The guy's got a way of looking at things in general, and at Army life in particular, that I could never dream of. It's bold, it's brave, and most importantly, it's often hilarious.* "You wish," he shot back, before getting his body to follow his eyes, and then to fold and unfold into a wobbly perch on the edge of his bunk. *My interpreter of all things American. His capacity for hanging in there, for surviving despite all the bullshit, is certainly worth something. Not his fault Waverly committed suicide. We all let the guy down.*

"You can't help Waverly or that Japanese kid no more," Conroy told him, "so whyntcha fahget it . . . ? If you want sumpin' to worry about, worry about us."

"Hah!" Gower's eyebrows jumped at the notion. "We're in *Medical Replacement*, Danny! What've we got to worry about besides running out of cotton swabs and iodine?"

"You kiddin' me? When we're busy tending the wounded out there on the battlefield, we'll be sittin' ducks! And if we got those helmets with the white circles and the red crosses painted on 'em, it's sumpin' extra for the Japs and the Krauts to aim at! We oughta get a medal for just showin' up, for chrissake!"

It took a while, but Gower realized his buddy was right—though not about the medal part. He needed to buck up. And if any additional motivation was required, it was right there in the daily news.

"Russian Army in General Retreat."
"Rommel Stymies Brits in Egypt."
"Japs Take Guadalcanal, Threaten Port Moresby."

There was no news but bad news. "The Forces of savagery and enslavement" were winning. And before anything got any better, it very likely "could get wuhse" as Conroy kept insisting.

The "Nurse Nancy" Battalion isn't exactly what I had in mind for "defending against all enemies," but like Mugsy says, "Ya gotta play the hand what you been dealt widt." For inspiration, Gower needed only to recall a few things Mrs. Bailey told them, some things about their mother they hadn't realized.

"Your mum come down all that way from the far north of Wales, she done! As a lass! A girl alone in those days?! That were sumpin' all by itself, it were!"

How Mom ended up a student nurse in a faraway town full of strangers—likely not very fond of the Welsh. Took a lotta courage and belief in herself. Hope I can come close to following her example—with a dash of Sid Bailey's advice thrown in—"Jump and tumble."

So, here goes. Gonna be the best damned Medical Replacement trainee there ever was, and make Mom proud by out-bandaging, out-splinting, out-compressing, out-healing everyone else in Company B, if not the whole damned Medical Battalion!

Next morning, the "new and improved" Gower began his crusade. As he and others waited for their Battlefield Aid instructor to show, some guy appeared at the back of the room and approached a few of his classmates. *Looking for someone? With that armband . . . A messenger of some sort?* A couple of the other guys pointed in Gower's direction.

"Gonna be setting splints so good," he was telling Conroy and anyone else within earshot, "guys'll be breaking their own bones just to watch me operate!"

"Save it for later, Dr. Kildare," the runner said, coming up alongside and serving Gower with a document. "Right now, you better bust your own ass by hightailing it over to Classification. Captain Mennur wants to see you on the double!"

Mennur? Captain Cabbage? Gower stared at the piece of paper. *Of Classification? Hmmm.* He knew from early on the Army didn't always describe things the way civilians would. Shovels were "entrenching tools." Undershirts were "vests." But in this case, he hoped *classification* actually meant "classification."

Hah! They've finally realized assigning me to Medical Replacement was a mistake! Going to be training with Bucoda and McCleary, after all! Christ! Even Kelso made Infantry—and my scores were better than his and *McCleary's!*

"Private Gower reporting as ordered," he announced, snapping to attention and saluting when he arrived in the Classification Office's reception area. Though the reception clerk's face was aimed at the keys of his typewriter, Gower recognized "Sgt. B. Fitch"—according to the nameplate—as the same sergeant from the "beets inspection" at the mess hall.

B. Fitch didn't look up. Gower held his pose. The sergeant pawed at his machine until several keys got themselves in a jam. "Damn!" he cursed the machine before finally addressing the visitor. "Got here pretty fast, didn'tcha, Cower. Gonna be a while, though. So, whyntcha have a seat."

"Cower"? Did he call me "Cower"?

2

Leaning forward to peer into the throat of the paralyzed Remington, B. Fitch resumed ignoring the visitor. His salute never answered, Gower surrendered the gesture and sat down. "The runner said I was to report on the double, Sergeant. So, I did."

Fitch continued to poke and pick at the tortured keys until *click, click, ca-clack* announced their release. "'On the double,' eh? Well," he chuckled, finally looking at the visitor, "maybe it was a finger of speech, or something—'on the double.' Anyway, it don't matter, cuz the captain's still busy, so . . . how about some coffee, Cower?"

Since the office brew smelled strong enough to serve itself, Gower declined. "By the way, it's *Gower.* Private Mervyn *Gower,* with a '*G.*'"

"Says 'Cower,' widda '*C*' in the report, though," the sergeant said, cranking himself up out of his chair and heading for the pot of java sitting on a side table. "And I ought to know, cuz I typed it myself!"

Jeez! Is there some guy named Cower in Combat School who should be with the Nurse Nancys instead of me? If this Mennur guy's got any pull at all, maybe he can correct the mistake on the spot! Maybe that's why he called me in here!

Gower sat back, feeling a lot better about things till he realized reversal of his "misplacement" would mean separating from Conroy. *Really going to miss that guy . . . But, just like Corporal Pierce always told us, "Don't get too chummy with other guys, 'cause they might be the next to go." And in this case, that guy's going to be me!*

Back with a fresh cup of joe, B. Fitch resumed his place behind the hulking gray word-trasher and let out a whale-worthy sigh. He stretched. He cracked his knuckles and stretched again before returning to hunt-and-peck his way through another form.

After Gower had watched the clerk for a mind-numbing twenty minutes, his gaze fell to his lap, where his thumbs had set themselves to twiddling on their own—something they never did before he joined the Army. Soon bored with watching that, he gazed around at the unremarkable surroundings, including, finally, the ceiling, where he spotted a couple of flies. Instead of circles, they were flying in squares. *Maybe it's a different species than we've got in LA. Maybe nobody else ever noticed. Maybe I could end up in a future copy of Dad's* National Geographic *for discovering it.*

"Fitch!" At last came a call from an inner office. The sergeant quickly got up and disappeared behind the door marked "Classification Officer."

"Captain Mennur's ready to see you, now, Cower," Fitch said, returning from the other room.

"*Gower,*" the private corrected one last time as he passed Fitch going the other way.

Fitch shrugged. "Tomato. Potato. Suit yourself, Cower."

Gower knocked. "Enter, *see voo play*!" the unmistakable voice invited. Gower went in and saluted Captain Cabbage. The contents of a manila file were spread on the surface of the largest desk Gower had ever seen. Set to one side of it was the nameplate "O. D. Mennur, Cpt., Classification." Captain Mennur sat poring over a document. Gower guessed the file was his.

Without looking up at his visitor, the captain motioned Gower toward the only other chair. From the way he was greeted, the private assumed Mennur wasn't much interested in formalities. This suited Gower just fine. He dropped his salute and sat down. With high hopes for reassignment to the Infantry, he began working on ways to break the news to Conroy. He put on his thinking cap while he tried but failed to get comfortable in the straight-backed wooden chair. He thought maybe this chair was lower than the one his butt had just left or Mennur's desk was higher than Fitch's, or both. In any case, this chair didn't sit flush on the floor, and rocked a bit whenever Gower's weight shifted. He looked down for the source of the problem. *Fresh saw marks. This chair* is *shorter. To make the captain appear taller than he actually is?*

As Gower resigned himself to more waiting in a slightly rocking chair and with no end in sight, his attention wandered around the room until again settling on the ceiling. *The same flies from the other room? Or two different ones? And, if anybody asked, could I tell the difference?*

After several more minutes, the captain sighed, put the document down on the blotter in front of him, looked squarely at Gower, and nodded solemnly a couple of times before pulling open a drawer in the desk. He took something out and set it down between them.

Gower could hardly believe his eyes. *Mugsy's brass knuckles!*

3

Without a word, Mennur proceeded to slowly nudge Mugsy's token of friendship toward Gower with the tips of his fingers. He did it in spurts, all the while staring not at the knuckles, but at Gower, as if watching him for a particular response. *Returning them? I'm probably not supposed to have them. So . . . blackmail? Evidence for my court-martial?* He feigned disinterest.

When the brass knuckles had been pushed to the halfway point, the captain stopped, sighed, and withdrew his hand. Arms folded, he leaned back and sighed again. "Hostility, Private Gower," he said softly.

Crap! Called me Gower. There goes the "wrong name" theory. So . . . why am I here, then?

"I'm feeling nothing but . . . *hostility* from you, Private. *Why* am I feeling this from you—toward me, toward Sergeant Thornton, toward the Army—because of something in your childhood, *put tet*?"

"I-I don't know why you're feeling that, sir—hostility, I mean. I wasn't aware I had any in particular, sir. Boots like to complain—"

"Complaining is one thing, Private. But according to your file, I'm afraid you have gone *way* beyond that. Oh, yes. *Sawns doot!* And apparently, from Day One. 'Questioning a noncommissioned officer's fitness for duty,' et cetera and et cetera. It's all right here, in great detail," he added, tapping a fingertip on the folder, presumably containing the entirety of Gower's Army life—not quite three months.

So, I was called in here because I rubbed Sergeant Thornton the wrong way? No wonder Hogjaw pretty much ignored me the last few weeks. The Forrest's "Classification Officer" is in his pocket! Even with qualifying scores, the sergeant already knew I wouldn't be classified Infantry! All he had to do was tell Manure here what he wanted, and that was that!

"Professionally, Sergeant Thornton is nothing if not thorough. A little careless privately, perhaps—a pity about that boy down in Texas. . . . Houston, I think it was, awful place, Houston—but thorough."

Beat up some kid or something? "Woon't surprise me," as Conroy would say.

Mennur pressed forward, leaning his chin on knitted hands. "You don't feel it's your patriotic duty to follow orders, Private Gower—to serve without question and, if necessary, defend your country with your life?"

"Yes, sir. It is my duty. I do feel it, sir," Gower said, hesitating for a second before adding, "I don't know—"

"Don't know *what*?" The captain cut him short. "Despite what you may say to deny it, Gower, Sergeant Thornton tells me you are a habitual shirker, a troublemaker—a veritable *blaggu-rur*, if you will."

Gower wasn't sure what Mennur called him was even English and suddenly felt a tightness around his neck. *Better choose my own words wisely.*

"With your permission, sir," he offered up. "I'm afraid the sergeant is mistaken. My actions might possibly fit that last word you said, but definitely not the other two. . . . Did the sergeant really call me a . . . *bla. Blag* . . . ? Excuse me, sir, but what did you say the sergeant told you I was, sir?"

"Blaggu-rur." Mennur repeated the word, exasperation singeing the edges. "It's *French.* In words you can understand, Private, it's someone who's full of bull. Of course, the sergeant didn't actually say *blaggu-rur.*" The captain's eyebrows hopped as high as anatomy allowed. "Oh, no . . . ! *Bien sûr!* Sergeant Thornton is a fine soldier. Unlike you, he does what he's told. But, let's face it, he's not very well educated." Mennur chuckled at the thought. "No, indeed! But an excellent disciplinarian . . ." He leaned back in his chair before turning to stare wistfully out the window, as if savoring a memory.

After an extended pause, the captain suddenly swiveled back around to face the private. "Sadly, despite Sergeant Thornton's wishes, I've decided he's unfit for combat. Too old. And, I'm afraid, too prone to engage in . . . ? Let us call them *lapses*, shall we? *Faux pas,* as they say—particularly with subordinates. Instead, I have recommended him for something more suited to his temperament and abilities—the Military Police—with immediate promotion to head of the force, as well as the stockade. The camp's *commandant,* if you will. General Flagg has already approved the change. Sergeant Thornton should do very well in that position, wouldn't you agree?"

Gower had no idea what to say, or what was expected. "I'm sure he will, sir."

"Of course, he will. He has to," Mennur said, and then went silent. He steepled his forefingers at his nose, tapping it a couple times as he stared at Gower, as if sizing him up. "Speaking of *lapses*, Private Gower, you haven't witnessed any noncommissioned officers—any officers at all, for that matter—take certain . . . *liberties* with enlisted men, have you?"

"Liberties, sir?"

More nose-tapping. A longer pause. "Yes," the captain said. *"Liberties."*

4

Mennur gazed at Mugsy's knuckles on the blotter between them, then sighed and leaned forward, motioning for Gower to do the same. "We're making a considerable investment in the sergeant, Private," Mennur whispered. "You see, General Flagg has known Thornton practically since he enlisted. They served together in Mexico with Pershing, and then again, a few years later, during some nasty business right here in Arkansas—some local coloreds got out of hand, so to speak. You might say the careers of those two soldiers are intertwined. And if the sergeant were to fail, not only my future but that of the general could also be at risk."

And now he wants me to support the guy who torpedoed my best chance to see combat. Give me a break! Gower's response was likewise a whisper. "I'm not sure I follow you, sir."

"Not sure?!" Mennur leaned back in surprise before a sort

of smirk seized his face. "*Bien joué, mon ami!* Well played, Private! I may have underestimated you!"

Did he just pay me a compliment?

"It can't have escaped you, Private Gower, that we've been adding busloads of colored soldiers to Camp Forrest—practically on a daily basis. Oh, yes! Already they number in the thousands. The locals resent us for it. We need to try and appease them, PDQ! Let's face it. Many, if not most, of the colored troops are, frankly, *mizerawb-lay,* illiterate sons of bitches." Mennur folded his arms, leaned back, and slowly wagged his head a few times while lifting his eyes toward the ceiling. "With less sense than . . . than those flies buzzing around the ceiling fan! Fitch!" The captain suddenly shot forward, shouting at the wall separating him from the sergeant's desk. "*Why* isn't the ceiling fan *on,* Fitch?! Get in here, on the *double!*" There was no answer. The captain emitted a low-pitched kind of growl toward the supposed location of his unseen subordinate. "I may have misinterpreted your motives *once,* Fitch, but *never* again! Do *not* test me! *Set-oon grave er-ror!*"

Not knowing what else to do or say, Gower got up and went over to the ceiling fan's wall switch. "Allow me, sir," he said, turning it on and returning to his seat.

Mennur shrugged and nodded approval. "Thank you, Private." He then made a quick notation in Gower's file before going on. "Where was I?"

"Sons of bitches, sir," Gower said and then immediately regretted it. The conversation was clearly veering further away from his own status and his desire to have that status changed.

"What? Yes! Exactly! Those colored sons of bitches simply shouldn't be here. They aren't fit for fighting. All my testing bears this out! And the large numbers of them have the locals upset. Upset? Hah! They're *terrified*! Community leaders have confided in me privately, Private. There are rumors.

The good people of Little Rock fear an armed uprising. Oh, yes! Renegade Black soldiers, fanning the flames of revolt. Roaming bands of them. With weapons! With *intentions*, if you get my meaning. Think of the women and children, Gower. Especially the women!"

The poster I put up for Mr. Scobbs on my last day at the Y—the Japanese soldier threatening a white woman on a darkened street.

"There are rumors. Credible rumors. Black mutineers with tanks! *Tanks*, Gower! Can you imagine?! And they say they've already done things out West—terrible things, unspeakable things—in Arizona, or one of those other places nobody ever goes." The captain nodded solemnly. "According to highly reliable sources, they're headed in this direction, traveling at night so as not to be detected. Oh, yes! And adding more rebels along the way!"

There were tanks on that trainload of colored soldiers that passed us in the desert near Yuma. But that was in broad daylight! Some of them waved back. Pretty friendly for mutineers, if you ask me. And how could they steal those tanks without anyone noticing?

"Of course, these are only rumors," Mennur said, as if reading Gower's mind. "But it pays to be safe. It could happen. *Certain mont.* In fact, it already did—an uprising of Blacks! Oh, yes. Mere months after the last war. Not too far from where we sit. Right here in Arkansas!" He emphasized the point by tapping a forefinger on his desk. "General Flagg and Sergeant Thornton were both there, in fact—a town named Elaine—to help restore order after most of the mayhem had ended. Returning colored soldiers got the local Blacks all riled up about their *rights*, and other nonsense. Hundreds were killed during the violence because of it! According to what General Flagg told me, the bodies of the dead and wounded were everywhere!"

Gower was shocked. With that many dead, he couldn't believe he hadn't heard about it in history class. "Hundreds of *white people*, sir?"

"Whites? Oh, no. Heavens no. Only a handful, thank goodness. But it could have been worse. Oh, yes. Much, *much* worse. Just imagine, if those rebellious Blacks had been *armed*, who knows what could have happened? Which is why we can't trust the colored troops with bullets, Gower. You may not have noticed, but we don't allow them to train with loaded guns."

"*Cartridges*, sir, and *rifles*," Gower corrected the captain, then immediately regretted his knee-jerk reference to Corporal Pierce's constant reminders regarding the Army's preferred vocabulary for those items.

"What?"

"Oh, sorry, sir. Force of habit, I guess. We were taught to call them *cartridges* and *rifles*. Also, sir, as far as I know, no one—white or Black—is authorized to have loaded weapons, sir, unless they're on guard duty, at the firing range, or serving as MPs."

The captain eyed Gower skeptically as he leaned away and shook his head—as if trying to clear his thoughts. "Be that as it may . . ."

"Yes, sir."

"Back to why I called you in here."

"Yes, sir. Thank you, sir." *Jeez! Is this guy nuts, or what?*

"Think of it, Gower. You and me caught with our pants down."

He's nuts.

5

"This war has taken us completely by surprise, tearing us, kicking and screaming"—Mennur grasped, two-fisted, at the air between them, as if to illustrate his point—"from the bosoms of our families. From the very *teats* of complacency, innocent lips still dribbling with the milk of our carefree civilian lives, before *thrusting* us," he added—along with a more-or-less appropriately illustrative gesture—"headlong into service, during our country's darkest hour. Citizen soldiers, *all*—from the humblest, most ignorant lout, to the more . . . *junsay paw* . . . refined among us, unfamiliar with the brutal arts of Mars." The captain leaned back, a self-satisfied smile on his face.

"Well, except for fossils like Flagg and Thornton. They were already here—and now, 'dead wood,' as they say. When the war started, we didn't have enough qualified officers, Gower—commissioned or otherwise. We still don't. I myself was an aide to a member of Congress when duty called. Oh, yes. As it happens, he represents this part of the country. Pure coincidence, I assure you. Having experienced the region firsthand, I can't say I'm very impressed. But I'm a glass-half-full type of guy, Gower. I'm always looking for opportunities—including right here, at Camp Forrest. And, if we play our cards right—yes, even you—we could move up the ladder and come out of this war in much better shape than when we went in."

Wants me to be his partner? In what? Or is he just trying to put the squeeze on me?

The captain leaned in again, beckoning the recruit to join him. "Washington has its eye on us, Gower. Exhibit A"—Mennur ticked it off with a finger—"the government needs to save money, and B"—up went another finger—"help reduce the hardship on communities near new or expanded replacement depots—like Camp Forrest, here in Little Rock. As you should know by now, Mrs. Roosevelt has taken a personal interest in 'my boys'—as she calls us—eating a healthy diet. Vegetables, Gower, right here in Arkansas. Beets are big, Gower. Oh, yes. Very big." He nodded and leaned back. "I personally find them disgusting, but there you have it. By the way, are beets a vegetable?"

"I'm not really sure, sir."

"*Neesee, neelaw.* No matter." Mennur waved a hand dismissively in the air above Mugsy's knuckles, still sitting on the blotter, before coming in close again. "Can you keep a secret?"

Gower silently thumbed through the catalog of candidates already stuffing his noodle—the Japanese boy, Mugsy's knuckles, what Pierce said about Sergeant King, his suspicions about Waverly and Hogjaw—before a nod and a sigh. "Yes, sir. Several, sir."

Apparently assured of Gower's confidence, Mennur leaned back and continued with his story. "Word is, Gower, the first lady is planning on paying us a visit. At this point, it's all very hush-hush, you understand. Not even General Flagg knows! But *I* know." He nodded, grinning ear to ear. "I shouldn't even be telling you this, Gower, but it could mean quite a lot to us after the war—to me, to you, to all of us here at Camp Forrest—besides the coloreds, of course—if we play our cards right. But I flatter myself."

"Yes, sir." *Where the hell is all this going?*

"Think about it, Gower. If we want to succeed, if we want the Army—the government—to succeed in mustering support for the war effort here in Arkansas, we *must work* with the locals—*play ball* with them, as they say—relieve their fears about having so many soldiers around—especially the Black ones—and show them we can be a positive part of the community—in solidarity with these fine, upstanding citizen-patriots, many of whom are, let's face it, complete idiots. Like this beet farmer I met the other day—Benton or Buntson, or something. *Sheesh!* What a clown. But I digress. It's toward that end, Gower, that I have made, that is, I have *nominated* Sergeant Thornton to head the Military Police here in "The Forrest"—as you dogfaces like to call it. He's only been at it a week or two, but he's already organized our MPs into a real *fighting force*. Oh, yes! And he's placed a twenty-four-hour guard at key positions surrounding the *darker* parts of the camp, if you get my meaning. If we ever do have to face colored renegades, in tanks or otherwise, he will not fail us, Gower. He's a good man, with a bit of flair for the dramatic, as it happens—who knew?"

"I was unaware of that, sir. Of Sergeant Thornton's flair." *Off the deep end.* That's *where this is going.*

"Oh, yes! Recently Thornton led a tour here for some local leaders—under my direction, of course—and capped it off by letting them shoot the machine guns he recently had mounted on those new, *kuh-voot-dear*? The 'jeeps' the MPs are driving around in these days. Great fun, really." Mennur punched repeatedly at the air between them. "*Rat-a-tat-tat!* Have you tried it?" The captain leaned back in his chair, folded his arms over his chest, and stared out the window. His reflection in the glass was all smiles. "*Rat-a-tat-tat,* indeed!"

"No, sir, I haven't." The private gave out with a weary sigh. "Only *Infantry* trainees are allowed to be machine gunners, sir—which is why I thought you sent for me—"

"And by all indications, the townsfolk had a *wonderful* time." A suddenly more somber Mennur swung back around. "I take my responsibilities very seriously, and if I do say so myself, I have Thornton *perfectly* placed. Sergeant Fitch, on the other hand . . ." The captain suddenly sat up straight as if remembering something. "You *do* know what my job is here, don't you, Private?"

Gower looked again at the nameplate on the captain's desk just to be sure he hadn't imagined it. "Classification Officer," it continued to read.

"Classification Officer?" he ventured.

6

Mennur couldn't contain a chuckle. "Yes, yes, that's what the *sign* says I do. What I actually *do* do—before, during, and after Basic Training—is perform detailed analyses of the backgrounds, abilities, character, and—oh, yes—even the *diet* of every young man and woman who passes through our gates—except the colored ones. That would be a complete waste of my time."

The only Black soldiers I even sorta know are Eberley, the model airplane maker, and Johnson, the crooner who sings with Lacey. Based on what little I know about those two guys, I'd say they're worth any amount of investment the Army would care to make.

"I aim to place our young warriors within the Army's vast fighting machine *precisely* where they will do the most good, help win this war, and send us all home victorious, to the bosoms of our families."

"Do you miss them, sir?"

"Bosoms?"

"Your family, sir. I sure miss mine."

Mennur turned away. "My wife and son went to live with her parents in Trenton. My folks retired to the Adirondacks. I never see any of them."

"Sorry to hear that, sir, and excuse me for interrupting, but, if you don't mind, may I ask you something about *my* classification?" Mennur shrugged, then gestured for Gower to go ahead. "Based on what you've told me, sir, despite having combat-related scores near the top of my platoon, I was wondering why I wasn't assigned to the Infantry. Was it because I am a certified lifeguard? And if so, were you thinking I'd be more useful to the Army in a medical unit?"

"*You* were a lifeguard?" Mennur flipped through the private's file. "Ah! So, you were! No," he shrugged. "That's not it. Despite what you may know about certain *private* matters, Private, it's because you're a slacker, and that's what we do with slackers—you and that good-for-nothing pal of yours, Conroy. If we find recruits who won't play ball with us here at Camp Forrest, we place them in the 'Bedpan Battalion,' as Thornton likes to call it. Clever name for it, don't you think? Frankly, Gower, I'd say you two clowns are lucky I didn't assign you to one of those miserable colored units on the other side of camp. Yes, very lucky, indeed." Apparently deciding any further discussion would be a waste of his time, Mennur deliberately swung around to face the window. "That is all, Private," he said over his shoulder. "Dismissed," he added with a brief wave of a hand when he realized Gower hadn't moved.

What the hell was the point of all this anyway, if not simply to humiliate me? "Yes, sir," Gower said, rising to leave. Before going, he cast a last, longing glance at Mugsy's shiny brass going-away gift, still sitting where the captain had left it.

Mennur suddenly turned back around, grinning broadly. "A-*ha*! They *are* yours, aren't they! Sergeant Thornton told me he got them from Waverly, who told *him* he took them from some Japanese kid, who took them from you during your ride out here from California!"

"So, Waverly had them, after all. Anything else the sergeant told you about the boy, or about Waverly?"

"That all depends. What did you have in mind?" After the brief defensive stand, Mennur took a step back. "Listen, I know I can't always believe what Thornton tells me, Private, and yes, he's been known to have a drink, or two, now and again." Mennur chuckled. "But then, who doesn't, now and again?" He winked before going on. "So, I've learned to take some of the things he tells me with a generous grain of salt. The story about the knuckles is one of them. The information I have gathered regarding him and Private Waverly, on the other hand . . ."

Gower looked hard at the captain, trying to read him. *What* is *this all about?*

"And then, the private's suicide. So very sad. . . . It happens, of course. The pressures a young man faces—away from home for the first time, alone among strangers, trying to fit in. They say he hanged himself in the showers, I think it was. Oh, yes. Very sad, indeed."

"Yes, sir," Gower agreed. "Very sad."

"Did you know Waverly well?"

"Not as well as I thought, as it turns out."

"Coincidentally, I was about to recommend Waverly be dishonorably discharged for his behavior, which was, well, *dishonorable*, let's face it. Somehow, he learned of my plans before I could carry them out and decided to take matters into his own hands. Regrettable. Otherwise, who knows? He might still be with us."

Gower felt something crucial draining from the center of himself—replaced by an ill-fitting sadness, forcing itself into place, giving rise to an urge to reach over and punch Mennur in his self-satisfied face.

"Take them," the captain said, waving vaguely toward Mugsy's brass knuckles. "Nothing will be said—nothing, that is, as long as you do the same—say nothing you may know concerning certain *liberties* taken with Waverly by the sergeant. We want you to keep the weapon," Mennur added when he realized Gower wasn't biting. "Thornton told me so himself. Let's just call it a little *teet oh taht*—that's French for 'tit for tat'—just don't ever use them. The knuckles, I mean."

"I'm sure I don't know what you mean by *dishonorable*, sir, or *liberties*, either. Waverly seemed like a fine soldier to me. But I don't think any of us treated him very fairly."

"What are you trying to say, Private?" Mennur asked, raising his voice.

"Nothing," Gower answered. "Nothing, sir," he said, then saluted and turned to leave. "Thank you, Captain Mennur. I learned a lot here today."

"Wait," Mennur said, indicating the brass knuckles still on the desk. "Aren't you forgetting something?"

"No, sir," he said. "Not forgetting anything . . . ever again," and left empty handed.

CHAPTER SEVENTEEN

Smooth Operators

1

On his way back to the classroom, things Mennur said bumped up against stuff already crammed inside Gower's head, throwing him off balance. *How come he knows so much about Waverly, anyway? Hogjaw tell him? And what's Mugsy's knuckles got to do with any of this? Did the Japanese kid take them? Or was it actually Waverly? And why's it so important I don't tell anyone about . . .* what? *I don't even know what it is I'm not supposed to blab! Guess the message is, "Play ball with us, or I can make things even tougher." As if he works for the Buffone brothers or something! One thing for sure, me and Conroy were cheated out of rightful placement in the Infantry.*

When the Battlefield Aid class broke for lunch, Gower led Conroy over to a quiet table where he could spill some pretty disturbing beans by summarizing Mennur's rambling monologue as best he could. ". . . and sounded like he was trying to blackmail me, or bribe me not to say anything about something. But what? And why?"

"You still don't get it, do you."

"What? Don't get what?"

"Waverly and Hogjaw were . . . you know . . . *doing* stuff."

"Stuff?" With a helpless shrug, Gower pleaded for more information. "What stuff?"

"The Pigeon was *queer.*"

"Queer?" Gower stared at Danny till the picture came into focus. "Oh! So, Waverly and Thornton . . . !" *No wonder Mennur threatened Waverly with dishonorable discharge. Poor guy!*

"Yeah, 'Oh.' Also, *ex cetra,* and so on. Sounds like Mennur's trying to save Hogjaw's butt. Maybe his own. Maybe General Flagg's butt, too. Who knows? Who cares?"

"*I* care. About Waverly! He paid the price for Hogjaw's . . . *liberties*!"

"I feel kinda sorry for the guy, too, but, I dunno, seems like he musta made some choices along the way, don't you think?"

Gower shrugged and shook his head. "Just wish things had been different. That's all."

"Who don't—sometimes? But, hey, Medical's not so bad. Could mean giving the WACs a little *treatment,* every once in a while, if you know what I mean. Lacey's a nurse, right? Offer to cure a certain *itch* or sumpin' sometime." He winked. "Could be wuhse."

Gower had to agree. For soldiers in Medical there was the added benefit of access via proximity, which men on the Infantry side of the coin could only experience when they were likely too sick or injured to take full advantage of it. He decided to apply himself to the study and practice with renewed energy—occasionally spending some of that energy on Lacey after Friday rehearsals and Saturday dances. *Even though she still seems more interested in Wendell's nonexistent friendships with Mugsy Levine and the Buffones than in me. At least she appreciates what I can do on the dance floor—maybe the only place where I got my brother beat.*

Nothing much changed till the day Conroy burst in with a news flash. "We hit the jackpot, Gowah! Sergeant Rodri-, Rodrig-, you know, *that* guy. Got himself assigned to Medical Replacement HQ—in Supply!"

"Yeah . . . so?"

"Dontcha get it? Lemme spell it out for you. Al-ka-h-a-l-l! We use a lotta alcohol, right? Sometimes a little's left in the bottle. There's a lot of bottles. A lot of medical-grade ethanol's just lying around, or gets wasted—unless, you know, someone *takes care of it.*"

"Yeah, OK. Got it. Still can't hear the difference, can you. 'Rodrigues. Rodriguez.'"

"Won't talk to me till my version's close enough to suit him. The guy's a pain. But he's been dealing hooch since before I got here, so whaddya gonna do? *'Fucking gold mine,'* he says. Didjya know ethanol's only a hop, skip, and a few juniper berries from a bottle of gin?" Gower did know, based on his dad's history, and nodded, unenthused.

"We're right in the middle of it!"

Dabbling in "surplus supplies" didn't interest Gower very much, but he figured as long as war casualties weren't pouring in, he was willing to look the other way. Gower understood that having Rodrigues-Rodriguez "directing traffic" should mean improved quality and quantity of the end product. Conroy told him some of the other recent arrivals and a few of the noncom orderlies were also playing ball.

"Waste not, want not," the Phluffian added.

Meanwhile, studies intensified. As medics in training, they were given minor procedures to perform in The

Forrest's hospitals, with access to supplies they needed for tending to the sick, injured, or wounded. They were also allowed to practice on actual patients—if any happened to be available—but only while under the supervision of senior staff. For what everyone assumed were obvious reasons, prisoners of war were the preferred objects of trainees' attentions.

Next up for Conroy and Gower was how to administer an enema. Looking forward to their final, qualifying "purgation," Gower wondered aloud whether they might somehow be violating the Geneva Convention by performing enemas on captive German soldiers.

"You kidding me? The Krauts never had it so good!" Conroy reassured him with a wink. "We'll be doing the guy a favor!"

When a subject turned up who fit the bill, the two students reported to the scheduling desk at the camp's main hospital on a Saturday, just before lunch. Conroy handed Gower the chit they got detailing the assignment.

"Hang on to this while I check on a rumor I heard from You Know Who." When no one was looking, the Phluffian flipped through a list of current patients. "Whaddya think, Gowah?" He showed a particular name and room assignment to his buddy. "Instead of some Kraut, how'd you like to operate on *this* guy—if we had the chance?"

Gower smiled grimly and nodded. "*If* we had the chance."

2

After lunch at the mess hall, they picked up a Mason jar full of "something special" they'd requested from Cookie. "You gonna be drinking that?" he asked them. "'Cause if you are, I don't wanna be standing anywhere near you when it crosses home plate!"

"You kidding, me? Mother's milk! We love this stuff." Conroy placed the jar of reddish liquid in a satchel, and the two "Nancys" set out to perform their first enema on an actual patient.

"You're late!" the clerk at Hospital Command barked when they got there. "The instructor's already at the guy's room, waiting for you two birds to show up! So, get a move on!"

They were issued gloves, gowns, masks, caps, an enema bag, tubing, a nozzle for the purpose, and the requisition form confirming the name and room number. After donning their whites, including the masks, they set off in search of the POW they'd been assigned to treat. "In case somebody asks, the guy's name is Schnitzel or something, isn't it?" Gower asked.

Conroy squinted at the form. "Looks more like 'Pretzel.' But whadda I know? I never took Nazi in school." They wandered down a long hallway in the camp's main hospital until they came to a corridor connecting them to an annex for officers and VIPs.

"This way, I think," Conroy said as they made the turn.

"You sure he's still here?"

"Unless they let him out early—you know, for good behavior or sumpin'."

A bit farther down the corridor was a large printed banner over a door.

"Whaddya think, Gowah? Should we stop in and say hello?"

"Hunh. Whaddya know? Mennur told me nobody knows she's coming, but him."

"I guess *somebody* else knows—or do you think he put that up himself and hoped nobody'd notice."

"Welcome, Mrs. Roosevelt!" the large banner read.

Gower tried the door of the room reserved for the first lady. It was unlocked. There was nothing special inside. "Doesn't look like she's coming anytime soon."

"Maybe *she's* the one who don't know she's coming." Conroy shrugged. "It's the gubberment, so woont surprise me."

"Well, if anyone knows, it's Rodrigues," Gower added.

"Wait a minute. Are you sayin' his name the same way I'm sayin' it? Sounds different."

Gower shrugged. "Maybe."

They continued down the hall, Conroy mumbling to himself along the way, "Rodrigues. Rodriguez. *Rodriguez. Rodrigues.* Crap! Now *I'm* not even sure which one I'm trying to say!"

"Hold it!" Gower abruptly placed a hand over Conroy's masked mouth. "This is it!" Cautiously and quietly, they entered the dimly lit, two-bed room. Only one of the stations was occupied. According to the duty sheet, the patient was suffering from "poisoning, alcohol, mild."

They tiptoed up to the bed and put on their rubber gloves. Gower snapped one of the fingers inadvertently. They anxiously eyed their guinea pig. No response. His breathing was steady but a bit labored. Otherwise, he was out. The pair went back to work. Conroy unscrewed the enema bag and emptied some of its contents into a bedpan. Gower took the jar they got from Cookie, topped off the enema solution with the contents, then shook the bag for good measure.

"You think he likes beets?" Conroy whispered.

"No problem. He won't taste a thing. . . . Come to think of it, though, the guy does do a lot of talking through his other end. So . . . ?"

Conroy shrugged and nodded before going to work. He hung the bag of solution from an IV stand and wheeled it closer. Gower pulled back the top sheet and gently rolled the man over so he rested on his side. "Looks ready to me," Gower announced. "What do you think?"

"You're the boss," Conroy said in lowered tones. He grabbed the nozzle at the end of the bladder's hose and rubbed it liberally with mineral oil. "Would you like to do the honors?"

"I *would,* as a matter of fact!" Gower took the applicator and proceeded to insert it gently into the patient's anus. The man appeared to smile.

"Sorry in advance if we mess this up," Gower whispered to the unconscious subject. "Ordinarily, we wouldn't be doing this sort of thing, you see, but, by an ironic twist of fate, we've been misclassified as medical replacements, instead of infantrymen, by some asshole."

Gower turned to his buddy. "You may proceed when ready, Private."

Nodding solemnly, Conroy undid the hose clamp, and let gravity do its thing. The patient moaned softly, but didn't appear to be experiencing any pain. After giving each other a congratulatory nod, the two trainees disposed of their gloves and slipped silently from the room with their jar of the red elixir.

"Wait!" Conroy said, outside in the hallway. "I got it! *Rodrigues*. Not *Rodriguez*."

"Ah!" Gower told him. "*Now* I hear a difference."

"Great!" Conroy beamed with pride before challenging his friend. "Which one's which?"

"Hullif-ai-know," Gower said, mimicking his friend's Philly accent.

"Very funny." They'd gone only a few steps when someone yelled from behind them.

"Hey! You! Hold on there!"

3

"Been looking all over for you two mugs!" It was their instructor. "Take a wrong turn or something? Thought you wanted to learn how to perform an enema! Well, you're too late. We got tired of waiting and did it ourselves. What a mess! Those POWs eat like pigs! Better hope we can schedule you for another time." He looked past them to see if anyone else was around. "By the way, I wouldn't be hanging around here in the officer's annex, if I were you. The sawbones get their noses bent out of shape if they think us lowlifes are butting in."

As he turned to leave, the noncom orderly caught a glimpse of the duty sheet for the room the two trainees had just left. "*Mennur*," the orderly chuckled. "Well, well. *Captain Cocktail* has alcohol poisoning. What else is new?" he added sarcastically. "See you Monday. You'll be drawing each other's blood."

"Speaking of butting in," Gower asked his buddy as they walked on, "do you remember how long it usually takes for an enema to work?"

A captain in whites emerged from a doorway up ahead of them before Conroy could answer. The pair of masked privates saluted. The medical officer gave them a surprised look before returning their salute and disappearing into Mennur's room. After a few seconds, they heard someone shout, "Sh-i-i-i-it!" from behind the closed door.

"Offhand, I'd say right about now," Conroy said with a shrug. "Woont surprise me."

Gower nodded. "Thought it might take a little longer. But whaddya know! Time *does* fly when you're having a good time! Probably better get along now, though, don't you think?"

They hurried back to the scheduling desk, returned the hospital wear, and went back to their barracks. It was

Saturday afternoon. There was a dance at the Service Club that evening.

"Hey, ya know what? Since Mennur had alcohol poisoning," Conroy said when they returned from evening chow, "if we'd put booze up his ass, 'steada that red stuff, it coulda killed him."

"I'll keep that in mind," Gower said as they started getting ready for the dance. "By the way, you finally manage to round up a date for tonight?"

"I got a plan," Conroy reported while posing in the mirror. "Still working on it."

"Haven't seen Kelso in quite a while. Maybe he's available if she doesn't show."

"Ha! Good one, Gowah! And here's a little sumpin' for you to chew on—Johnson's not allowed to sing with Lacey no more on account of he's Black and she's white, and Mrs. General Flagg don't like the idea of 'em being together on the same stage—especially singing romantic stuff. Maybe their 'Love Walked In' duet's what did it! Woont surprise me. So . . . you know what *that* means, dontcha? Fewer breaks for Lacey 'cause she's gonna be too busy singing, which means you're gonna be spending most of your time moping around the stage, like before she gave you a spin. Better bring some *Rodri-guess Special* along with ya so's to take some of the sting outta the deal! And you're right about Kelso. Heard he's been looking for that *certain someone*. Maybe you and him can cut a few rugs tahgethuh." He turned again to go. "See ya around the punchbowl—*if* my squeeze wants to take a breather!"

The news about Lacey stopped Gower dead in the middle of cinching his tie. The mug staring back from the mirror said it all. *Maybe it just wasn't meant to be.*

"Tried to tell ya, Kid." He could hear Mugsy piling on. *"Back off before ya get hurt."*

Too late. Already hurts. Thought she might be the one—taking my heart to where it's never been.

"Face it," the mirror seemed to be saying, *"Lacey's too glamorous, too attractive—too whatever it is that drives men crazy—to settle for someone who isn't handsome or smart or talented."*

Meaning, anyone not Wendell. Gower cinched up his tie and looked around. He was the only one left in the barracks. He retreated to his bunk, where he parked his butt on the edge of it. Elbows on his knees, head in hands while twin Gowers moped up at him from shiny shoe leather. With only frustrations and regrets for company, he was reminded, somehow, of Waverly and decided he preferred being with other people, even if they weren't named Lacey Lane.

He showed up at the dance about an hour into it and decided he could resist the urge to press up against the stage and moon over Lacey if he simply kept moving. Wandering over to one of the refreshment tables, he considered some punch but pointed instead at a USO cookie. "Chocolate chips. With nuts!" the local girl in charge said between smiles.

Gower nodded, grinned, and took a bite. The cookie—his favorite kind—was surprisingly good. Despite rationing, it had plenty of chocolate. About to congratulate himself for choosing it over the peanut brittle, and for having the strength to turn his back to the stage, the bluesy piano intro of "If I Didn't Care" drifted his way. All the chocolate chips in the world couldn't have cured him. He turned and stared at Lacey Lane the rest of the way through the cookie, and all the way through her rendition. He thought maybe she winked at him but was willing to admit it could have been something in her eye. Arms folded, watching her through two or three more songs, he decided Conroy was right. Without Johnson to spell her, and given her popularity among "the boys," even a single spin with her figured to be rare. He could only hope for an instrumental or two to save the evening.

A few minutes later, she did him a favor. *"Green Eyes." Never really cared for that one.* Grateful for the excuse to stop feeling sorry for himself, he let the cheerful USO girl serve him some of the punch. It wasn't nearly as satisfying as the cookie, so while Lacey sang another couple of numbers, he had a couple more of those, motivating the USO girl to move them closer to her, so she could do a better job of equitable distribution. He nodded an apology and buried nervous hands in his pockets. Lacey sang something else. He had some more of the punch. *Shoulda followed Conroy's advice and spiked it.*

Staring at the thin red liquid in his cup, which somehow managed to taste like beets, reminded Gower of Mennur. That only made him feel worse. *What we did to the guy . . . Hope he's OK. But, man, the bastard had it coming! Scaring poor Waverly into hanging himself . . .*

"Shoulda juiced it, hunh." Conroy squeezed out of the crowd, alone, and sidled up to his pal.

4

"So . . . Danny . . . where's your date?"

"She'll be here. Don't worry," Conroy said, nervously scanning the Service Club's foyer.

"Kelso hasn't showed yet, either." Gower tried serving up a little humor to flip the mood.

"Hey, look, McCleary!" Bucoda's voice cut through the music. "A couple of Nancys with no one to dance with but each other!" The almond farmer was a few steps behind.

"At least *I* got a date," Conroy insisted.

"Yeah?" Bucoda said, looking around. "Well, you're hiding her pretty good, Conroy. Ours are in the powder room . . . powdering. Yours wearing camouflage or something? She's blending in pretty good."

Conroy eyeballed the foyer again. "She oughta be here any minute," he assured them.

"What about you, Gower? What's your excuse?" McCleary asked.

A song ended. Gower shot a glance toward the stage, hoping Lacey would be begging off. Instead, she remained at the mike, already snapping her fingers to the beat of the next tune. The band struck up "Deep Purple," a little more up tempo than the radio usually played it. "Guess I struck out," he told the others when he realized Lacey wasn't budging.

"Dames," Bucoda said. "Whaddya gonna do, hey?"

"Yeah," McCleary chuckled. "Whaddya gonna do?"

"Drive ya crazy, hey?" Conroy added.

"You can say that again."

"Can't live with 'em. Can't live without 'em."

"Ain't that the truth."

Already at a trickle, the small talk soon ran dry. With nothing more to add, Gower surveyed the room—refreshments table, stage, dancing couples—and from the looks on his buddies' faces, he assumed their dates remained agonizingly MIA. But while the two Infantry guys slowly stewed, Medical Conroy fairly bubbled in his own pot of frustration over a partner gone AWOL.

Time's either speeding by or dawdling, I guess, depending on what you're waiting for. With Lacey out of the running, only The Welsh Kid was able to avoid the anxiety.

"Field exercises in a few weeks." McCleary broke the silence. "Won't tell us where, but with gas rationing, and with trains reserved mostly for freight, has to be close by."

"So, maybe even here?" Gower asked, hopeful of somehow being involved.

Bucoda shook his head. "'Just us and the gators,' Sarge told us."

"Yeah," McCleary added. "So, I figure it's gotta be Louisiana, you know, 'cause nothing makes me think of North African desert battlefields like the swamps of Louisiana."

"Is he joking?" the geographically challenged Bucoda asked the assemblage.

"I never joke about funny stuff," McCleary deadpanned.

"The Army finally issue you a sensayumah, McCleary, or what?" Conroy asked.

"Too bad you Nancys won't be joining us," Bucoda added. "You'd be swell to have along, Gower. Conroy, too, maybe—if only you'd speak English once in a while."

"Yeah, yeah." Conroy ignored the slight, and instead stared puppy-lovelorn toward the entry in search of his gal.

Gower jumped in. "Who says we won't be going along? When you miserable sacks skin a knee or get a blister, who's going to patch you up?!" A sudden silence from the stage stopped him short. The musicians appeared to be taking a break. Lacey was nowhere to be seen.

The eventual appearance of the Powder Room Twins was underscored by *we told you so* grins from Bucoda and McCleary. Their dates gave Gower and Conroy polite but coy nods before leading their own men away from the small talk and out onto the dance floor to await the music's return.

Conroy went AWOL about the same time as Kelso drifted by, complaining to no one in particular about how bad the punch was compared to what his mother used to make—simultaneously accepting a cup of it from the USO girl. With Kelso at his elbow, grousing about how hard he had it training for the Infantry—"with Bucoda always on me for being stupid and clumsy"—Gower stood searching the hall for Lacey.

"Do they let you guys do surgery?" Kelso asked between sips of the punch he kept insisting was worse than horse piss, without explaining how he knew. "Those cookies look pretty good. But chocolate makes my face break out. How about just tonsils? Can you do that? I ought to have mine out, that's for sure. My nose is running something awful. Ever since I got here it's been like this. Makes my throat sore and my eyes water. All these weeds are doing it. Didn't have them like this back in LA. Did *you*? You lived on Poppy Peak, so I guess you had poppies. Are poppies weeds? Do they let you guys practice on real people? If they do, then I volunteer. But just for tonsils. Tonsils aren't fatal, are they? That reminds me, have you seen any dead guys yet? Saw my uncle when he died. He was just lying there—like he was asleep or something, but you know . . . *dead*."

It was getting toward eleven. The dance party was nearly over. Gower hoped Kelso would turn into a pumpkin or something as he watched him stare soberly into his cup of the scarlet punch, as if for inspiration. "I don't think I could actually *kill* anybody, though, do you?" the pimply-faced kid was saying, when Lacey suddenly glided up unseen and tapped him on the shoulder.

"I don't think *I* could kill anyone, either, bub," she said, "unless I was really jealous—so please excuse us, before I have a change of heart."

5

The suddenly silenced Kelso backed away, sloshing his punch as he did so. "Crap! This won't come out! Will it? Not going to pay for a new uniform! Wasn't *my* fault!"

"Hello, Mervie. Mind if I cut in?"

Gower felt a grateful smile take command as Lacey led him toward the dance floor. "Hold it a sec," he told her. "Let me set you straight about my brother and Mugsy Levine."

She looked him in the eyes. "Later, doll. Right now, I just wanna feel your arms around me." She led him past several other couples, awaiting the final tune. They let Lacey and her beau pass by before closing in around again. "Told John I'm on a mission and I'm not letting anyone else spoil it. This last one's just for you and me." She winked, then turned to signal the maestro, apparently waiting on her cue. The band struck up the instrumental version of a fairly recent hit.

"'Love Walked In.'" Gower chuckled when he recognized the song.

"Yes," she said, giving him the side-eye, a little concerned. "Don't you like it?"

"I do," he said, pulling her closer. "I was just thinking about it this afternoon."

"Well, then, there you go," she said. "It was meant to be ours." She leaned in, her cheek next to his, holding him tight, as if waiting to be swept away. At first, Gower felt overwhelmed, but then his footwork simply took over, and they moved as one around the floor. He got lost in the moment, while Lacey made good on her promise—rebuffing all attempts at cutting in. All of it was wonderfully warm and exciting—but so strange.

Paired with this incredibly glamorous woman, as if suddenly, somehow completely alone. He imagined all the other men wondering, *"Why that little guy with the broken nose, instead of me?"*

Meanwhile, Lacey was uncharacteristically silent. Gower wondered whether it had anything to do with what the general's wife said about her and Johnson. He decided to offer a little sympathy. "Too bad you can't sing with Johnson anymore. You two sounded so good together."

She pulled her head away. "You heard about that?"

"Conroy told me. But it is kinda obvious. . . . A lot of your regular numbers are duets. You got no one to . . . duet with," Gower added before immediately regretting he'd unintentionally made it sound like a come-on.

"It wasn't working out," she said curtly, before burying her head on his shoulder. "Anyway, I don't want to talk about him right now. Let's enjoy the time we have to ourselves. All I want is for you to hold me tight and not have to think—about that, or anything else."

A little confused, but not really interested in hearing any more, Gower lost himself in the feel of her, in her beauty, in being completely and pleasantly overcome by the willingness, the openness of this woman to accept him. He hoped to heaven it was real. *Is this it?* he asked himself, not really sure what "it" was, though knowing now what it wasn't. *Not those painted, made-up broads hanging around the Jungle Club. But why me?*

"Quit trying to figure it out, Kid," Mugsy would surely say. *"For some dizzy reason, she thinks you're swell. Nothing else matters. Enjoy it while you can."* As they danced, cheek to cheek, he could feel her breasts press up against him, her thighs meeting him more than halfway. *Here is a* woman. *Nothing withheld. No hesitation.* She nuzzled his neck. It made him feel warm, but then also embarrassingly urgent, and aroused.

"Oops," Lacey whispered. "Seems like Mervie Junior wants to come out and play."

"Sorry," Gower said. Ashamed, he tried to step away.

"Sorry for what?" she asked, reeling him back in. "For

wanting me? I'm flattered," she cooed before adding, "Where can we go?" Gower had an idea.

The corridor of the hospital annex was deserted. "Do you think she'll mind?" Lacey said when he opened the door to the Eleanor Roosevelt room and led her inside.

"There's two beds. If she shows up, we can share," Gower told her. Lacey giggled at the thought.

He locked the door behind them, but didn't turn on the lights. From buildings nearby, there was enough illumination through the shaded windows to see vague but sufficient detail. Imagination could fill in the rest. He reached for her blouse and fumbled with the buttons. "We don't have all night, Mervie," she whispered and, gently pushing away his hands, finished the job on her own. Quickly peeling off her other garments, she let them fall to the floor. Gower was doing the same, until she took over, soon having him naked as well.

She held him gently by his renewed salute to her affections and led him toward the nearest of the pair of beds. She pulled aside the covers and then lay easily down on her back.

"Mount up, soldier," she purred, slowly spreading her thighs.

Gower, hard pressed to contain himself, got down, too, on his hands and knees. He was hovering over the waiting woman when the door handle was given a heart-stopping jerk.

"Shit! It's locked!" They heard someone outside, in the hallway. Gower recognized the voice. It was Conroy.

"Shoulda known you couldn't deliver, GI Joe," a female could be heard dismissing him.

"Wait! Babe! Don't *go*!" Conroy called after the woman, apparently leaving down the hall. "I'll make it up to you, sweetheart!" Conroy said, his voice trailing in the distance. "I know a guy . . . !" After a suspended moment or two, all was quiet again.

Deflated by the interruption, Gower shifted to a sitting position on the edge of the mattress. "Well, I guess that's the end of that."

"Not necessarily, honey," Lacey whispered, sliding over next to him. He felt her warm, willing hands draped around his waist. "Pretty sure I can fix you right up."

CHAPTER EIGHTEEN

Und Apple Pie

1

A pair of boots stomping across the floor had Gower prying open a wary eyelid. Afternoon sunlight slicing through a window slapped him across the face, so he quickly zipped it shut again. *Ah . . . Barracks.* Not *Mrs. Roosevelt's room. That explains it. Woulda preferred to still be lying next to Lacey, but whaddya gonna do?*

"Hey!" someone yelled. "Any of you bunk jockeys wanna go for a chicken dinner with a local family? Two spots just came open!"

Gower saw a hand rise up from the next bunk. "Me," Conroy managed "And my buddy," he added, pointing, no-look, in the general direction of Gower's bed.

"OK. So that's *Conroy . . .*" Gower could hear the guy as he scribbled something. "And, uh, *Gower . . .* Got you down. Bus leaves in an hour. Be on it, or it's latrine patrol for a week—orders from General Flagg's office."

Several minutes passed. *Have I been dreaming about some guy with an offer of dinner, and am I still in the middle of that dream, or am I actually awake now and just thinking about dreaming about dinner?*

"*Latrine patrol?!* Shit! Gowah!" Conroy shouted. "Wake up! We gotta go!"

Somehow, they made it to the bus on time. The shuttle took them and a couple dozen other soldiers south, across the river, through Little Rock proper and on out toward farmland to the southeast. During the ride, neither one said much till Conroy offered up.

"Stopped by Missus Rosaveld's room last night. But whaddya know! Door was locked."

As he felt Conroy's stare bore into the side of his head, Gower responded without turning from the window. "Really? Hunh."

The bus full of soldier dinner guests stopped at a church in the middle of a small town. A group of locals was there to greet them. "More like a village, I'd say," Conroy offered. "Too measly for a town."

"Welcome Camp Forrest GIs!" was painted on what looked like a bedsheet strung above the sanctuary door. The soldiers got off the bus and stood around waiting for someone to tell them what to do next. Apparently, it was all arranged. When the driver read off the men's names, local folks stepped up and greeted their guests for the afternoon.

"Anyone here for Crowley and Stearns?" the bus driver asked the steadily dwindling crowd.

A tall, overweight man approached. "They're for me, son," he said. "Tom Bentson."

"Sorry, Mr. Bentson, but they couldn't make it," the driver told him. "We got, uh . . . Conroy and Gower, instead," he said after consulting his clipboard.

Looking a bit apprehensive at the switch, Bentson

nevertheless offered his hand in greeting as the two hungry privates met him halfway. "Tom Bentson. Pleased to meet you. Glad you could join us. Please call me Tom. Mrs. Bentson's back at the house, cooking something special," he added. "Hope you like chicken. The car's over there," he said, leading the way. "Oh, by the way, I hope you're not of the Jewish persuasion," Bentson added after a couple of steps toward the car. "We specifically asked for a couple of good Christian boys. Mother fries her chickens in bacon grease, you see. So, it wouldn't work out."

"No problem," Gower said.

"Catholic," Conroy added.

"Catholic?" Bentson thought about it for a moment. "Oh, well, that's good enough, then," he said with a grin. "*Conroy* and *Gower.* Irish and British, I assume. And may I know your Christian names and hometowns?"

"Sorry we're not the GIs you were expecting, Mr. Bentson," Gower offered after he and Conroy introduced themselves. "But thank you for inviting us into your home all the same."

"Yeah. Ditto," Conroy added.

"Thank *you*, boys," Bentson countered. "Not only on behalf of me, my wife, and our two children, but on behalf of the whole country, really, for defending our way of life."

"Thanks for your support, sir," Gower said, "but we haven't done much of anything so far except train."

"That's OK, son. We do as we are called to do, even if it only means standing at the ready. As the Good Book says, 'Let your loins be girded about, and your lights be kept burning.'"

"God knows I've been trying, Mr. Bentson," Conroy confessed. "But Private Gower here's definitely got me beat in the loins department. Speshly lately." Out of Bentson's view, he elbowed Gower in the ribs to emphasize the point.

"Well, I'm not worried. I'm sure you both will do well and

make us all proud—if and when the time comes. By the way, Melvin, excuse me for saying so, son, but you seem somehow familiar. Have we met?"

"I don't think so, sir, unless you've been to Los Angeles. And by the way, it's *Mervyn.*"

"*Los Angeleeze?!* Oh, Lord, no!" Tom Bentson dismissed the notion with a disdainful sniff. "Too close to all that Hollywood hoo-hah for me, I can tell you that!"

The two soldiers followed their host to a four-door sedan waiting at the side of the road—a late-model Packard Clipper. "That's quite the chariot you got there, sir!" Conroy blurted out.

"Thank you, young man. The Lord has truly blessed us." Somebody was waiting behind the wheel. Bentson steered Conroy toward the front passenger seat, Gower, the seat behind the guy driving.

By the "P"s and the "W"s on the man's denims, Gower realized the driver was a captive German.

2

"Boys, this is Rolf."

"Glück, Rolf," the German said, starting the car. "At your surfiss. It is *mein* happiness in meeting *mit* you. Much better here, than at the field of battle, I do think it."

The Packard pulled away from the tiny cluster of modest buildings surrounding the church. Soon, they were bouncing down a road Gower assumed had been graded and graveled at least once during its history, though maybe not since the first Roosevelt was in office.

"Rolf is a sergeant. An airman," Bentson explained.

"Not longer," Rolf said, plainly embarrassed. "Now, I am *ein* prisoner for the United States of America. *Ein* vonderful land."

"Shot down over Libya," Bentson added. "Had no idea what or where that was, till Rolf showed me on a map."

"Luckily, I am surwived." The POW shrugged. "Many, not."

"Your camp sends Rolf and a couple other prisoners over a few days a week," Bentson explained. "What they call 'work furlough.' A whole lot more reliable than the coloreds working for us prior. Worthless as the day is long, those boys we had. Heard some of them got drafted. Why the Army wants 'em, I wouldn't know. What do you fellas make? Twenty dollars a month? Hope they're not using our taxes to pay colored boys that kind of money. What a waste *that* would be!" he added, shaking his head. "Well, enough about them. They're gone now, so it don't matter. In the meantime, we can't thank Rolf and the other POWs—that's what you call 'em, isn't it? POWs?—can't thank 'em enough for helping out on the farm and around the house since our boy, Jacob, was called up. Luckily, he got an appointment back there in Worshington," Bentson added with pride before something else took over. "Almost wish we hadn't called him Jacob, though. Turns out a fair number of names from the Bible sound *Jewish* to folks back East!"

Wait a minute. The Jews wrote the Old Testament. So, isn't 'Jacob' actually a Jewish name?

"You boys ever see Rolf over there at Camp Forrest?"

"Haven't had the happiness," Conroy butted in. "But it's a big place. Lots of prisoners. Hopefully, there'll soon be a lot more to keep Rolf and his buddies company." He turned to the driver and grinned. In the rearview mirror, Gower could see Rolf roll his eyes ever so slightly.

"You're telling *me*, Camp Forrest's a big place!" Bentson

agreed. “It’s *huge*! Me and some other community members were invited over there a while back for a tour—by a captain, name of Mennur. Interesting fellow. Didn’t know a captain could have the level of authority he seems to possess. Waltzed us right into the general’s office without so much as a howdy-do! I don’t suppose you’ve run into the captain over there, either, then.”

“Actually, we *do* know the captain,” Gower said, brightening at the memory. “Saw him just yesterday, as a matter of fact.”

“A real gentleman,” Bentson added. “No wonder they made that man an officer.”

“We got to see a side of the captain few people ever do,” Conroy added.

“He used to work for our congressman. That connection helped our Jacob get his Worshington job. Quite the stroke of luck, really. Where was I? Oh, yes! The tour of Camp Forrest! It was really something. Unfortunately, Captain Mennur couldn’t be with us the whole time. Apparently, something urgent came up over at the Officers’ Club. So, the commandant of the Military Police took over. Hey, *commandant*! That sounds kinda German, doesn’t it? Thornton’s his name. A sergeant. Had his men drive us around in those, whatchamacallems? *Jeeps*. That’s it. ‘Jeeps.’ They got machine guns—‘stingers,’ Sergeant Thornton called ’em—mounted in the back. Thornton told us the Military Police gotta be ready—*on high alert*, he called it—because there’s been these rumors, you see, about a mutiny, or some such, by colored soldiers out West! And apparently heading this way! Not sure I’m buying it. But these days, with them drafting so many colored boys? Who knows?

“Come to think on it, a similar thing did happen! Right here in Arkansas, not long after the Great War, and not far from here! What was that place called? Elaine. That’s it. Pity to spoil such a pretty name with the disgrace those coloreds brought down on that poor little town."

Didn't Mennur mention 'Elaine'? And 'Bentson', too. Called him a 'clown'?

"People were murdered!" the farmer went on. "Heard it was colored soldiers—outsiders—come back from France! Stirring up the locals. Going on about their *rights,* and whatnot! What a bunch of bull! Just goes to show—you never know what some folks might be up to. Especially outsiders like them colored soldiers what started it! It's always outsiders what's causing the problems, you see. *Agitators* is what's wrong. Always agitatin' and whatnot. Never satisfied with what's what, you see. *That's* the problem. And so, that sergeant over here at the camp decided the MPs ought to have more firepower, just in case, you see, and had them 'stingers' mounted on the jeep things. And, by golly, he let us shoot one of 'em! Quite something, it was, too, I do say. Must be how 'tis when you get a Jap or a German lined up in your sights, and let 'em have it, hunh, boys?! *Rat-a-tat-tat!*" Bentson shouted from the back seat of the Packard as he pretended to mow down a line of advancing Nazis.

"Oh, sorry, Rolf," he said, catching himself. "Present company excepted."

Rolf nodded curtly once in Bentson's direction. Gower guessed he was used to hearing things like that being said. *Small price to pay for being out of the war and still in one piece.*

The road threaded a seam in the gently rolling patchwork of cultivated fields, tucked in at the edges by rows of brilliant green trees. Some of the squares contained a farmhouse, or a barn, a few scattered sheds. Many of the buildings Gower could see out his window were leaning toward decline. They turned off the main road onto a dirt-and-gravel affair ending in a circular driveway. The Bentson place was an exception, newly painted and reroofed.

"What do you grow here, Mr. Bentson?" Gower wanted to know.

"Beets mainly, since the government buys all we can give 'em—at the government price, mind you—but I guess you could say it's beets that keeps us in clover!" He laughed at his own joke as the Packard rolled to a stop. "Welcome to our humble home."

3

Rolf came around to open Bentson's door. "Don't have to tell *you* boys we're at war," Bentson said. "If the Army wants beets, that's fine with us. Like to think of beets as our own little way of giving Hitler the raspberry!"

The POW drove around to the back of the house after the others got out. They climbed the steps to the veranda and went inside.

"Make yourselves at home, boys. My nose tells me we're almost ready to eat. Wash up down the hall, if you care to. If not, pull up a chair at the table and make yourselves comfortable. Mother," he called out. "We're back." Bentson was seating himself as Rolf entered the room from the kitchen. Without saying a word, the German walked up to the table and sat down. Gower couldn't resist a private moment of sarcasm to describe the scene. *As if the guy's just coming home from a day's work in Düsseldorf, or wherever he's from.*

"In a minute, Tom," a woman called out. "My hands are all covered in bacon grease!"

Tom gave his guests an *I told you so* look before responding to his unseen wife. “Take your time, Mother. The wait will only make the meal that much more worth the while.” He winked at Gower and Conroy. “I have to tell you though, Mother,” he added. “I have both bad news and good news about our guests for this afternoon.”

“Oh? What is it?”

“The bad news is, the boys we originally invited couldn’t make it.”

“Oh, Tom, that is such a pity.”

“I know! It is, isn’t it? But the good news is, *these* boys aren’t Jewish, either!”

Rolf looked over at the two young Americans, smiled, and nodded.

“Well, that is good news,” his wife replied. “Praise the Lord!”

Bentson leaned in to confide in the two GIs. “Although we asked specifically for two good Christian boys, we know how it is these days,” he explained, “and of course we have to open our hearts and our homes to our boys in uniform no matter their beliefs or backgrounds . . .”

Mrs. Bentson appeared, and set down a large platter of freshly fried chicken pieces. “Just not the colored ones,” she said, finishing her husband’s sentence. “So pleased to meet you!” she added with a smile, then headed back to the kitchen. “Excuse me while I finish serving.” Rolf went with her to help bring out biscuits, beans, okra, potatoes, beets, and gravy to go along with the chicken.

“Let us pray,” Bentson said when the table was fully loaded, and his wife and Rolf were settled in. “Heavenly Father, as we partake of Your bounty, we humbly ask for Your blessing. Thank You for sparing Rolf, and sending him to us in our time of need. And please bless these fine American boys, Melvin and Danny, willing to lay down their lives in defense of our liberties, and the freedoms we so cherish. Finally, Dear Lord, bless America, where men of such vastly diverse backgrounds as these—German, Irish, and British—can break bread together, accepting each other in peace and understanding. Amen."

Vastly diverse? *Well, in another setting, we'd be trying our best to kill each other, so* "diverse" *in that sense, you bet.*

Everyone dug in. Having slept through breakfast and lunch, Gower and Conroy were more interested in eating than adding to the conversation.

"Wonderful dishes, Mother. I wouldn't have thought it possible, but you have truly outdone yourself," Bentson said. Gower and Conroy nodded and smiled politely, mid-chew.

"Wunderbar," Rolf added through a mouthful of beans.

A full hopper of grub didn't keep Bentson from a favored theme. "Say, did you boys know that if Camp Forrest was a city, it'd be the second-largest in the state? No one can argue, that's a whole lot of soldiers. And did you know nearly a third of those soldiers are colored?"

"Mmmph," Gower and Conroy said and smiled and nodded.

"That's a lot," their host went on. "More coloreds than we already had in Little Rock, all told. More than all of Arkansas combined, I heard say. And mostly illiterates." Bentson punctuated his words by jabbing his fork at the air in front of his face. "Captain Mennur told me the other day. So, you tell me how those boys can be expected to fight? How can they be expected to do much of *anything*, if they can't read?!"

Gower thought of Kelso. *It's a good question.*

"And even if they could, what kind of soldiers would they be? I ask you. No-account, shiftless, lazy—would you mind passing the gravy, please?—run away at the first sign of a fight!" Bentson shoveled in another load of potatoes and chicken fixings.

Gower remembered Johnson and his buddies "getting in some work" as the colored private put it, even though no one was telling them to do anything. "Haven't met that many Black recruits," Gower offered. "But the ones I have were anxious to do their part. Word is, they need more colored drill instructors in order to train the newcomers faster."

Bentson gave Gower the squirrely eye. "Be that as it may . . . Heard half of 'em hail from up north, like your Philadelphia, Danny. That's just not going to work. Northern coloreds haven't the slightest notion what's expected of 'em hereabouts—how colored folk ought to behave, so as to get along. Your northern boys got their city ways, their airs . . ." Bentson twiddled the space around his free hand with the tips of his fingers. "Maybe that's fine and dandy for all y'all up north. But it's not going to sit well with folks 'round here—not white, nor colored. Won't have it. No sir."

Bentson paused to take a healthy bite from a fried chicken leg, then proceeded to wave it around for emphasis. "What the Army's doing to us—bringing in so many soldiers, 'specially so many *colored* boys, so fast! It ain't right. And I said so, right to the government man's face when they came here in January—invitin' us to hear all about their grandiose plans for expanding the camp. Well, sir, that was only *after* they'd already decided what to do, with or without our say-so. Didn't I tell him that, Mother. 'That's too many soldiers and way too many Black ones!' Right to that government man's face."

Gower stared at the piece of poultry Bentson continued to brandish—grease oozing from between the farmer's fingers—occasionally aimed straight at his half-Welsh head.

"Yes, you did," Mrs. Bentson nodded. "That's *exactly* what you told me you said to him."

"'As it is,' I told him, 'we can barely keep the coloreds we already got here in line. And now *this*!'" Kinetic emphasis on the word *this* sent the thigh half of his chicken leg high above the table, before it landed with a grease-and-gravy-muffled *thud* on the floorboards behind ex-Flight Sergeant Glück. Obviously embarrassed, the farmer gazed at the orphaned drumstick in his hand. "Never mind," he finally said, chuckling. "The dog'll eat it . . . Soon as we get a dog!"

4

"He never tires of telling that joke." Mrs. Bentson laughed as she pushed away from the table and retrieved the flying piece of poultry. Gower could see Rolf's eyes loop-de-loop.

"All kidding aside, boys," Bentson leaned in and confided. "I know we've all got to do our part in support of the war." With a cuke-sized pointer finger, he emphasized his every second or third word by thumping the tabletop. "I know we've all got to make sacrifices. There's simply no two ways about it! All of us around here agree. We *just* don't *want* to be *told* how to *do* it! But I wasn't the one most upset about it there that day." The beet farmer leaned back, as if relishing a remembered moment. "Was I, Mother."

The way Bentson said that last bit struck Gower as not so much a question as a declaration.

"No," she said. "You weren't. You told me there was this other man."

"Darned right I wasn't—oh sorry, Mother. Forgive the impropriety." Mrs. Bentson blushed while offering a brief nod of tolerance.

"Not by a long shot, I wasn't. There was this other fella at the meeting, owns the dry goods down on Van Buren—or maybe over on Lee . . . Don't matter. He stands up and says to the government man, right there in front of everyone at the meeting, he says, 'That's way too many soldiers to begin with. And iffen our congressman voted to allow any n***** soldiers in here along with 'em,' he says, 'well, to begin with, I will personally shoot the first n***** soldier I see,' he says. 'And then, after *that,*' the fella goes on, 'I will think on what I'm going to do about that back-stabbing weasel we sent to Worshington, 'sposed to be representin' us!' And a lot of the folks there in the hall applauded. But I didn't. No, sir. I didn't. Threatening a United States congressman? That's where *I* draw the line. And anyhow, our man in Congress helped us with Jacob, and with the beets deal. Which is pretty sweet," he said, while helping himself to another serving of the red vegetable. "If I do say so."

"Yes, you do," Mrs. Bentson agreed. "You do say so."

With Rolf's help, Mrs. Bentson cleared the table and then soon returned with dessert. "Apple pie," the woman confirmed. "With rationing and all, there's no sugar to speak of. But I used honey from our hives, so I hope you boys find it sweet enough for your liking."

"A fine dish, *apfel* pie," Rolf said as Mrs. Bentson served each man a hefty slice before retiring to the kitchen to do the dishes. "And you know," he went on, "your American *apfel* pie is to our *Deutscher Apfelstrudel,* ein, uh . . . cousin. Do you not think it?"

"I'm with ya there, Rolf!" Bentson said. "And excuse me while I make room for it." Leaning back, he loosened his belt and trousers before belching to put a bullfrog to shame. "I had some of that stu-*ru*-del stuff up there in Hermann, once. They got a kind of German town up there, in Missourah. It *is* just about the same thing, isn't it."

"Vat ist you Americans are saying?" the prisoner asked, grabbing a fork, but stopping short of digging in. "'Fight for Mom, und *apfel* pie,' isn't it?" The Nazi then stuffed a large forkful into his mouth.

5

"And 'for baseball'!" Bentson added. "They say 'for baseball,' too!"

Conroy nodded. Gower shrugged. The Nazi's face lit up. "Ah, yes! The baseball! I haff vatched your soldiers play zis game at Camp Forrest, and children play it near to here. There is no limit time, *ja*? *Es ist so faszinierend*—sorry—so *fascinating* to me, zis baseball. Played as a team, is it not? Yet zuccess is depending zo much on ze batter and ze pitcher."

"Yeah. I guess so." Gower nodded. He wasn't much of a fan. *Played a little pickup at Brookside, just to kill time, waiting for the pool to open.*

"*Mom?* Sure, I'd fight for Mom," Conroy said. "*Apple pie?* Maybe. But *baseball*? No way! Definitely not fighting for the Phullies. They stink . . . *again!* Woont you know it."

"Zee, uh, Fillies uff your Filadelphia, yah?" the German confirmed.

"We get the Cardinals on the radio," Bentson explained, "and we let Rolf listen in."

"I *love* ze Cardinals of Zaint Louis!" Rolf gushed. "Musial, Walker, Slaughter. An amusing name, 'Slaughter,' is it not? *Und* I should not to forget Kurowski! They call him 'Whitey'? Aren't all players off the major leagues white? There are no Black players. *Jah*?"

The others nodded, mouths open. *How come this guy knows so much about baseball?* Gower wondered.

"In Berlin, uh . . . *bei den Olympischen Spielen* . . . in the Games of the Olympics, I remember your fine Black man, Jesse Owens. And alzo, of course the famous, um, you say *boxing matches*, isn't it . . . ? Between the Black Joe Louis, *und* my kinsman, Schmeling."

Gower perked up a bit when the discussion moved on to boxing.

"Because of *die schwarzen manner*—Jesse Owens and Joe Louis," the German continued, "I know of Black Americans who are *wunderbare athleten*—excellent at sports. And yet, you do not include *die* Black man in your teams of ze major leagues of baseball. Zis is, to me, zurprising—if teams desire ze best off players only."

Thoroughly amazed by Rolf's knowledge of something not very German, the Americans sat there nodding like a trio of carnival dolls, then finished their slices of pie in silence. Conroy broke the spell by pulling out his Luckies to share. Tom and the prisoner couldn't conceal their delight in the prospect.

"Rationing," Tom said, grateful for the chance at genuine tobacco. "All we can get, when we can get 'em, are Picayunes, or Ramses. Can't even rightly call them cigarettes. More like rolled up horse manure, if you ask me."

"Tom!" Mrs. Bentson called out from the kitchen.

"Sorry, Mother," he said, sheepishly. "You weren't supposed to hear that."

He turned to the men. "Why don't we retire to the porch, where we'll be out of earshot?"

Once regrouped and seated on the modest veranda, Rolf gratefully accepted a cigarette from Conroy. Gower lit the tip of the Nazi's Lucky with Wendell's Zippo. *"Danke sehr!"* the POW exclaimed, obviously very pleased. He drew on the burnt offering, long and slow, then pulled it away from his face by pinching it lightly between thumb and first finger—the other digits faced forward, as if making the sign for OK. *In the European style.* Gower remembered seeing it in the movies.

"Vee getten zometime zese at Camp Forrest," Rolf told them. "I zuppose it *ist ein privileg* off *ein* prisoner."

"And you've earned it, haven't you, Rolf," Bentson said, blowing smoke. "Being shot down and all. We can't begrudge him that, can we, boys."

Tired of responding with feigned politeness, Gower defaulted to a slight shake of the head after catching Conroy in a lip-biting eye roll.

Another draw on the cigarette and the ex-lifeguard felt himself slipping free of the SS *Tom Bentson*'s undertow. The bountiful meal and the pastoral surroundings had come to the rescue. Working fields spread away from the house toward a rank of bright green leafy trees crossing the mid-distance, crowned by the tops of gently rolling hills far to the west. The slightest of breezes played with the wisps of smoke from the men's cigarettes, bringing with it the sounds and smells of the countryside. *Freshly tilled soil, blooming flowers, the song of a meadowlark.* The stinging whiff of cow dung herded Gower back to reality. *If they ever find out what Danny and I did to Captain Manure . . .*

"But I'm forgetting about the Cubs!" Bentson suddenly said.

"Chicago?" Conroy asked.

"Little Rock!" the farmer told them. "There's the *colored* league! We've got the Little Rock Cubs. Or at least we did have. Not sure if they were even getting paid. Not that it matters. Who would pay to go see coloreds play baseball, anyhow? Beats the tar outta me. Maybe that's why I don't hear about 'em anymore."

"In *mein* true mind, Tom," the captured Nazi offered up, "I zink it wise to keep out *die schwarzen*, ze Blacks, from bazeball. *Und* keep zem alzo from everyzing you kannst. When you are able. Or," he went on, "zey will feel . . . um. *Ermutigt.* How is it? *More bold. Und* you vill not longer be able to control zem, I zink."

"Well, there's no way they're ever going to allow coloreds

to play in the major leagues. You can bet on *that*," Bentson said.

"*Apfel* pie *und strudel*." The POW blew a cloud of smoke out and over their heads, then smiled the smile of peace and contentment. He joined his cigarette-holding hand with the other, into an inclusive gesture, as if to conjoin the four of them, there on the veranda. "I zink, not zo wery different, you *Amerikaner, und* we *Deutsche. Ja*?"

CHAPTER NINETEEN

Along for the Ride

1

While the four men continued to sit, smoke, and relax on the Bentsons' front porch, a two-and-a-half ton, "deuce-five" Army truck ground toward them most of the way up the Bentsons' long gravel drive before getting stuck part way through a U-turn just short of the house, where it settled into a loud, shuddering idle. Owing to the warm weather, Gower supposed, the canvas sides of the truck bed had been rolled up, exposing bench seats packed with POWs. *Work-furloughing Krauts—like Bentson's pet Nazi?—collected from surrounding farms, I guess, done for the day and heading back to Camp Forrest.*

The driver honked the horn.

Bentson got quickly to his feet. "Jesus, Lord God Almighty!" The farmer tossed the butt of his gifted Lucky angrily away and stormed down the steps toward the impatient iron beast. "I thought I told you not to honk that infernal horn, young man! You're gonna wake the dead with that thing!"

A freckle-faced soldier leaned out the driver's window. "Sorry, sir. I didn't know. First time for me on this route, sir."

"Well . . . Anyhow, aren't you a little early, son?" Bentson fumed. All the driver could do was shrug. Bentson dug in, pointing vaguely back toward the porch. "I'm supposed to have this prisoner till sundown. I thought that was the agreement with your commanders."

While the farmer continued arguing with the driver, Gower saw Rolf carefully snuff out his cigarette and put the dead butt in a breast pocket. He got up and excused himself before disappearing into the house. He returned a few seconds later, wearing his regulation gabardine POW jacket and holding his matching clamdigger hat. He stopped, faced the two GIs, and snapped to attention.

"Auf Wiedersehen, meine Herren," the German said, grinning. "Goodbye, sirs." He then added with a bow, *"Die Freude war ganz meinerseits.* Uh, you are . . . uh . . . *mein* pleasure." He then descended to the gravel drive and headed for the truck. Gower watched him seem to stay on Bentson's blind side, as if to slip by unnoticed.

"Sorry, sir. I'm only doing what they told me," the kid behind the wheel was saying.

"Well, since you're here, I guess it *is* time for Rolf to be going," Bentson added, reluctantly accepting the obvious. By the time he turned to beckon his hired hand forward from the porch, the German prisoner had already reached the passenger side door of the cab and was mounting up. Bentson appeared a bit miffed but gave in with relative grace. "Thanks for helping out today, Rolf," the farmer offered as he went around to the other side of the transport and placed a hand on the German's protruding elbow. "Much obliged. Oh, and don't you forget about next Sunday's VFW social, like I told you. Our daughter . . . Well, I don't think I'm speaking out of school by telling you that Becky's looking forward to seeing you over there." Rolf nodded and smiled. With a wan grin and a nod of his own, Bentson backed away from the truck.

"You know what, Danny," Gower said as they watched the drama unfold, "unless we're dying to let Bunsen Burner there talk our ears off on the way back to that little town . . ."

"You mean that village? Way aheada ya, Gowah. Come on. Let's ask the deuce jockey for a ride back to camp."

"Got room for two more in there, buddy?" Gower asked when they got within earshot. "We oughta be getting back soon ourselves."

"It's still a bit early for your bus, isn't it, Melvin?" Bentson protested. "Shouldn't be due at the church for nearly an hour!"

Gower pressed the GI behind the wheel. "It would save our host, Mr. Bentson here, the trouble of driving us . . . Not to mention the money for gas."

"You mean that church in the little town?" the kid asked.

Conroy nodded. "Pretty sure it's only a village, though."

"OK, I can take you that far, but no farther, and you gotta ride the fenders," he told them. "Got a full house here, and if they catch me giving rides to anyone but Krauts, it'll be *my* butt in a sling, not yours."

Mrs. Bentson came out for the sendoff as Conroy and Gower said their thank-yous and goodbyes before hopping on the fenders and riding with the prisoners as far as the little church. Compared to how it looked when they arrived by bus, the village appeared to be deserted. They dismounted and waved goodbye to Rolf and the others. For the next half hour or so, they stood on the same spot where the deuce-five left them.

Conroy broke the silence first. "Interesting guy, that Rolf. I'd almost regret having to shoot him during a battle . . .

Whaddya think, Gowah. You think we're still too early for our bus?"

"Despite what Bentson said about the schedule, I'm pretty sure we're too late."

Three young women happened by on the other side of the road, smiling and giggling. The GIs whistled and waved. "You seen a bus go by here?" Conroy asked. The women giggled and shook their heads. "How about a ride, then?" Conroy added. More headshakes and giggles erupted from that side of the road. "Wouldn't mind riding that redhead," Conroy said when the women were out of earshot.

The two privates walked over to a bench in front of the little church and sat down. They talked about Rolf and wondered what it would be like to be American prisoners of war in Germany. They smoked. They laughed about their chicken dinner episode at the Bentsons and the flying chicken leg.

"Whadda jerk!" the Phluffian guffawed.

Gower nodded with a chuckle before a sobering thought crossed his mind. *The more I heard Bentson talk, the more I thought his voice sounded familiar.* As he sat there, he tried to imagine what the beet farmer might look like in a white gown and matching hood.

2

"One thing about Rolf, though," Conroy said, after blowing a smoke ring. "Sure knows his baseball."

Gower nodded. "A lot more than me."

"You're British. You know much about—whadda they call it?—cricket?"

Gower shook his head. "Mom said her brother, Albert,

used to play. Guess maybe they're sorta similar." He remembered a photo she showed him once, of players and spectators breaking for tea in the middle of a match. "But maybe not."

They smoked some more. Another several minutes passed. "Guess you're right about the bus," Conroy finally admitted.

They played catch with a kid who happened by with a glove and a ball. They petted a stray cat. They sat down on the front steps of the church. The sun was all but gone.

"Pretty sure we missed it," Gower said.

"Woont surprise me," Conroy added. "Smoke?" he asked.

"Are you kidding?! I already feel like a chimney. Had more cigarettes today than I usually have in a week."

After another several minutes gone, they could hear the church door behind them open a crack. They turned to look. A thin, older man wearing spectacles peered out, saw them, looked surprised, and then ducked back inside and closed the door.

"Didn't think we looked that scary."

"It's a church, Gowah. I think he could tell we aren't well acquainted."

The man opened the door again. This time he came part way out from behind it and consulted a piece of paper in his hand. "Stearns and Crowley?" he asked.

"Nope," Conroy said. "That ain't us. But I got a feeling we wish it was us right about now."

"Ray Ferguson," the man said, stepping away from the building and extending a hand. The GIs met him halfway and shook. "I'm one of the lay pastors, so just call me 'Reverend Billy.' Evyone 'round here does."

Conroy did the honors. "I'm Danny. And this is Mervyn, but you can call him Melvin, everyone around here does," he said, grinning at Gower, who was anything but pleased by the reference to the name Bentson had tagged him with all afternoon.

"You boys—I mean them other boys—was crossed off the list, so I had a hunch you wahn't them," Reverend Billy added. "Bus left over a hour ago, 'cause they thought they had evyone 'counted for." The stranded soldiers confirmed their last names before explaining what may have led to the mix-up.

"Now, if you boys can wait here just a spell longer, me and some other fellas is headin' over to Little Rock—soon's we get our sweet char-i-ot running again. You can catch a bus on the way to where we going."

"Whaddya think, Gowah? Can we wait a spell?"

"Sure. Why not?"

"OK, then. Don't go nowhere. Be right back, Lord willin'." Reverend Billy slipped into the church, and from the sound of it, locked the door behind him. They sat down again and waited for another twenty minutes or so.

"How long is a *spell*, anyway?" Gower asked his buddy.

Before Conroy could answer, a muffled *bang!* from behind the church had them snapping to attention. An older-model pickup, missing a headlight and spewing plumes of black exhaust, came crow-hopping out from behind the sanctuary. Reverend Billy was driving. A man about the same age, but much bigger, sat with him in the cab. *Leaning to that side because the other guy's so fat?* The two GIs wandered over. Three younger men occupied the bed of the truck. At least two of them had shotguns. Four of the truck's five occupants appeared to be either too old or too young to be drafted. The one man who might have otherwise qualified was missing the first two fingers of his right hand and at least as many teeth.

"Climb on board, boys," the Reverend Billy yelled over the sputter and backfire of the low-powered engine. "We're on a mission of glory, in the name of the Lord!"

Gower and Conroy looked at each other before reluctantly taking up the offer and climbing aboard the Model T, easily as old as they were. They squeezed in among the three men in the back, causing limbs and a butt cheek or two to spill over the sides. While passengers sorted themselves out, the truck jerked into gear, nearly dumping Conroy out the back as the tin lizzie bucked and bounded toward Little Rock. To the *pop* and *putt* of the engine, Gower could hear Reverend Billy and his saddle buddy belting out "Rock of Ages" against the fading day. *We'll be lucky to be in bed by curfew.*

3

They were several miles down the uneven road, holding on to the truck bed walls and bracing themselves with their legs against the neck-cracking ride when one of Billy's friends leaned over and said something to Gower. Or at least Gower thought the guy said something. Engine noises and the relentless tattoo of gravel kicked up under the fenders conspired with local accents to render conversation a challenge. The two GIs resorted to their tried-and-true strategy of nodding and grinning whenever they guessed someone was addressing them and hoped they weren't committing themselves to anything they couldn't or shouldn't deliver.

Soon, a bottle of something alcoholic made the first of several journeys around the Ford, including the cab, and it wasn't long before the GIs felt considerably less apprehensive, if not ready to join Reverend Billy in hymns and prayers. At one point, another one of the riders tapped Gower on the knee, winked, grinned, and held up something strung on a lanyard around his neck for the soldier's appreciation if not approval.

Gower was tempted to shout, "Thanks, but I'm already

spoken for," over the din, but thought better of it, since, after all, the guy had a shotgun cradled in his lap, and he didn't want his attempt at humor misinterpreted. Instead, he poked Conroy in the ribs to get him to turn and look at the thing the guy was displaying, apparently for their benefit. It was about the shape and appearance of a rather large, dried fig, but seemed to be made out of old leather. It bounced erratically up and down with the motion of the truck. That, and their increasingly inebriated state, made a more accurate identification of the object problematic. Whatever the thing was, the guy was obviously very proud to show it off. Gower and Conroy smiled and nodded.

Seemingly satisfied with their reactions to the prized possession, the guy tucked it back under his shirt and pointed over the shoulder of a comrade toward a small, roughly built cabin coming up rapidly on the other side of the road. As the GIs watched in disbelief, the man lifted his shotgun, turned, and fired a blast in the direction of the hovel as they passed it, clearly to the delight of all the truck's passengers not in uniform. Swinging back around to face the two GIs, the local man broke out another yellow tooth–baring grin.

Did this clown actually shoot at someone's house?

Gower wondered whether his hearing had been permanently damaged by the blast. He supposed the good news was he was no longer able to listen to Reverend Billy's off-key renditions of gospel songs.

"Nice shot!" Conroy yelled. Or at least Gower thought he did. Lip-reading seemed to confirm it. He scowled at his friend for the implied encouragement. Conroy shrugged. More of the booze was circulated.

They rolled into Little Rock a bit after dark and well after Gower's hearing returned. Reverend Billy steered the wheezy little pickup toward the curb of a fairly major street, left the motor running, and hopped out. "This's 'sfar's ya go," the pastor told the two GIs. "Don' wanna get you boys inta any kinda trouble, so we'll say our gubbyes, and leyya off right here." Free of the butt-busting ride and exhaust fumes, but not the effects of strong liquor, Gower and Conroy not so much climbed as tumbled from the bed of the truck to the pavement, where they bobbed and weaved while jelly legs tried to cope.

Whatever it is they gave us to drink's starting to kick back pretty hard.

"Got some things ta take care of over'n n***** town," Billy told them, shaking their hands. "Main bus runs 'long this road, so, pretty sure you can catch one back ta camp 'round here somewheres. Jus' keep headin' thadda way." He pointed to his left before realizing his mistake and pointed right. "Thadda way."

Apparently lacking a parking brake, the truck began slowly rolling away. "Hey! Looka there! Lizzie's getting anxious ta crack a few nappy heads!" The spry older man of faith ran to catch up before scrambling into the cab with a practiced dexterity. "God bless you, boys!" Reverend Billy shouted out the window and hit the gas. As the old Ford pulled away, the shooter smiled and waved from the bed with his three-fingered hand at the two snockered, saddle-weary soldiers as they headed unsteadily for what they hoped was a bus stop.

"You know what?" Conroy said after several wobbly yards down the sidewalk. "That guy with the thing 'round his neck? I think he likes you."

Gower turned and sneered at his friend. "'Nice shot,' you said. They don't need any 'couragement, Danny. You heard Reverend Geezer. Gonna go beat up some Black people."

"Yeah . . . Maybe shoot 'em . . . Who knows?"

"Yeah, who knows?" Gower asked, waxing philosophical. "*I* dunno. *You* don' know. *Anyone* know? Maybe oughta report those guys ta the cops." They staggered on a little farther, in stupored silence.

"Mebbe 'swhat white people do 'round here on a Sunday," Conroy offered. "*I* wouldn't do it. *You* wouldn't do it. Maybe *they* do it. S'maybe's OK 'round here . . . Maybe cops'd laugh in our faces if we tol 'em."

Gower nodded. "Scary people."

"Yeah," Conroy agreed. "But you ain't been ta Sout Phully."

They found a bus stop, studied the schedule, picked out the bus they'd be looking for, sat down on a bench, and waited.

"'Nice shot,'" Gower groused again after a while, slowly shaking his head in disapproval.

"Hey, they were giving us a ride. Jeez! Was just trying ta be, ya know, neighbor-ror-ly."

They sat in silence for quite a while before Gower spoke again. "What'd you think of that . . . *thing* the one guy had around his neck?"

"Your boyfriend? Looked like some poor Black guy's dried ear," Conroy said after giving it a little thought.

"Yeah." Gower jerked his head around to nod—nearly toppling off the bench in the process. "It did, didn't it."

4

Well after the posted arrival time had come and gone, Gower and Conroy were awakened by the toot of a horn. Shocked into action, the two inebriated dogfaces scuttled awkwardly to the waiting bus and pulled themselves aboard. Standing next to the driver while fumbling in their pockets for change, listing precariously to one side and then the other, Gower noticed a few of the passengers begin to fidget. *You try fishing for nickels when you're this drunk!*

"These boys're here to defend us, driver. I'll pay their way," a man said, and did so.

They mumbled thank-yous, saluted, and staggered down the aisle in search of somewhere to light. The bus took off before they had a chance to settle into any of the few empty seats remaining, nearly knocking them off their feet. They received a smattering of smiles and approving nods as they worked their way unsteadily toward the rear.

Gower thought about saying, "Still got both our ears, too," but didn't.

Being in the lead, Conroy was about to pull himself into a window seat toward the front, where a good-looking woman sat dozing on the aisle, when a heretofore hidden kid popped up, aimed his toy gun at the interloper, and woke his mom. She smiled when she saw the uniform and, embarrassed, bowed her head. The private saluted, then slipped into an empty aisle spot a couple of rows beyond her.

Close behind, Gower pulled his way past his buddy, aiming for the only other empty seat he could see, much nearer to the back. He got there as the bus was lurching through a turn. The sway and the alcohol knocked him off balance, sending him partially sprawled across the lap of an older Negro man separating the drunken soldier from the seat he had in mind.

"Oh!" he said, excusing himself. "Sorry, sir! You OK?"

The man bristled but seemed to be more upset than hurt. Gower apologized a couple more times, regained his legs, stepped over the gentleman's knees, and sat down at the window.

A few more minutes on, he sensed the old man begin to fidget, alternately turning to glare at him and craning his neck anxiously forward as if looking to the front of the bus for some sort of rescue. *Upset because he's sitting next to a drunken GI? Do I look like I'm drunk? Maybe he can smell it. I can't smell a thing—probably 'cause I'm drunk.*

Since there was nothing Gower could do about being drunk, he decided to ignore the guy, act as if he rode the bus around Little Rock every day—sober or not—and blend in with the rest of the riders. It was while attempting to blend in that Gower noticed there were only Black people seated in the rest of his row, as well as from there to the rear of the bus. Glancing toward the front, he could see that some of the white passengers had turned to stare. They didn't seem as happy with him as they had been when he came down the aisle. He sat there worrying whether he'd actually made the crack about still having both his ears out loud or not, and whether that was why they were angry.

"The nerve!" he heard one of the white women say.

"Just *who* does he think he *is*?!" a man seated toward the front of the bus angrily added.

Another few seconds on, it seemed to Gower as if everyone but Conroy and the driver was staring back at him. Soon, even those two could no longer resist the urge to see what was up. The coach lurched over to the curb and stopped.

The aisle quickly filled with a thicket of passengers trying to get a better look. As the driver snaked his way through the crowd to find out what was going on, their rubbernecking heads bobbed and dipped, like cattails parting for a polecat on the prowl.

"Excuse me . . . Pardon me . . . Sorry, ma'am. . . Excuse me, folks," the driver said as he approached. Sweat had long since stained his hat above the band. The yoke and the underarms of his gray uniform shirt were likewise several shades darker than the rest of it. When he arrived at Gower's row, he briefly apologized to the elderly colored man before leaning in to speak with Gower at a more intimate distance. Gower assumed it was the smell of spirits on his breath that sent the driver instantly backward. *As if stung by a bee.*

"You haven't been drinking, now, have you, son?" the driver asked.

Gower looked up. "Not for a spell, I reckon," he offered with a smile, still trying to blend in with the locals.

"Well, drunk or no, I can't let you sit back here," the driver said. "This coach is full, so I'm afraid you're gonna have to get off and walk to the next corner and wait there for another bus to come along. I 'spect one in about half an hour or so."

Trying to digest what the driver told him, Gower looked down between his legs at the leather-covered bench and then around in disbelief. *If the bus is full, then how come I can be sitting in a seat?* He turned to his elderly Black seatmate. A few beads of perspiration were making their way slowly down the side of the man's head. *Impressive!* Despite having his point of view severely restricted by the driver's sweat-soaked, cotton-covered flank, the older Negro man continued staring stoically straight ahead. *As if there was nothing more interesting in this world than an overweight bus driver's uniformed gut. Or maybe this particular Black man has managed to see beyond this world and so, to consider it from a different dimension, like Flash Gordon, or some sort of holy man in the Himalayas—like the ones in Dad's* National Geographics. *Maybe gone to a place far away, where a drunk white boy in the next seat couldn't possibly exist, and so . . . doesn't.* Gower leaned over a bit and sniffed at the guy. *Or maybe he's been drinking, too.*

"Well, son," the driver persisted. "What's it gonna be? You getting off here, or not?"

Gower rolled his eyes everywhere but in the driver's direction before looking him smack dab in the puss. "Not," he said.

5

"Teach that Yankee boy some manners, driver!" a woman shouted.

"We gotta be getting on home, now, driver," a male passenger added. "*Do* something!"

"What's wrong with the seat I'm sitting in?" Gower asked, surprised by how lucid he suddenly sounded to himself. "No one sitting here when I got on. Am I bothering anybody?"

"Get rid of a row of n*****s and let the soldier boy ride, why dontcha?" someone yelled.

"Yeah!" several white passengers shouted. "Let the soldier ride!"

"Kick the n*****s off! Kick the n*****s off!" three or four others chanted.

The driver turned toward the front of the bus and raised his hands. "Hold on, now, folks, just a minute there, please. You know, a lotta these Army men ain't from around here. So, lemme 'splain a few things to this soldier boy, first. Then we can settle this affair and be on our way." That seemed to satisfy most of the other riders, at least for the moment.

Reaching up over his head, the driver snatched a large placard from a rail running down the middle of the bus's ceiling and showed it to Gower. "Colored Only," it read. "You're sitting in the colored section, son. And, far as I can tell, you ain't colored. So, you can't sit here. And the white folks' section is already full, so you gotta get off. City ordinance."

Gower, head wobbling as the alcohol sloshed gently back and forth inside it, studied the sign before speaking. "That's nuts."

"Be that as it may, it's the law," the driver told him.

"Doesn't make it any . . . nutslesser." The response momentarily puzzled even Gower, who silently repeated it to himself just to be sure those were the words he actually said.

"Listen to me carefully, son," the driver said, clearly beginning to lose his patience. "At the present time, the 'Whites Only' section on my bus extends only so far as to the row in front of you. As you can plainly tell, there are no more unoccupied seats in the 'Whites Only' section of this coach. Howsomever, it is within my authority to move this sign forwards or backwards, depending on how many white folk want to ride on my bus. If *you* want to keep riding on my bus, that's just fine. I will move this marker back one row, and have these three folks here get off, for your accommodation," he said, indicating the elderly man next to Gower and a couple of gray-haired Black women on the other side of the aisle. "So, what's it going to be?"

Gower considered again the old man and then leaned precariously around the driver to have a look at the two women passengers in the same row, staring anxiously back in the white GI's direction. He took their silence for agreement, and winked at them in acknowledgement.

"Forget it, Mac!" Gower said, leaning back in his seat and folding his arms. "I'm not going anywhere, and neither are they." This time, the horrified gasp among the passengers was unanimous, including all eleven colored riders—in and behind Gower's row.

Some of the white riders were a bit more expressive. *"Get that drunken sonbitch offen this bus, right now, driver, or we'll throw him off!"* was one of the more accommodating suggestions Gower could make out.

"Well, that's it, then," the driver said, shaking his head. "On the next corner, I believe there's a call box for the poleece," he announced as he headed back toward the front of the coach. "Will someone please step over there and send in an alarm? I'm not supposed to leave my bus while passengers is aboard."

As a man sitting near the door got off to fulfill the driver's request, Conroy stood up and faced toward the back of the coach. "Wait a minute! Wait a minute! You don't need to call the cops," he shouted over the growing chorus of curses aimed at his friend. "Come on, Gowah. Let's blow this cracker wagon and leave it to the hillbillies."

With that, the bus erupted. Two or three white men leapt from their seats, got a hold of Conroy, and attempted to wrangle him out the door without benefit of opening it first. Other passengers swung at the Philadelphian with their fists and kicked at him when they got the chance. A woman wearing a feathered hat started beating on him with her parasol.

"Gowah!" his buddy yelled. "Do sumpin'! They're killin' me!"

"Excuse me," Gower said to the colored man sitting next to him. "Gotta go." He stepped unsteadily over his seatmate's lap and pushed his way down the aisle, past the driver, toward his friend, and into the melee. As soon as he got within range, riders grabbed and kicked at him, too. Reaching out for one of Conroy's attackers, Gower grabbed him by the shoulder and spun him around so as to deliver a punch, straight on. Owing to the crowded confines, when The Welsh Kid drew back his arm, he struck the parasol-wielding woman in the jaw with his elbow instead, knocking her out from under her feathered hat, and apparently, cold.

The two soldiers eventually ended their evening well before Camp Forrest's Sunday curfew, their intention all along. "Good night, Gowah," Conroy said from his bed. "Thanks for saving me from that lady with the umbrella."

"Don't mention it," Gower told him. After thinking it over, he added, "Seriously, don't *ever* mention it. Hope I didn't break her jaw."

"OK—I won't say nothing, but only if you stop needling me about saying 'nice shot' to that guy in the truck."

"Deal," Gower agreed. He rolled over on the surprisingly

ample mattress and sighed. “Never thought I’d see the inside of the Little Rock city jail,” he said. “Not as bad as I would have thought.”

“Certainly seen wuhse,” Conroy confessed.

CHAPTER TWENTY

Fitting End

1

Gower's nose told him more or less what time it was. *Coffee . . . and bacon. Burned it.*

What was more difficult to understand was the tight-skinned tom-tom thumping and pumping inside his skull. *And why my brain wants to leap through my ear holes and bounce around the bed screaming bloody murder . . . Where* is *my head, by the way?!* He felt around frantically in the bedding. *Ah-ha! I have buried it beneath, I guess, a pillow—cranial escape thus prevented. Very clever.* Satisfaction quickly dissolved into panic when he realized he had no idea where he was, or how he got there. *Can't be the barracks! No one ever offered to make coffee or bacon in the barracks!*

Owing to the high probability of more pain, and of losing whatever was yearning to be free of his stomach, Gower decided that standing, let alone raising his head to have a look around, was out of the question. He continued to lie facedown on what he assumed was a mattress—*Is that vomit I smell?*—and shuffle through the memories of what he hoped was only a single missing day, searching for a winner. *Ummm . . . Nazi chauffeur . . . Fried chicken dinner . . . Reverend Billy's jug of something highly alcoholic . . . Old Black man on a bus . . . Feathered hat . . . Yes! Like the one Mom wears to church! Bingo!* Instead of providing solace, however, the insight only added more drumbeat-accompanied mystery. *But where does that leave me?*

Beyond the pounding in his head came a murmur of distant voices—one appreciably higher than the other. "Mom? Dad?" he meant to say but wasn't sure if he actually did. The voices stopped. Keys jingled. A latch clicked. A metal door somewhere creaked open briefly before groaning in agony and then abruptly slamming shut, accompanied by appropriately creepy echoes. Gower winced in response to the jarring shock of the sounds, as well as an epiphany as to their most likely source. *Oh, yeah . . . Jail.*

Two pairs of leather-soled footsteps tap-attacked both a wood plank floor and Gower's eardrums, ever louder as they approached. *Taking forever! Jeez! Where was that door they opened? In the next county?!* When the footsteps reached a spot directly between Gower's ears, they stopped, leaving him to the relative peace of the more familiar, if still annoying, throb of blood banging away against the back of his eyeballs—soon interrupted by someone literately rattling their cage.

"This here's that Early fella come down from the camp to see you two birds," a man said.

"That early fella." Gower repeated the phrase to himself. *This messenger guy sounds bored. Must not be that urgent. Anyway, said the other guy's early, so . . .* "Can he come back later, then?" the private muttered through the pillow. "Not feeling too good right now," Gower added. "Might improve, given enough time . . . You never know."

"Lieutenant Early," the other, higher-pitched voice insisted.

Gower shot to a sitting position. Icepick jabs to the forehead froze him in mid-grimace—a stone-solid gargoyle on the edge of his bed. He sensed someone stirring in the adjacent bunk. Fighting pain-shuttered eyelids, he decided it must be Conroy. Or anyway, he hoped so. Whoever it was joined him in a studied effort to achieve a more or less standing position on shoeless feet and to salute this *Early fella* after an obvious and dearly won struggle over gravity and distress.

"Sorry, sir," Gower moaned in the lieutenant's direction. Despite having trouble with his focus, the private decided the stern expression on this Early fella's face belied a man who looked too young to be a lieutenant—possibly younger than either him or Conroy. There was no evidence the officer had yet started shaving or had otherwise entered puberty. He was carrying a large valise, perhaps weighing as much as he did. Joining him on the better side of the bars was a man not wearing an Army uniform. *Must be the jailer. Sounded bored. Looks bored. Maybe this is routine for him—drunken GIs under his lock and key.*

"All right, then, you men. At ease!" The "ease" part of the command apparently put an untenable strain on the young officer's voice, as that's when it broke into squeaky little pieces, reminding Gower of a certain cartoon mouse.

"Thank you, sir," Gower whimpered. "I only wish that were possible, sir."

"*What* did you say?!"

"Sorry, sir. No disrespect meant, sir. It's just that we're hungover, sir."

"Very well, then. Sit down, if that helps."

They did, and it did.

"Thank you, sir. We owe you, sir."

"As it happens, private"—the lieutenant grinned as he said it—"that is exactly why I am here."

2

The slowly sobering Gower could see Lieutenant Early say something to the bailiff. The jailer nodded and moved a small table closer to the cage where the two privates had spent at least the previous night. The smooth-faced young officer set his bulging briefcase down on the borrowed furniture and withdrew a file, fat with documents. *Please, Lord, not a repeat of the meeting with Captain Mennur. I beg you.*

"As I say, private, you men do owe me. More correctly, you owe the Army, which in this case, I am authorized to represent. And, on behalf of Major Wright, commanding officer of C Company, Medical Replacement Battalion, I am prepared to offer you what we consider an attractive way out of your current . . . shall we say . . . *predicament*?"

"Yes, sir. 'Predicament,' sir. It appears we are in one," Gower agreed. *And please let there be nothing in that file about an enema.*

Conroy finally joined the party. "But we're assigned to *B* Company, sir," the Phluffian managed. "At least last time I checked. Which I guess was, um . . . *yesterday*?"

"For the moment, that is true, Private Conroy," Early said. "But why don't we wait till I tell you what Major Wright has in mind, and then we will see what you have to say about your current assignment, shall we?"

"Excuse me, sir," Conroy added, "but howdjya know I was

me?" Gower looked over at his cellmate. His buddy's right eye had sprouted a shiner. *Oh, yeah. Fight on the bus.*

"I know a Philadelphia accent when I hear one, private. I graduated law, from Penn."

"Got it, sir." Conroy offered a misery-accented nod. "Thank you, sir."

Early proceeded to explain their dilemma, as the Army saw it. Both privates were facing charges of disturbing the peace and misdemeanor assault. "In addition to *those* charges, Private Gower"—the officer consulted a document from the file—"you, alone, have been charged with . . . 'interfering with a city employee in the performance of his duties,' as well as 'failing to abide by a municipal ordinance establishing and enforcing race-designated public and private facilities and conveyances' . . . Congratulations," he added sarcastically. "If I'm not mistaken, that second charge is a first for a white soldier stationed here in Little Rock." For confirmation, Early glanced at the bailiff, who responded with a noncommittal shrug.

"Excuse me, sir," Conroy protested, "but *we* were the 'saulted ones. *They* started it."

Early lowered his gaze before turning again to the bailiff. "Excuse us, jailer, if you will." The lieutenant eyeballed the keeper until the guy got the hint and reluctantly retreated down the hallway. Once satisfied the deputy was out of earshot, Early fed Gower and Conroy the scoop. "Yes, actually. According to the majority of witnesses willing to talk to the police at the scene, that charge should have been dropped."

"Then, excuse me again, sir, but why are we the ones in jail?"

"Because, Private Conroy, most of the witnesses supporting your version of the story are identified as colored in this report." The lieutenant returned the document to the folder. "Even assuming those colored riders supporting your case would agree to testify in court—which they likely wouldn't—who would believe them? I'm pretty sure you wouldn't stand a chance. If the passengers who attacked you had been Black, however, you likely wouldn't have been arrested. Who knows? These crackers might even have held a parade in your honor."

To Gower's curious amazement, Early then tsk-tsked. Gower couldn't remember anyone actually doing that except in the movies. The lieutenant pulled more papers from the file and gave them a cursory glance before setting them aside.

"Instead," Early added solemnly, "here you both sit—in jail and possibly facing dishonorable discharge, if not court-martial."

3

Dishonorable discharge! Court-martial! Early's assertion of punishment beyond a night or two in jail was a literal eye-opener. Gower stared out from behind the bars with renewed interest as the lieutenant tested a fountain pen on the document's cover folder.

"I therefore urge you to accept what I think is Major Wright's very generous offer as your most favorable alternative—ensuring your freedom and certain privileges. To wit, not only am I authorized to arrange for your immediate release from this facility, but I am carrying orders, signed by General Flagg himself, which will keep you out of the Camp Forrest stockade. As they may have mentioned when they brought you in here, as soldiers—US government property, if you will—they can only hold you in city jail a maximum of twenty-four hours before the Army takes custody."

News to me. Maybe somebody told us something when we got here . . . Too drunk to remember.

"You men need to understand something," the lieutenant went on. "The civilian population is hardly thrilled the Army is here—especially in such large numbers, and particularly with such large numbers of colored troops. The president—the federal government generally—takes maintaining a positive, peaceful partnership with local communities *very seriously*—and at nearly any cost. Punishing a couple of white privates for breaking local law and decorum is a small price for the War Department to pay for keeping the peace."

"We were only defending ourselves, sir," Gower offered.

"Yeah! And we were drunk, so we didn't really know *what* we were doing."

"With due respect, Private Conroy, I wouldn't use that in your defense if I were you. And as an attorney, I suggest signing Major Wright's offer is your best option out of all of this."

With that, Early extended the forms through the bars of the cell, along with his Parker pen for the purpose of signing them. "But here's the best part. The Army needs you. There is a severe shortage of colored noncommissioned officers available for training and leading Black recruits. To fill this need, white soldiers are the only alternative. Unfortunately, very few have volunteered," he added, his voice trailing off. "So, anyway, after your transfer to C Company, you will be immediately promoted to the rank of corporal and each given command of a squad of a dozen colored privates. They've gone through Basic Training, but the majority of them are illiterate, or close to it, making them more or less unfit for combat—practically guaranteeing you won't ever see combat, either!"

Gower stared anxiously at the papers and the pen, wondering what he should do—and whether never seeing combat was a good thing. *Promoted to corporal's nice, but if I never set foot on a battlefield, how's that going to help me prove anything? Or defend against "all enemies, foreign and domestic"? Or* Unum *my* E *in the* Pluribus, *for that matter*? Despite residuals from Reverend Billy's moonshine still ringing in his ears, he could hear Mugsy Levine offering him a little more of his unsolicited, but often useful, advice. *"Listen to me, Kid, if somebody makes you an offer what seems too good to be true, you can bet the house it sure as hell is."*

While the caged canaries thought it over, Early pressed the issue. "A lot of men in your shoes would be *dying* to get out of combat," he insisted, abruptly thrusting his Parker and the documents closer, for effect.

"Excuse me, sir," Gower started. "That all sounds very generous, but why would Major Wright want to help *us* out?"

"Yeah," Conroy added, "what's the catch?"

At those words, the arms extending the major's offer slumped to rest on a crossbar, leaving both the deal, and the pen with which to sign it, hanging precariously in the balance. The lieutenant cocked his head in earnest before trying once again to persuade the two jailbirds of the benefits of providing their John Hancocks. "You both will be promoted to corporal, resulting in an immediate pay raise, backdated to the first of the month. I can't see how that could possibly be interpreted as a 'catch,' as you put it, Private Conroy."

"But we didn't earn it," Gower said.

Early couldn't hide his disappointment. "Then, is that a 'no' . . . ? From both of you?" Neither man replied.

"Very well, then," the lieutenant added, literally withdrawing Wright's offer. He put his pen back in his pocket and the documents back in the folder, then stood up and made to leave. "Jailer!" he shouted before turning again to the prisoners. "I hope you'll reconsider. In a few hours, the MPs will come here and escort you both to the Camp Forrest stockade. I'm told the stockade is now run by a Staff Sergeant Thornton, a very thorough and thoroughly disagreeable disciplinarian whom they call *Hogjaw*. I understand you two may have already made his acquaintance. Please give him my regards. Goodbye and good luck."

Gower stared at the back of freedom making its way down the hall. *Dishonorable discharge . . . Stockade . . . Hogjaw Thornton.* A cold sweat welled up and out of his pores before panic grabbed him where it hurts. "Lieutenant!" he shouted while launching himself at the wall of their cage. "Uh . . . Lieutenant Early, sir? A moment, please, sir?"

4

"One more thing," Early told the slowly sobering dogfaces squinting against the bright, sunny Monday morning as they left the Little Rock city jail. "If you mess this up—if even *one* of your men, in either squad, gets out of line—the charges against both of you will be instantly reinstated and, at the very least, you will be reacquainted with Sergeant Thornton, if not dishonorably discharged. Get it?"

"Yes, sir! Got it, sir! Thank you, sir!" *Fear is a powerful motivator.*

"Then mount up. We've got a war to fight." He ushered the two toward a jeep waiting at the curb. The driver, a corporal, was standing by. After situating the lieutenant and his satchel of documents in the jump seat, the corporal stepped around to greet the pair of ex-privates. "Corporals," he said, nodding, but without answering their salute.

Oh, yeah, we're two-stripers now, too. Guess we don't have to salute another corporal . . . That'll take some getting used to. After an aborted first shot at mounting up, during which

Conroy took a bit of a nosedive into the side of the jeep, the ex-jailbirds climbed gingerly into the back seat, Gower directly behind Lieutenant Early.

"You'll be coordinating with Corporal Ski, here, from C Company HQ," Early told them. "And no, 'Ski' is not his real name."

"Polish," Ski offered up. "Lotta letters to get through before you come to a vowel. So . . ."

"So, everyone calls him 'Ski.' He'll be your right-hand man. And that reminds me. You two need to understand something about C Company. Despite what I said about you likely not seeing combat, depending on how badly the war goes—and right now, it isn't going very well—it could happen. In any case, C Company has a reputation to uphold."

Ski had them heading back to camp with a neck-snapping release of the clutch that gave Gower other things to think about. *Uh-oh. Tastes like Mrs. Bentson's fried chicken dinner is thinking about flying the coop.*

". . . may not be the best educated, but, for the most part, our men work hard and go the extra mile. As Major Wright says, it's not the colored recruit's fault if others in uniform don't trust him to become a good fighter as well as a good soldier. In C Company, we certainly do. You should assume, therefore, that you and your men could one day come under fire. So do everything you can to prepare them. Our top kick is Sergeant King. He's rarely, if ever, satisfied. He's tough but fair. I suggest you study his example and follow it."

At the mention of Sergeant King's name, Gower brightened a bit. *So, still in the Army, despite the rumors.*

"Sergeant King was our guy, sir," Conroy said, "before some shi . . . , well anyway, before. We liked him a lot."

While trying to tame his bubbly gut, Gower's mind skipped ahead to his new assignment. *Even if my guys do well—really well—would that be good enough?* He could already hear Bucoda and McCleary laughing at them. *"The babysitters!"*

They passed through the drab north side of the city—mostly a Monday-morning-hangover blur—where nothing much demanded Gower's visual attention beyond the several "Whites Only" signs on the way to the river, and the bridge to The Forrest beyond it. *And what* about *the guys I'm supposed to be leading? The way they treat them down here—and maybe in most places. . . . They really wanna fight for a country that doesn't seem that much interested in fighting for* them*?*

When they neared the river, the ride got notably rougher. And after the jeep abruptly veered onto the bridge, Gower and Conroy nearly got bucked out the back. The Welsh Kid's stomach took an even more drastic turn. *Uh-oh! Gonna spew some of Mrs. Bentson's "chicken and fixins" all over Lieutenant Early's jeep, if not the back of his head! Do I dare even open my trap to ask them to stop the jeep so I can dismount and let fly?* He looked to Conroy for assistance. Despite bouncing around like a rag doll during most of the ride, his buddy had passed out. And before Gower could get Early's attention, the lieutenant ducked down out of the wind to light a cigar. A cloud of the smoke caught the queasy new corporal square in the face. And that did it.

5

Gower tapped urgently on driver Ski's shoulder. The specialist corporal slowed the jeep as he turned toward his panicky passenger. Gower made the universal gesture for *"I'm about to lose it,"* prompting Ski for a rapid pull to the side of the bridge-mounted road before the jeep lurched to a stop.

Gower scrambled the few feet to the railing, leaned over it, and let go. He watched as most of the load hit the water, far below. But some dribbled down the girders, where it startled a nesting pair of doves. The spent, rubber-legged, bent-over immigrant from Poppy Peak gazed past the birds to the river rolling by underneath them. Graceful surface rings and ripples soothed his mind but not his gut, and it wasn't long before the speed of the river's passing had him fighting a repeat of his performance.

An encore apparently averted, he reconsidered the water, curious as to what it would feel like. *Have it take me, save me from explaining all this to Mom and Dad. . . . Maybe Waverly was thinking the same kind of thing, there, at the end.* Tightening his grip on the top rail, Gower planted a foot on one lower down for leverage, and started to pull himself up and over. He stared again, down at the river. *Maybe I wouldn't die, though. Pretty good swimmer . . .* Through the taste of soured chicken gravy, he managed a cynical grin. *But only half a Taffy . . . So, maybe somehow, I'd make it back and have to tell Mom and Dad what happened . . . How I let them down. . . . Only one way to find out.* He raised himself high enough for the weight of his head and upper body to send him over the rail, stopping only when he could hear his mother's voice repeat a favored hope for her youngest son.

Mervyn! You must *fit in. Please, now! You* must*!*

Gower relaxed his grip on the railing and returned both feet to the bridge. *Guess I failed at that, too, Mom. Still not sure what that means, "fit in." How exactly should I do that? "Fit in" to what? As far as the Army's concerned, instead of fitting in, feels more like I've been* taken *in—stuffed into the wrong box! Serving like some kinda glorified nanny for a bunch of colored guys with pretty long odds against joining the fight against . . . oppression? And by the way, doesn't the Army see the irony in that? Talk about "fitting in"! I mean, come* on*! Those guys were born here! They're literally more American than I am! But they're not allowed to "fit in," even if they wanted to. Nobody looks at my face and doubts my loyalties, my determination, my right to be here—or even my right to exist—simply because of my complexion! I'm a white guy. All I gotta do is show up. No questions asked. Guess I "fit in" to that role pretty well. All I had to do was be the right color!*

Am I an American, now? Instead of cowboy heroes fighting bad guys, ever since leaving home all I've seen is a country at war, apparently, with itself—bayonet-wielding soldiers forcing other Americans from their homes because they happen to be of Japanese ancestry—escorting them away to . . . prison camps, *I guess . . . And from the train taking us "defenders of freedom" directly into the heart of this same America, I saw a burning cross! Days later, met a band of hooded vigilantes, roaming freely around The Forrest—self-appointed crusaders for hatred! And, well, all around me, ever since I got here, reminders that Black citizens can't even share in the most basic of public conveniences, if not the rights and freedoms supposed to be granted to* all *Americans.* He thought of the old man sitting next to him on the city bus. *The suffering and humiliation that must surely come with that . . . Poppy Peak is a dream world compared to much of what I've sworn to defend. And I admit it, Mom, I was a dreamer. What was it Mugsy used to say? "If you keep worrying about stuff what ain't actually there, Kid, you're gonna miss the stuff what actually is."*

The deep-throated growl of heavy vehicles transported Gower from self-pity back to the bridge on the Arkansas River. *Stuff what actually is.* He peered down the road, back toward Little Rock. *Deuce-five? Troops! Don't want anyone I know seeing me like this. Hell, I don't want anyone seeing me like this, period!* He staggered back to the jeep. Corporal Ski had dismounted. He was leaning against the driver's side fender, having a cigarette. Arms folded, he afforded the approaching convoy a casual glance. Lieutenant Early continued to sit where Gower left him, working his cigar, going over a document, seemingly oblivious to the approaching trucks. Conroy—head back, mouth open—was still out.

Swaying slightly, Gower parked himself behind the jeep and braced against the rear-mounted spare tire. He stood as straight as he could manage and saluted as the first of several transports roared on by. *Colored troops. From C Company? Maybe some of them're gonna be mine . . . Could I lead them? Am I fit to lead* anyone*? Haven't done that great leading myself, come to think of it . . . "Come on, Gower, fit in!" What else can I do but give it a try? Me. Them. Black men. White men. Takes* all *men and all women to make this country. It'll take all of us to win this war.* He remembered what his dad liked to say about choosing America over class-conscious Britain. *"No matter who your father was, no matter what you look like or where you came from, none of that should matter here." Nobody cares where I was born, or who my father was. And it* shouldn't *matter, should it. E pluribus unum.*

The GIs in the last truck to pass by the lieutenant's jeep were neither Black nor white. *Japanese?* One of them seated at the tailgate looked familiar. As if having a similar thought, the soldier stared, open-mouthed, back at Gower. *Hey-Gee? Hey-Gee Nakamura?!*

To be continued in Book Two—*Mud Men*.

AFTERWORD

The early years for both my father and me were spent in very white environments with very few, if any, people of color sharing them. I was born and raised in a very white suburb not far away from my father's boyhood home. And when a few "colored" people started showing up at the bus stop in front of our house, unapologetic, racially discriminating Mom must have panicked, pressed Dad, and had us move to a neighboring, nearly all-white unincorporated community where she believed we would be safe from the "other"—meaning, of course, the people of color gradually moving into the middle class.

As a small boy in the early 1950s, I loved visiting my very British grandparents' house on Poppy Peak, as the area is known. It was so different from any other. The way it had been decorated, the food I could eat only there, the strong Welsh tea, and the voices—the heavy West Suffolk accent of my grandfather and the lilting, singsong cadence of my grandmother's North Wales–inflected English—made it feel like another world. It was a neighborhood where everyone was trying to "fit in," become a "real American," learn English—American style—and "Make it snappy, Mac!"

Even the cellar of that house, full of old, sweet-smelling empty wine barrels, offered a glimpse into former times that I would later read about, including Los Angeles during Prohibition. While making "bathtub gin" and wine for illegal distribution, my grandfather developed peripheral connections to the local underworld. (It would have been impossible not to.) In those times, and in that version of the City of Angels, my wannabe boxer father and his bandleader older brother, too, occasionally bumped up against gangsters and their minions, including men like my novel's compulsive gift- and advice-giving Mugsy Levine (part-time boxing coach, but full-time mobster) in their natural habitats—the bookie joints, the swank downtown clubs, and the side-alley speakeasies wherein the likes of my angel-voiced character Lacey Lane would have sung—as they all chased after the elusive "good life" beyond.

By the time I came along, my father was a few years a veteran of WWII. True to his nature, he fit the stereotype of not wanting to talk much about what he did and what happened to him while in the service—beyond confirming he had come out of it a changed man. But while I was doing chores with my foreign-born, "too British!" (according to his childhood and adult acquaintances alike), low-key, "stiff upper lip" father of mine, he would suddenly share a non-sequential, offhand snippet of his unusual experience as an immigrant draftee in the US Army—the ranks of which were at that time, and until the Korean War, officially segregated by race. (To my surprise, I learned only while doing research for this novel that the Army's official designation for Black American soldiers and indeed, their separate units at that time, was "colored," with a capital "C.")

The tidbits of Dad's GI experience whetted my appetite for more. They were often funny and self-deprecating. But a few of them were puzzling—delivered as they were without context—and even a little scary. I dared not ask him to elaborate without risking a prolonged, stony stare and the end of his reminiscences altogether.

As I grew older, with sports, driving, and girls—roughly

in that order—on my mind, Dad's stories were no longer as appealing. During high school summer weekdays, I would borrow Mom's car every morning and drive myself to my first "real job"—working at the Los Angeles City Schools central textbook warehouse downtown, not far from the fictional location of this novel's "gym on Figueroa," where, fighting as "The Welsh Kid," Gower suffers coach-slash-gangster Mugsy Levine's harsh critiques.

Working in that textbook warehouse and taking inventory on site at the district's far-flung junior and senior high schools, I loved hearing "growing up in the South" stories my mostly Black supervisors would tell me and the other summer hires. One morning, in August 1965, a shockwave hit our particular crew. After driving myself to the designated high school where we had been assigned to take inventory that morning, we learned that the Watts riots had broken out a couple of blocks up the street from the campus. Fearing the worst, the African American managers of our team organized a car caravan and led me and the other young, mostly non-Black crew members out of, and safely away from, the riot zone. High school graduation was only months away. We all spent the rest of that summer working only within the walls of the warehouse downtown.

I had never personally witnessed any acts of racial discrimination until my freshman year at a small, conservative, and nominally "Christian" college east of Los Angeles. Early in my four-year stay, I ventured into the lobby of our twenty-four-man dormitory and saw one of the two Black residents participating in what appeared to be a friendly game of cards. As I stood watching, a couple of older, white dormmates suddenly addressed the Black student participant not by name, but simply and crudely as "Chocolate." I noticed the student's face flush, but he said nothing in response. He simply finished the hand in silence and quietly left the room. The

Civil Rights Era had barely begun. It did manage to nudge that college forward at least a little. The number of non-white students eventually increased dramatically during my time there, and I grew close to several of them. But I never saw a Black dormmate play cards with white students in our lobby again.

After college, with dreams of someday becoming a novelist, I won a fellowship in literature and headed off in my '67 VW Bug to Southern Illinois University's Carbondale campus, which I assumed was somewhere below Chicago. It turned out to be much farther south than I realized—farther south than most of Missouri, Kentucky, and both Virginias. Everyone in town spoke "Southern." Another assumption I'd made was that civil rights had also ushered positive changes into that part of the country. But seeing a "Colored Only" sign on a public drinking fountain in northern Arkansas and a burning cross on a hillside one evening in southern Missouri seemed to validate a particular Faulkner quote I'd become familiar with: "The past is never dead. It's not even past." There were many nights while trying to sleep when I could hear the sound of the ongoing gun battles between local white supremacists and Black Nationalists.

After graduating from SIU with an MA in literature, I returned to California and landed a job in educational TV as a production assistant not far from the same warehouse full of textbooks where I used to work. One day, to my pleasant surprise, I ran into one of my Black former supervisors and chatted with him about old times. Meanwhile, I struck up an acquaintance with a guest producer in the next cubicle—a Japanese-American woman working on a series about Japanese folktales. We hit it off immediately and ultimately established a friendship that lasts to this day. Before then, I'd had little knowledge of the plight of Japanese-Americans during the Second World War. And though

I remembered hearing Dad once offhandedly reminisce about going fishing with a Japanese guy during his days in the Army, I assumed he meant a Japanese POW, and I had wondered, *How could he go fishing with a prisoner?* But over time, talking with my newfound Japanese-American friend, I learned about "relocation" and the exemplary service of Nisei GIs, including her father, and, to my great surprise, the fact that her mother had been held for a time in an internment camp not far from where Dad had been stationed!

Still interested in TV, but tired of LA, I accepted a job at a local station on California's Central Coast. Soon after my arrival, however, everyone was laid off when the station lost its license due to anti-Semitic comments by the licensee. Luckily my master's degree qualified me to work as a community college instructor, so I taught English as a second language to recent immigrants, immigrant GIs, and foreign exchange students. Eventually, I fell in love, and the next thirty years found me busy with marriage, child-rearing, and a marketing- and promotions-related business career in government and private industry, which afforded me related experience in twenty-five countries. It wasn't until I was laid off during the Great Recession that I had time to do some thinking about my dreams of becoming a writer. And while going through some of my late dad's effects, including a few photos of him and his buddies in uniform, I awoke to the possibility that all those disconnected bits and pieces he'd shared with me about his time in the Army, if strung along a framework of thoroughly researched history, might make quite a tale.

And, while the reader may find some of the words and deeds of a few of the characters presented in these pages shocking and even offensive, that was, and unfortunately still is, too often the reality. But I believe that ignoring or downplaying this reality does society a disservice. The first time I encountered an example of the raw hatred behind this fear was in the hills not far from that small Christian college campus I attended. Someone had set up a target range consisting of grotesquely disfigured faces meant to represent African Americans, spray-painted on several bullet hole–riddled sheets of discarded plywood. I was horrified. Since that day, thankfully, I have also witnessed much in the way of positive interracial relationships occurring through conscientious outreach and thoughtful attempts at understanding. There remains much work to be done.

ABOUT THE AUTHOR

J. A. Nunn was born in Pasadena, California. He earned a BA in literature at a small Baptist college in a small town east of Los Angeles and later won a full fellowship in literature at Southern Illinois University. After living in Carbondale, Illinois, and then teaching in Berkeley, Pacific Grove, and a few other California cities, Nunn accepted a teaching position in Tokyo. He later switched to marketing and was ultimately appointed as the Japan-based trade representative for the State of Washington. Currently Nunn lives in Seattle, making ever more memories with his wife of forty-plus years.

www.ingramcontent.com/pod-product-compliance
Ingram Content Group UK Ltd.
Pitfield, Milton Keynes, MK11 3LW, UK
UKHW030621270525
6089UKWH00002B/289

9 781964 721484